Truly Madly Royally

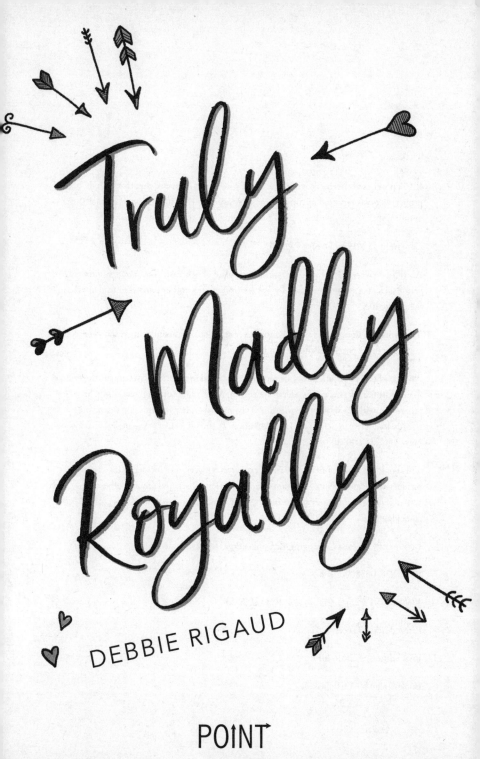

Truly Madly Royally

DEBBIE RIGAUD

POINT

Copyright © 2019 by Debbie Rigaud

All rights reserved. Published by Point, an imprint of Scholastic Inc., *Publishers since 1920*. SCHOLASTIC, POINT, and associated logos are trademarks and/or registered trademarks of Scholastic Inc.

The publisher does not have any control over and does not assume any responsibility for author or third-party websites or their content.

Library of Congress Cataloging-in-Publication Data available

ISBN 978-1-338-33272-8

10 9 8 7 6 5 4 3 2   19 20 21 22 23

Printed in the U.S.A.   23

First edition, August 2019

Book design by Yaffa Jaskoll

To teens who lift up their communities in tiny and tremendous ways. We got you.

You never walk alone.

Chapter 1

FOR CENTURIES, the famed halls of Halstead University have echoed with expansive dialogue, provocative debate, and poignant questions. Or something like that.

But not at this moment.

"Yes," I repeat to the incredulous faces around me. "I really do commute in every day."

There's an audible gasp among my fellow students.

"So, y-you're a local?" says the obvious It girl of the group. People lean in when she speaks and agree with her before she's even made her point. She probably owns the yacht they all look like they've just stepped off of.

"Well, local as in fifty minutes by train and light-rail," I joke.

"Is it safe?" the girl sitting catty-corner to me asks, extra earnestly. I look away before she feels compelled to give me a sympathy hug. On an unrelated note, she's the same person who used the term "third world" earlier.

Deep sigh. Why did I come to class fifteen minutes early today? If this were one of the common lecture halls, I'd be fine. But in a room that can barely fit the oval conference table we're all seated around, it's tough to zone out these Yacht Club kids.

"You don't drive?" It Girl will not let this go.

"I won't be seventeen until September," I say. "Until then, I'm saving up for a car."

"Why don't you just . . . ask your parents for one?" a wide-eyed boy asks.

Blocked.

My answer is to busy myself with my phone. There's too much awkwardness *not* to live-text this situation to my best friend, Skye Joseph. Since my summer program started a few days ago, I've been sending daily text-isodes of my "Overheard at Halstead U" series for Skye to binge-read.

Ready for this? I type, and then quickly summarize the conversation I've just had.

Ugh. Sorry, Skye responds right away. *But that's what u get for taking the bait.*

I chuckle to myself. It's true. This all started when some student asked another what the driving age is in New Jersey. (Everyone else at this program seems to be from out of state or even overseas.) I never miss a chance to rep my home state, so I jumped into the conversation with the answer. Serves me right.

Skye sends a follow-up text. *Don't let them stress you. The brave, get-things-done Zora Emerson I know would just keep moving.*

Easy for Skye to say. While we both got accepted into college-prep summer programs on actual college campuses, she's at a welcoming HBCU in Atlanta, and I stayed in New Jersey to attend snooty Halstead University. That's like the difference between going to a house party and going to a club. Or getting a ride from your ride or die, and a lift from Lyft.

"I almost wrecked the new Tesla," the It girl is saying now. She tucks her sleek gold strands behind a pearl-studded ear.

"You should practice on the family car next time," says a guy with that pink whale logo on his cap.

"That *is* the family car," she answers with a titter.

Guffaw.

The more she talks, the more I gather her star sign is Snob rising. But at least she inspires new material for my next text-isode of "Overheard at Halstead U."

I never thought I'd be so happy to see the professor walk in.

After class, I plug in my headphones and resume the audiobook I need to finish for another class. For a while, the memory of my annoying exchange with It Girl and her friends buzzes louder than the narrator's voice.

It's true. You won't see many people from Halstead U schlepping anywhere on a train, unless it's to Manhattan. There's even someone on campus so loaded, he has a security detail. I've seen his sleek fleet of black town cars, but I've never run into Richie Rich myself. I overheard someone refer to him as royalty, so he's probably a spoiled corporate heir or something.

As out of place as I feel just being in class with these students, I can't imagine how uncomfortable it would be sharing a dorm room with one of them. I've convinced myself that *that* is the bright side of receiving a scholarship award that doesn't cover room and board.

Days like this make me happy I get to leave campus. And today I'm leaving earlier than usual. This afternoon at 3:00 p.m. is the Appleton Summer Soak & Arts Fest at the local summer camp. It's like Water Day and an art presentation rolled into one. Some of the grammar school students from Walk Me Home, the after-school chaperone service I started freshman year, have enrolled at the camp. Thanks to Walk Me Home, I've become an adoptive big sis to lots of Appleton kiddos. I promised the kids I'd come to the center today to help hang their final artwork. I can't wait to see their proud little faces.

Just one quick stop before I head to the train station.

Halstead U has an impressive campus, but no architectural star shines brighter than the school's acclaimed library. It looks like a legit castle. Gothic and majestic, some sections are almost three centuries old! But as ancient as the library's exterior structure is, the interiors have been recently renovated. And talk about modern and cool. It makes Appleton's public library look like a clunky, old-school iPod.

I reach the castle doors just as my audiobook's chapter on digital philanthropy ends. I have half an hour before my train home, which should be more than enough time to swing by to pick up the book I reserved.

The twisting grand staircase that slices through the cathedral-ceiling entryway leads me right to the reference room. But just as I scan out the book, my cell phone rings. Loudly. *How could I have forgotten to turn off my ringer?*

I silence it as quickly as humanly possible but still get glares from people quietly studying at large oak tables. In sending the caller—my mom—to voicemail, I somehow call her back. On speaker! I hang up just as soon as the call goes through. Of course, my mom takes this as her cue to ring back. Even my phone's buzzing manages to sound loud. Heading down the echoey stairs to the main entrance is too risky. So I slip out of the reference atrium and hang a right into an area with rows of tall bookcases. It's a carpeted room, which absorbs the sound of the incessant buzzing. There doesn't seem to be anyone in this area, so I answer the call to find out what Ma's emergency is.

"Hold on," I say.

In my half a dozen visits to the library, I've never ventured to this part. Even though the maze of bookcases is clear of any other students, I still work my way to the back.

"Ma? Hi."

"Are you okay?" She sounds worried.

"Yes, I'm fine. I'm at the library."

"Oh, good. Your day went well, then? Now that you're nearly a week in, you feeling better about being there?"

"It's getting better."

5

"Are you sure, baby? I don't want you to be so stressed out about this."

"I know I was nervous about coming here, but your constant checkups are making my anxieties harder to shake off."

"What anxieties? You have anxiety?"

"Mother, I didn't mean it like that. It's just a little hard to feel comfortable here. But I'm sure it'll get better."

"Yes, of course it will get better. Maybe you'll find another student you can relate to?"

"Ma, I'm like the only person commuting, so I don't get to hang out with kids at the dorm. And to be honest, it's like half these people are speaking a different language. I could barely follow this one guy's presentation in class earlier."

"I'm gonna pray you find a friend there you can relate to. You know God always listens to a mother's prayer," she singsongs.

"Yes, Ma, okay." She is like a broken record sometimes, but it's sweet of her. "I gotta go. See you tonight."

I hang up the phone, rest my forehead against the bookcase, and sigh.

"Great, now I'm worrying my mom," I chastise myself out loud. "Not cool."

"At least you know which way to look as you cross the street."

The guy's voice comes from the other side of the bookcase. He is obviously reacting to my private conversation. I try to look at him, but the shelves are so well stocked, I can only see flashes of his steel-blue shirt through the rows of books.

"And as for another language," he goes on, "be grateful you haven't been caught referring to the last letter in the alphabet as 'zed.'"

He has a distinct British accent. Who is this guy? Normally, an unabashed eavesdropper would be my least favorite person. But something about him doesn't set off any alarms or piss me off . . . yet. Maybe it's his refreshing lack of smugness, which is hard to come by in this place. Still, I can't let him off the hook that easy.

"Have I stumbled onto some library stand-up comedy routine?" I ask, slightly annoyed.

"I'm sorry. It was my poor attempt at lightening the mood." He's clearly embarrassed.

"Maybe next time don't base your jokes on eavesdropping?" I say.

"Right," he says, sounding sheepish. "Sound advice. Pun intended."

I smirk to myself.

"Anyway, you wouldn't want to swap problems," I say, thinking back to that morning's pre-class chitchat. "If you really heard what I've been going through, you'd decide you'd be better off 'zed.'"

He chuckles. "Aah, I see what you did there. What sorts of problems keep a clever pun artist like you awake at night?"

I play along. Something about this anonymous church confessional setup makes me spill the tea.

"Let's see—the classes here are twice as accelerated as my high school's most advanced ones. I feel like I'm in a foreign world every time I step on campus. Oh, and there's a whole community of people I'd let down back home if I don't do well here."

I can't believe how honest I'm being about this, at last. And it feels easy doing it.

"Well, it sounds like my lonely world now has a population of two," the guy says. "I'm barely keeping up with my classes, I am a foreigner everywhere I step, and, oh, there's a whole *country* of people I would let down if I didn't do well."

"How are *you* coping?" I ask. He seems so okay with it all. I have to know his secret.

"Oh, I hide out in the library, for one," he answers with a smile in his voice.

I'm smiling, too. I rest my elbows on the bookcase, not even trying to see his face through the spines now. "I get it. I have a bookish hiding place, too. Weekend mornings at Ingrum's Books out on Route 42. That's my escape."

"I found you!" says a girl who does not have a British accent. I recognize the voice—it's It Girl herself. She's on the other side of the shelf. I feel an eye roll coming on. "Have you been avoiding your fans again?" she's asking the British-sounding guy.

"Nothing like that," he tells her. "I just need to stay here in this spot. I'm getting the best Wi-Fi signal and I don't want to lose it, nor do I want it to go away."

I can tell by the way he says it that that remark is meant for me.

It Girl seems to take the hint and leaves. I'm relieved.

"Was that your girlfriend?" I ask. "She sounds . . . thoughtful."

"She is a very thoughtful person, but no, I don't have a girlfriend."

"Not that that was my pickup line or anything," I tease. "Just so we're clear."

"Oh, we're clear." His voice is smiling again. Pause. "Do *you* have someone?"

"Me? Nah."

The only boyfriend I've ever had moved to Philly three months ago and doesn't bother keeping in touch like he'd promised. I guess for him our relationship is out of sight, out of mind.

"What did your not-girlfriend mean about all your fans?" I ask the boy behind the books.

I can practically hear him shrug. "Just that I have a pretty hot ticket to a big event at the end of this summer, and I suppose a few different girls want to be my plus-one."

"Who would you take if you didn't have to worry about expectations?" I ask him.

Again, I catch glimpses of his steel-blue shirt between the books. Sunshine from the skylight bounces off of it as he shuffles around. He moves closer to the bookcase, and I get a whiff of spearmint candy. Is he chewing gum?

"Well, there is this girl I've seen on campus a few times this week."

"What is it you like about her?" I ask.

"She's beautiful. And I don't know, there's this self-possessed air about her that makes her stand out."

"Sooo, why don't you ask *her* to your event?"

I come short of patting myself on the back for single-handedly solving his problem.

"She's never noticed me. She's always zoned out, plugged into her music. I don't think I'm her type anyway."

I don't like hearing about yet another campus princess making someone feel small.

"She sounds kind of self-*obsessed* if you ask me," I tell him. "If she won't even acknowledge you, you're better off without her."

His silence means he isn't ready to give up his dream girl. Poor guy.

He changes the subject. "What's the toughest part of being here for you?"

"Are you recording this?" I ask. "Because if we're going for this anonymous real-talk confessional, I don't want what I say to get out."

"Noted and agreed."

I smile at the charming way he speaks.

"If I may make a proposal?" he asks ultra-politely.

"No, I will not be the plus-one on your hot ticket. I barely know you!" I tease.

"Fair enough. Then my follow-up proposal will be that we

each place our cell phones in sight as a guarantee that no devices are recording what's being said."

"Noted and agreed," I mimic him. I am giddy. This is so much fun!

He slips his phone through two hardcover burgundy textbooks and rests it on the shelf. And then it seems like he is attempting to slide out the book to the right of his phone.

"Hey, no peeking!" I scold playfully.

"Never! Why would I mess up the great dynamic we've got going?" He chuckles. "I'm just making room for your phone."

"Fine."

I reciprocate by squeezing my phone in next to his. Once we're both eyeballing phones, the real conversation begins.

"So, are you a college student or in one of the pre-college programs?" I ask him.

"I am pre-college. I have the option of starting college here in the fall, but I'll be attending back home."

"Aw, well, congratulations on your acceptance to Halstead U anyway."

"Cheers," he sheepishly thanks me. "I'm curious—what is the hardest thing you find about attending classes here?" he asks.

"Not damaging my eyes from rolling them so much," I'm surprised to hear myself admit.

"How do you mean?"

"Well, it's barely been a week, and somehow I'm already feeling so over everyone and everything. Instead of hearing what

11

classmates are actually saying, whether it's 'I'm tired' or 'Sorry I'm late,' I just hear 'I'm privileged' or 'Sorry I'm privileged.'"

"Sorry I'm privileged," he confesses. "And not only just because I'm a straight white male. I'm a straight white male from a long lineage of privileged people in power—with the ridiculous bank accounts to prove it."

"Whoa, that's like coming straight out the womb Beyoncé," I say with my eyebrows practically at my hairline. "*Beyoncé* didn't even come straight out the womb Beyoncé!"

"That's like coming straight out of the womb Beyoncé, but without any of the talent or hard work, yet people are throwing EGOTs at you, following you in droves, and waiting with bated breath for you to do something amazing."

"Not that I feel sorry for you—which I don't . . . that much . . ." I can't decide. Rolling in dough or not, I wouldn't want to lug around expectations that heavy. "I can relate—on a much smaller scale."

"It's the quickest way to feel inadequate."

I like his way of making light of his worries. And his manner of speaking really is so cute.

"Are you British?"

"Not exactly."

"Same accent, though?"

"We do share accents and some lineage, but I hail from a bit farther southwest of the British Isles. In the Celtic Sea."

I can't picture it.

"I'm from Landerel," he says. "We are to the Brits sort of like Canada is to America, similar accents and all."

"Oh, cool!" Now I am impressed. Though I couldn't say exactly where it is on the map, I have heard of Landerel. "For a tiny country, Landerel has a history of exceptional community organizing at the grass-roots level. Sister's Keeper was founded there. It's a global model!"

He laughs. "O-kay, most people think of our mediocre cuisine or our hosting the Olympics four years ago, so I'll accept that as a fresh departure."

I can't stop smiling throughout this wild conversation. Then I happen to glance toward the far corner and that's when I see the clock face on the wall. I almost swallow my tongue.

Oh. No.

"Speaking of departure . . . my train leaves in six minutes," I say in one breath. "I'll be late if I'm not on it."

"Late for what?" the boy asks.

"The kids will be crushed if I'm not there to help set up."

When you're tiny, empty promises from big people are tough to stomach. I've had my share of let*Dads*—er, I mean letdowns—and I don't want to put any kid through that.

I hate to cut this short, but public transport waits for no one.

My arms are a blur they're moving so fast. In a tizzy, I grab my books and cram them into my bag, then slide my phone off the shelf and shove it into my back pocket.

Seeing his solitary phone sandwiched between books must be

13

a lonely sight, because there's a tinge of disappointment in my mystery friend's voice when he speaks next.

"Sounds terribly important. What time does—"

I'm just about to cut him off to say good-bye when It Girl's voice returns.

"What time does what?" she asks him sweetly.

While his not-girlfriend chats him up, I turn and slip out of the bookshelf maze unnoticed. Even if I had time to loop around and take a peek at my mystery friend's face, I couldn't. A small group of Men in Black types start snaking their way toward me and I wouldn't want an audience to my spying. Besides, catching that train is the only thing on my mind.

No time to take in the impressive sights while I walk-run my way through the grassy quad. But also, no study chapters droning in my ears. No mental review of every awkward moment I had today. Just me, and the summer sun, and a dash through what honestly is a pretty dope campus.

I take a few running steps onto the platform, and I arrive, panting, at the same time as the train. I slide through the train doors with a sigh of relief and plop into the first empty seat, taking my phone out of my back pocket. No disappointed kiddos in my future.

As usual I pop in my earplugs, and go to cue the audiobook on my phone.

That's when I notice it for the first time. I have Library Guy's cell phone instead of my own!

Chapter 2

I LOSE my cool. Any chill I have left is gone, immediately.

How could I have taken the wrong phone? Panic creeps up my chest like a big, hairy spider. Forget about the fact that I know where I'm going. I still feel hopelessly lost. Maybe I can get off at the next stop and head back to school? But without my phone, I can't even check the rail schedule to see if that's manageable. *Gah!*

I don't know how long I sit on the train in shock, examining Library Guy's cell. It is the identical size as mine and has the same textured black case. But the lock screen image is not a close-up selfie of me and Anaya, my first Walk Me Home student. It's of an unidentifiable skydiver midjump.

"Stan' clea-yah of tha closing door-ahs."

I look out the train window for the first time. Newark Penn Station. This is my stop! Thank goodness I'm right next to an exit. I spring out of my seat and in one catlike move, my shoulder bag is lodged between the sliding doors. As I'd hoped, the jaws of the door release my bag, then open long enough for me to slip out.

"Watch the closing *door-ahs*," the hidden conductor scolds as I run toward the staircase leading down to the light-rail platform.

The first car is too packed to get on. Thankfully, the second one is right behind it. No available seats, though. Just wall-to-wall commuters avoiding each other's eye contact. Finally in the perfect standing nook, I grab ahold of a crowded safety pole. It's just a seven-minute ride to my hometown of Appleton.

The cell phone vibrates. With a start, I reach into my back pocket, and narrowly avoid elbowing the person next to me.

It looks like a foreign number, but I don't answer in time. The buzzing stops and then starts up again. A different number pops on the screen. This time, it's from a New York City area code. Could it be Library Guy calling? I decide to pick up the call. Whoever it is can help me get my phone back. The moment I swipe to answer, the light-rail jerks as it changes tracks. I stumble to the side a few paces, stepping on a fellow commuter's foot in the process. It's the same man who almost got my elbow moments ago.

"Yo!" He frowns.

"Sorry," I mumble, embarrassed.

"Hello?" A girl's voice is piping from the cell phone. I almost forgot about the call.

"Hello?" I respond breathlessly. But quietly, because dude with the throbbing toe is giving me a death stare.

"Who's this?" the girl asks in an aggressive tone.

"Hi, I'm—"

"What's going on over there? I hear lots of commotion."

"It's just that I'm on a train. Listen, do you—"

"On a train, right. I see how it is. I guess this is what he means by single."

"Huh? It's not like that at all. Can you just slow down for a second?"

"No, really. I can take a hint. Sorry to bother him. If I were you, I'd take the fastest *train* away from that player."

The girl hangs up, and I'm left frowning and confused. The toe-hurt commuter looks satisfied by my reaction to the troubling call. As long as it makes his toe feel better.

Whatever just happened with that call, I want to avoid it happening again. I shut off the cell phone, stick it back in my bag, and rush off the light-rail when we get to my stop.

It's a long city block from the station to the community center. I'm crossing the street when I spot the center's director, Ms. Nelson, unloading her car. *Sigh.* An encounter with her is the last thing I need when I'm still in freak-out mode. God love her, but Ms. Nelson can talk a person's ear off. A few car lengths before reaching her, I zip across the wide sidewalk and pretend not to notice her. I'm about to walk into the center when I hear her trunk slam.

"Zora, is that you?"

Cover blown. My surprised-to-see-you expression isn't going to win any acting awards, but I give it a try.

"Hello, Ms. Nelson," I say innocently. I slow my pace but don't stop. "Exciting day. I can't wait to see the kids' artwork."

"Now, hold on just a minute—you young people are always in a rush." The stubborn cowlick on top of her bowl-cut hairdo trembles with her deep disappointment. "We're planning to live-stream the Metropolitan Gala ceremony next week, and folks are signing up to come to the viewing."

She knows just how to guilt folks into a conversation. The Metropolitan Gala is the Oscars of service awards, where the "Goodies" are awarded to do-gooders from our New York City metro area. I still can't believe I'm one of the teen nominees. When I started Walk Me Home, I just wanted to help out a couple kids in my neighborhood—some as young as five—who didn't have after-school chaperones. They either had an elderly grandparent who couldn't meet them at school, or adults who couldn't leave work in time. And when I submitted an application for the Goodies, it felt a little out of reach. But Walk Me Home has grown beyond my wildest expectations, and *influential people* agree we're doing great work. The upcoming Gala is a huge deal. Black tie, fancy dinner, honored guests, moneyed guests, and—if I win— enough grant money to fund the after-school program for another year.

"If you win it, I know every penny of that fifteen-thousand-dollar award would go to Walk Me Home, not like that fundraising fraud couple from the news they just arrested." Ms. Nelson shakes her head. "You started something special. Your kids look out for each other, and they talk about you all the time."

18

My heart softens. I can't imagine life today without my Walk Me Home kids. And that little group has become involved in a bunch of the activities at the community center. Coming here today is my way of carving out some time to visit my little fam. They help me just as much as I help them.

I still get choked up when I think about the moment the families of my Walk Me Home students gifted me with a New Jersey Transit rider pass that covers the entire month of July. That's been one less concern about my attending Halstead U this summer. It's overwhelming knowing that what I learn in my philanthropy class at the program will not only boost my academic profile, but also benefit the Walk Me Home kids and the affordable aftercare service I'm helping the community center launch.

"Aw, I miss them, too. I can't wait to go in and see them," I say. (Hint, hint.)

Ms. Nelson looks pleased to recognize a trace of the old have-time-for-everyone Zora, pre–Halstead U.

"And here I was just yesterday bragging to my hairdresser about how our Zora is going to make everyone in Appleton proud," she says, beaming.

I don't know what to say. Unfortunately, Ms. Nelson does.

"Who would've dreamed we'd be sending one of *our* stars up to such a fancy un-i-ver-si-ty?"

She over-enunciates, as if speaking of the Ivy League school puts her in its formal company.

"It's good that they'll know what *our* best and brightest kids are made of."

Great—now I'm the ambassador for the entire town? Still fidgeting, I shift my weight (which now includes the heft of all of Appleton's expectations) from one foot to the other.

"Go on in and see those babies before they head home."

I wave and jog inside, confused by how it comes to be that Ms. Nelson is shooing *me* away.

"ZORRAA!" Anaya runs up to me as soon as I step through the door of the community center.

I don't have to bend as low as I used to to give her a hug.

"How did you already get so tall?" I ask. "It's only been a few weeks!"

"Girl power!" she giggles, repeating the rallying cry I usually give her. The multicolored beads weighing down her cornrows chime with her gleeful sways.

"A to Z back together again." I hold up my fist, and she bumps it with as much seven-year-old girl power as she can muster.

"Ouch!" I pretend my knuckles are aching and shake out my hand.

"Come on! Everyone is out back!" Anaya says. She takes my hand and leads me away from the lobby. I manage to wave hello to Mr. Lance, the elderly man volunteering at the front desk.

"Miss Zora, you're the one who wanted to teach them to be leaders! Careful what you ask for next time," Mr. Lance cackles.

"I should've listened when you warned me," I shout to him over my shoulder.

Anaya's braids chime all the way to the outdoor playground,

where the rest of the five-to-eight-year-old campers are buzzing with Water Day excitement. They're too distracted by the sprinklers, Slip 'N Slides, and bubble machine to notice me at first. And then I get mobbed by the group as they take turns hugging me with dripping wet arms.

"ZORRRAAA!"

"Hi guys! I've missed y'all!"

I call out each of their names with every embrace. Reunion over, the boys and girls all scurry back to their play, except for Anaya.

"Don't worry about me, go change into your bathing suit!" I tell her.

"My grandma said she'll get me a swimsuit not this paycheck but the one after because she has to pay the light bill first," Anaya explains matter-of-factly in between reassuring nods.

I look through my bag. Between my laptop and my Grant Writing course text is the size-eight Popsicle-print swimsuit I bought on sale for her. Anaya squeals when I hand it over, and I'm even happier I came today.

By the time she emerges from the bathroom splash-ready and beaming, the pop-up gallery is poppin'. Over the next hour, with all the gallery hopping and water-games playing, I hardly have time to stress over the fact that my cell phone is missing.

But no doubt, as soon as I get home that evening, I bust inside like an unleashed Black Friday shopper. I tear past the kitchen, where my big brother, Zach, is eating a bowl of cereal at the table.

His tall, curly 'fro practically uncoils from the whirlwind I've whipped up.

I run straight to the entry hall console table, where the cordless landline can be found sitting like a museum relic. Ma and my stepdad, John, stand strong every time Zach and I clown them for keeping a landline. For which I am suddenly grateful.

I grab the phone and dial my own cell phone number over and over again. No one picks up. *Game recognize game*, my dad would say. I guess any player with a broken-heart rap sheet would avoid the drama that could come with picking up a call on someone else's cell.

Zach pokes his head into the hallway. It's like he's been overprotective and on patrol ever since I started my summer program. Even more protective than he was four years ago, when he thought Ma marrying John would be the end of our Triple Threat we called a family.

Having just completed his first year as a premed student at Garden State U, Zach doesn't seem entirely comfortable knowing his kid sister has to be on any college campus every day. He looks mildly concerned for me, but I don't tell him what's up. If he knew, he'd probably poke fun and, purely for his amusement, refuse to let me use his cell.

"You run out of cell phone power?" he asks.

"You run out of ChapStick?" I throw back playfully.

The creases across his forehead smooth out. He smiles and waves his finger at me, backing out of the hall.

"Point for Zora," he says. There's relief in his voice. At least for now, he doesn't have to hunt down some college heartbreaker on my behalf.

I smile back at him, playing up the role of carefree sister.

"I'm *always* on point!" I respond.

Once he's back in the kitchen, I sneak the cordless phone up to my room. I put down my bag and turn on the mystery cell, which already has a text message waiting for me.

*Hi, it's me, from the library confessional. This is the
number I will call you from. Please pick up if you can.*

He's sure to call now that I've rung my own cell a bunch of times. I wait for his call to come in on his cell phone, debating how I'll answer it. "Hi" or "Hey" is what I settle on. I feel like either one would strike the right tone of casual and not too self-conscious.

Seconds later, the expected buzzing begins.

"Hello?" I hear myself answer. I roll my eyes at my reflection in the mirror.

"Hello." He echoes my formal vibe.

Then silence.

"Delightful meeting you today," he says.

"I can't believe I took the wrong phone," I say at the same time.

We both chuckle at our awkward simultaneous chatter.

"Terribly sorry. You first," he says.

I don't want to go first, so I hesitate. Then a good question pops to mind.

"What's your name?

"Owen," he says. "Owen Whittelsey."

I don't know much about Owen, but I can already tell his tone is different from our first conversation.

"And your name?" he asks.

"Zora Emerson."

"Hi, Zora. Nice to match the face to a name."

How has he seen my face? Then I remember: my selfie on the lock screen. I wonder if that explains the low-key flirtation in his voice. *Does he think I'm cute?* Anyway, why do I care if he does? Haven't I been forewarned that he's a player?

I shake off the whirling thoughts. All of it is none of my business. I just need my phone back, so I stick to the script.

"I need my phone back, but I've already left campus," I say.

"Right. I'll be happy to meet you at the library tomorrow morning," he offers.

"What time is your first class?" I don't want to push, but I can't make it much longer than twenty-four hours without my phone. I only have one class on campus tomorrow, but I can come in as early as possible.

One Mississippi, two Mississippi. No response.

"H-hello?"

I check the phone. The screen is dark; it's completely dead.

24

This is a disaster! A growl escapes through my clenched teeth.

My first thought is to call Skye, but I can't remember her new number. Ugh. I plug the cell in next to my bed, but the battery blinks at me, refusing to charge yet.

Keep it together, girl, I tell myself. I can spend one night without my cell phone. Right?

I pick up the cordless, working up the nerve to call Owen back from it, when my mother's signature bubbly laugh percolates up the stairs. It's quickly followed by the baritone hum of my stepdad's voice. They're home, and suddenly right down the hallway from my bedroom door.

"Hey, baby, how did the camp event go?" Ma calls out to me.

I shove the landline phone under a faux fur pillow. They'd never let me live it down if they knew I used it.

"Great," I say as cheerily as possible.

My mother appears in my doorway holding one end of a rustic-chic shelf fitted with wire baskets. John, holding the other end, peeks his head past my doorframe and his glasses slide down his nose. Ma's shoulder-length locs swing into her face as he bumps the shelf into the wall. They rebalance the shelf between them.

"Looks like somebody's been shopping without me," I say, desperate to take the focus away from me and the day I've had.

"It's my fault," says John. "I should've stressed the 'digital' part when I suggested your mom get more storage."

"Don't hate," says Ma. "Congratulate. I scored this bad boy at half off."

It's tough for my mom to keep her social work *at* work. Every time she signs up for a class or training session, there's an avalanche of pamphlets, handouts, and other reading materials. And in the mix are the handouts and pamphlets she herself writes for her colleagues.

They place the shelf somewhere in their room and follow me downstairs to the kitchen. No use trying to deal with my own drama on an empty stomach.

"West Indian Wednesday in effect!" sings Ma.

"Is that a thing?" I chuckle.

"Tonight it is," she says. "We've got takeout oxtail with rice and peas."

"Yum," I say, my stomach growling, and I momentarily put my whole phone swap freak-out on hold, because, hey, *whaddyagonnado?*

We catch Zach hunched over the counter getting a head start on dinner.

"Uh-uh." I swipe the box of fried plantains from him. "Weren't you just eating cereal a minute ago?"

"That was an *hors d'oeuvre.*" He mimics the swag-erific way our dad would say it. Dad's a chef at a country club restaurant, so there are a lot of French culinary terms he says with '90s homeboy swagger.

"I take it we have to serve and eat the food with our fingers?" jokes Ma, eyeing Zach's table setup. She gives Zach a playful poke in his side, and he grins like a little boy. I taste a smack of bitterness in their sweet exchange, recalling the times they didn't get along so well.

"You know, that's not a bad idea, Yvette," says John. He reaches across the counter to hand me a few serving spoons to place on the table. "Maybe next week we'll eat family-style without utensils, like they do in some parts of the majority world."

"Well, it better be a day Zora's not working with snot-nosed kids at the center." Zach makes a grossed-out face that has me forgetting my troubles.

I howl out a laugh, taking a seat across from him. "*Holdupwaitaminute!* When did Mr. EMT-in-training over here become a bouncer at the germ-free club?"

Ding.

The front doorbell ring is a timely break to this round of verbal sparring.

Our classy one-note doorbell has been missing the "dong" ever since Zach banged his oversized travel trunk against it a few weeks ago. Ma asked him not to carry it from the car on his own, but *no*.

"Zach, you expecting somebody?" Ma freezes en route to the table, salad bowl in hand.

"Nope." A trace of oxtail gravy sprays from his mouth.

"Neither am I, if anyone is wondering," I say. "But I'll get it."

"It's just that we know Skye is out of town," John explains to me.

"I have more than one friend." I stop searching the table for my cell phone. Habit. Normally, I don't make a move without it, even if I'm just going to answer the door.

"Anyone older than ten? All your other friends aren't tall enough to reach the doorbell," teases Zach.

"Plenty of mature young people would love to have a friend who knows how to delegate," I hear Ma say as I head up the entry hallway empty-handed. The poor woman thinks she's defending me.

"Whose side are you on, Ma?" I shout over my shoulder as I reach for the knob.

I swing open the door, and there standing on our tiny front porch in my Appleton, New Jersey, neighborhood are the Men in Black from campus.

Chapter 3

"SORRY TO interrupt," says the square-jawed man on the left. "We're trying to locate Mr. Whittelsey's cell phone. We've traced it to this house."

It takes me a moment. At first I ponder the familiarity of the name, which almost sounds like a professor's. But, cell phone—

"Mr. Owen Whittelsey," says the man.

My heart drops to my toes.

What is going on? These are the same Men in Black types I'd seen earlier at the library. What do they have to do with my cell mix-up? Or with Owen? Am I in some kind of trouble?

"Are you the police or something?" I ask. Our neighbor Mr. Stanley is now suspiciously pacing the sidewalk in front of our home. When he catches my eye, he gestures to his phone camera to let me know he's prepared to start filming at any moment. I give him a weak wave.

"No, Miss," the man on the right finally speaks. He has the

same Landerelian accent as Owen. "We are the royal security assigned to Prince Owen of Landerel."

"Prince?"

Say what, now? The news literally knocks me back a step. My jaw is hanging off its hinge and practically swinging from the blunt force of shock.

Owen is a prince? Like, a legit *prince?* As in pick a year, any year—oh, say 1414—and Owen could probably *show* me what his ancestors were wearing, doing, saying? A legit prince, as in castle-living, crown-wearing, throne-sitting, country-conquering, people-subjugating on repeat . . . for centuries?

At Appleton High School, we've got princesses, royal screw-ups, a few noble souls, and definitely a ruling clique. And sure, I've been to Queens. Countless times. But up until now, the closest I've ever come to royalty is getting a crown put on my tooth.

I could *not* be more shocked if I stuck a wet finger in a janky outlet. The guy hanging out in the library, making anonymous wisecracks through bookshelves? My realest human connection at this school was with someone who . . . is a rightful heir to some throne?

I can't believe what I'm hearing.

Wait. Owen is THAT prince? The thoughts on my mental turntable go *zip-zip-zip* like a vinyl-record rewind. I recall my mom's excitement a few months ago when Landerel's royal wedding announcement made the news. It was reported that one of the princes was engaged to marry a biracial Landerelian woman.

People like my mom and her girlfriends have been losing their minds ever since, like "Gah! A brown-girl princess!"

What else? I know the royal family has three brothers. The eldest is already married with kids, the second is the hottie who broke hearts when he recently got engaged. He's the one I would recognize if I saw him on the street. His face has been all over magazine covers. You can't stand at a supermarket checkout without catching a glimpse of it.

But the youngest brother? From what I can remember, he was some gangly, awkward eighth grader the last time he made an official appearance that people in the States cared about. That was the Summer Olympics in Landerel four years ago.

"Yes, Prince Owen," repeats the royal guard, or whatever he is. "Do you have his missing cell phone?"

"Yeah—uh, I—I have it," I croak.

In a fog, I listen to their concern about privacy, and I answer that I have not accessed his phone details.

"No, we are not under foreclosure." Ma is on the phone and headed my way. "Nobody is seizing anything. Where did you get that idea—?" Her voice trails off as she eyes the imposing figures in the doorway. John and Zach are right behind her.

"Thank you for the call, Ms. June," she says to Mr. Stanley's wife on the other end. "Everything is fine. You have a good evening." Ma turns to me. "Zora?"

"Ma, there's been a mix-up, and these men are here for a phone I took by mistake. I'll go get it," I say. The truth is, I can't wait to be alone in my room so I can process this ... and maybe scream the shock and confusion into my pillow.

Shaky legs take me upstairs while the security duo talk to my family. When I get back, Zach stands at attention like he's wearing a suit of armor, John looks like he's conjuring some calming spell with his hands as he speaks to everyone, but Ma looks like she's on a game show.

"The actual prince? Ohmygod!" Ma shouts.

But then she looks at my face and back at the security. "Oh my God," she echoes more ominously, wraps a protective arm around my shoulders, and pulls me close. "Are you accusing our daughter of stealing this phone?"

"We'd just like to know how it is she came to have it in her possession," the square-jawed guard says as I hand Owen's cell back to him.

"Wait. Did he tell you it was stolen?" I ask. Forget shocked; now I'm pissed. Who do they think they are, coming to our home and accusing us? Who do they think *we* are? We're not their royal subjects, that's for sure.

The Men in Black glance at each other. Then one of them repeats, "How did you come in contact with it?"

"Zora, you don't have to answer that." John holds out his arm like a parking gate barring entry to any more info.

These men are lucky to encounter John and not my biological dad. The "one and only" Kenney Emerson doesn't do anything low-key when it counts. If he were here, he'd probably shame them for having the nerve to come to our door. Dad loves showing people up for kicks. "Some folks need to be taken down a few notches," he likes to say.

"I gave you his phone, so I don't owe you anything else." I rest my hands on my hips.

"Yo," says Zach with a gleam in his eyes. "Sounds like they don't even know where this prince even is."

Game recognize game, my dad would say. And Zach has played almost every game at one time or another.

No comment from the security duo, except to pardon themselves as they take what looks like an urgent phone call.

"Ma, got anything in your pamphlets about how to handle royal bullies?" Zach shakes his head.

"Gentlemen, I'm afraid I'm going to ask you to get off our property," says Ma.

The Landerelian man is off the phone now.

"Yes, madam. We would like to extend our deepest apologies for the intrusion. Everything has been sorted."

"Sounds like they've just located the missing prince," scoffs Zach.

"What about returning *my* phone?" I ask. "Owen has it."

"We'll be more than happy to retrieve and hand-deliver it tomorrow evening at this time, if someone will be home."

"Another twenty-four hours?" I cry after they've gone. Owen had said on the phone that we could meet in the library again. I have to try to find him there tomorrow.

"Keep your head up, Zo," says Zach.

"John, doesn't someone from church have a relative who works at Halstead?" Ma is already working her Amen Circuit.

"I'll give him a call," says John before he heads to the kitchen.

"Speaking of phones." Ma looks around. "Where's the cordless?"

Ugh, I'd forgotten to put it back. A fitting way to end a baffling day. Zach smirks at me. I pick up a white envelope from the mail inbox and wave it in surrender like a flag.

Chapter 4

ZACH DROPS me off at the train station the next morning. The whole car ride, he doesn't seem to suspect anything different about the way I'm acting. But I *feel* different. Something about me has definitely changed since yesterday.

I wear my usual go-to denim skirt with a tucked-in V-neck tee and my gladiator sandals. But as Zach drives, I consult the mirror for any wayward curls. The early morning humidity has caused my shoulder-length hair to look extra puffy, so I pin up the sides and leave the back down. This new hairstyle makes my deep-set eyes and high cheekbones look even more pronounced somehow. I refresh my magenta lipstick and smooth down the coils of my side-swept bangs before I hop out of Zach's car.

Once I arrive on campus, I feel even more lost without my phone. How could Owen just leave me flapping in the wind, knowing he's got his phone and I don't have mine? For every text I'm missing from Skye, I'm cursing him out under my breath.

Skye is spending the summer at her drama-loving relatives' house in Atlanta, so she probably has tons of juicy updates for me by now.

I take wider strides across campus. The sooner I start my search, the sooner I'll meet Owen—er, get my phone back. He better show at the library *first thing* with my phone (and explanations). I was too pissed off last night to call him back for details. Instead, I'd emailed Skye, letting her know I was offline without giving much more info. That was all the headspace I could give to the situation, considering all the homework I brought home last night. And then I'd fallen asleep with my lights on.

I'm greeted by stately archways, ornate iron gates, and centuries-old buildings covered in ivy as I make my way over grassy knolls and around Frisbee-tossing students.

When I get to the same section in the library where I met Owen yesterday, I'm annoyed. There's no sign of him.

I drag my busted feelings to Grant Writing class, still phoneless. Before everyone else shows, Professor Abdullah takes ten minutes with me to critique the proposal I've started writing for Walk Me Home funding. I show her the books I've picked up at the library, and she bookmarks a few proposals I can model mine on. After our discussion, I feel like I have a solid plan B and C in case I don't win that grant money at the Gala. My professor seems to think I'm on the right track, too. She even calls me out during class. In a good way.

"For example, Zora's chosen focus is Appleton, New Jersey, because of the connection she has to the city as her hometown."

Of course, this info piques It Girl's curiosity in me again. Right at the end of class, she and the whale-logo-wearing friend walk up to me. I'm so ready to shut her down. I need to get back to the library to look for Owen again.

"Wasn't Appleton recently in the news for their disproportionate number of misdemeanors?" she asks randomly.

It was a sample study in a tiny section of the city, but whatever.

"Not every person in Appleton is intimately familiar with the back of a squad car," I tell her.

"Zora Emerson?" I turn around to see a campus officer in the classroom doorway. "I'm Officer Kirkwood. Do you have a moment to discuss yesterday's events?"

I might as well be in a dentist's chair for all the discomfort I feel right now. In any case, It Girl's voice is as piercing as a tooth drill.

"My, my, how awkward is this?"

Everyone has paused in their book gathering and has their eyes glued on me, or at least that's how it feels.

I've seen this particular cop before. He always gives me a slight nod when he sees me in passing. I can't get over how much he reminds me of my uncle Roland—the heavy eyelids, the ample forehead.

I will not be shamed. I refuse. Why is he here talking to me rather than His Holy Majesty in Honor?

"Have you reached out to Owen Whittelsey?" I ask. "He's the one who has my phone."

My words suck the air out of the room for a few seconds before it comes whooshing back, blowing eavesdroppers' minds.

Okay, so maybe I shouldn't have name-dropped. And, okay, I'll admit that a large part of my flexing is an attempt to save face.

But It Girl and Whale Logo Guy each raise an eyebrow and loiter to watch my exchange with the officer. They might as well be munching on popcorn right now.

"We can discuss this at the station and include the other party. I'm here to help resolve this situation," says Uncle-Officer.

This time I *know* all eyes are on me as I take what appears to be a perp walk to the police station. I'm sure they expect nothing less.

"Prince Owen of Landerel is here under VIP protection, and his privacy is of the utmost importance to the university," explains Uncle-Officer on our walk to the campus police station. "Just be aware that during those times he can't be located, his security can track him to his phone."

I nod.

"I understand your family's concern, so I'll be sure this is settled quickly," he says.

Aha. Ma's Amen Circuit on 100. I instantly feel more at ease.

"The university won't keep a record of this incident, unless you file a report," Uncle-Officer says. "If you'd like, you can exchange contact information with Prince Owen, in the event you discover something wrong with your phone."

I nod.

The same Men in Black from last night are waiting for us at the police station. Officer Kirkwood ushers us to a private room.

"Is Ms. Emerson's phone present?" Uncle-Officer asks the Men in Black as soon as he closes the door.

As if on cue, the prince himself walks in, visibly upset at his security people. His face softens the second we lock eyes.

Owen looks way different than I expected. Far from the lanky kid of four years ago, he is lean but muscular. His angular face is dotted with a few freckles, and poking out from his vintage baseball cap are strands of ginger hair. His entire vibe is not at all stuffy, but approachable. Relatable. Cool, even. He looks like he'd feel right at home either traveling by subway *or* by yacht. And I can't stand myself for noticing all these details in the span of seconds.

"Zora, I'm sorry," he says, looking right at me. "I didn't mean for this to happen."

"But it *did* happen," I mumble under my breath as I snatch my cell phone he's handing me. I just want to go home.

"Is there anything I can do to make things right?" he asks, searching my face.

"Oh, so *now* you want to make things right?" I fume, loud and clear this time. "Not *before* you have security show up at my home, or *before* you decide not to show up at the library, or—oh yeah, before I get a police escort from my class?"

"I am so sorry you went through that," Owen says, sounding truly regretful.

"You know, for all your talk about the burdens of being privileged, you sure know how to use that privilege to get yours."

Owen looks at me pleadingly. "Please know that my security went to your house without my knowledge," he says quietly. "I would never have asked them to do that."

Even though I'm relieved to hear this, it's all too much to process right now.

"Well, you need to get on the same page with them, because what they did was intrusive," I say.

"My deepest apologies to your family," says Owen. "It's my fault for not being forthcoming with my security team. I will keep them better informed in the future. If I may have the honor to see you again, things will be different."

He wants to see me again?

I resist this distraction and command myself to hold firm. Refusing to acknowledge Owen any further, I thank Uncle-Officer and blow right past Owen out the door. I keep going, speed walking across campus, until I reach the train station so I can head home. At some point, *Prince* Owen gives up on following me with apologies. I can't remember exactly where.

Chapter 5

IT'S A sweet reunion with my phone! But I'm not going to front. On that train ride home, I Google the heck out of Owen.

Oh, the images. And the stories.

That Owen is a busy prince. Travel, parties, girls. So many girls. No wonder I got that angry phone call on his cell yesterday; I'm surprised there weren't more. The Landerelian rumor mill has him linked to actresses, singers—you name it. And to back up the claims, they have the pictures of him hanging out with them. At the beach. On party buses. In selfies.

But there's only one photo of him that I wish I could unsee— Owen with It Girl. Unlike the pics of him hanging out with girls on the town, they're together at what appears to be a formal, even royal, event. I spend more time than I want to admit studying exactly how they're standing next to each other. *Prince Owen and Kelsey Reston at the Queen's Annual Garden Party honoring veterans,* the caption reads. So It Girl's name is Kelsey. How does she even know Owen?

But what do I care?

I close out the window and I scroll through my messages. One missed call from Daddy. And only one text from Skye? I crack a smile watching the short "Hi, Zora!" animation she created with her young cousin Kyree.

The phone rings. It's my dad. Even if I didn't have the choice yesterday, he'll find it suspicious and even rude if I send him to voicemail a second time in as many days.

"Hi, Daddy," I answer, even though this is the last thing I need right now. I usually have to be mentally prepared to talk to my dad, but he's even tougher to tolerate if he's upset and lecturing me about not staying in touch. Better to avoid that scene by picking up his call now.

"I was expecting a call back from you, Zora."

"I know, and I'm sorry. The past few days have been unpredictable. I was juggling a few things at once." I do *not* want to explain a cell mix-up with a crown prince to my father.

"You know you still have a daddy. Or are you confusing me with that Artificial Intelligence robot John?" he asks facetiously. "You know, no matter how real they look, AI will never replace a human."

"That's not nice, Daddy, and you know that." I shake my head and try not to laugh . . . loud enough for him to hear. I don't want to encourage him. My dad knows I share his wicked sense of humor. It's not something I'm always proud of.

He, on the other hand, doesn't hide his laughter.

"It may not be nice, but I see you didn't say it's *wrong*." He barely gets these words out before he whoops and cackles again.

"I'm on the train and about to go in a tunnel soon, Daddy. How are you? Is everything all right?"

"I'm fine, princess, it's you I'm calling about. I saw your name mentioned in the *Appleton Weekly* for this fancy gala happening next week. Congratulations, sweetheart!"

"Aw, thank you, Daddy."

I hadn't told my dad about the Gala, because over the years, he hasn't taken much interest in my community projects beyond the flat "that's nice" response. I get the sense that he'd rather I go into a more exciting field. "Thankless jobs," as he calls them, are for invisible people, and my dad is all about staying visible.

"Go on to your do-gooding—we'll talk more about it when you call me back," he says. "You have a good day and keep making your human daddy proud."

That is so sweet of him. Well, aside from the insult to John. But I can't believe I actually got a small boost from talking to Daddy.

There's one more person I need to talk to. As soon as I'm home and up in my room, I call Skye.

"Zora, how you gonna call me during KATUNI? You know today is the elimination round," Skye says in one breath the moment she picks up my call.

I didn't forget about Skye's Thursday-afternoon rule. Watching Kenyan animators compete is her weekly obsess—er, ritual.

Not two months ago, as we had sat at a coffee shop mapping out our summer class schedules, she'd reminded me, "Don't forget to do something for fun, too, Zora. Look at it as your treat for working hard all week."

Now I tease, "Aw, come on, didn't you miss me?"

"Hmmph. You're lucky this is my second time watching it. The first time around, Kyree asked too many questions."

"Why are you treating that boy like your intern?" I ask, while removing the dug-in pins from my big hair and massaging my scalp.

"He's only ten and he's cooler than I am. He has *me* looking like the auntie and I'm barely seventeen. It just ain't right."

The girl is a perfectionist and believes she can do everything— from robotics to dance moves—better than most people. If I know Skye, she won't leave Atlanta until she's mastered every new concept she comes across. This can be a good thing because she mostly uses her competitive edge to benefit others. This means I won't have a choice in the matter: I'll be learning every animation technique, robotics idea, and dance move from her the minute she gets back to Jersey. And she can't come back soon enough. Her program runs through mid-August, so that means at least five more weeks before we get back together to map out our Appleton High senior year goals.

"You knew who you were dealing with when you flew down there," I remind her. "Atlanta is the new New York City."

"Yes," she whisper-screams in exaggerated shock. Knowing Skye, she's already unraveling her silk headscarf by now. After so many sleepovers over the years, I've gotten used to Skye's constant hair checks for any dents. If she sleeps on her signature blown-out do in some wacky way, she can pin it down flat in the morning, but I know she'd rather retie her headscarf a million times to try to avoid it. I imagine her retying her scarf just as quickly as she untied it. "Back in elementary school when I used to come down to Atlanta, saying you're from New York or New Jersey used to get you instant respect. Nowadays they expect *us* to bow down and kiss *their* ring. It's incredible."

"Funny you should mention bowing and ring kissing . . . I have something to tell you."

As I spill all the tea on my brush with Prince Owen of Landerel, Skye gasps, squeals, shouts, and emphatically orders me to shut up, several times. And then—complete silence.

Ring.

I haven't noticed Skye had literally hung up in shock.

"Hello?" I answer.

"Woo!" Skye still sounds shook. "I just had to let that sink in. But I'm good now."

"Good."

"I think . . ."

"Skye?"

Ring.

"Whew! This is way too much, but I'm glad you told me."

"You're the only one who knows, so please keep it to yourself."

"Of course," she says.

I hear a beep. I pull my ear from the phone to see a text from a number I don't recognize.

> *Hi, Zora. This is Owen. I hope you don't mind my reaching out to you here. My preference would be to call you, but if you rather I text or not contact you at all, I completely understand. I want to express my deep regrets for what transpired. I am sorry. You did not deserve that.*

"Zora?" Skye asks, and I realize she's been waiting on the line. I return to our call and tell her about the text I just got.

"Wait. What?" Skye says. "Okay, now listen to me carefully. Prince or no prince, if you feel you've been treated unfairly, you don't have to answer his texts."

"It's not even that, it's—" My voice trails off and gets small.

"You like him." Skye's words have that "aha!" tone to them. "My best friend has a royal crush on the prince of Landerel."

"Huh? I wouldn't say that." *Then why am I smizing? And remembering how cute he looked in that maroon baseball cap today?* "But I admit I kinda had a real nice time talking to him."

"And you could see hanging out with him again, and getting to know him better." Skye nails it.

"Well . . ." is all I'll give her.

"Why won't you admit it, though?" Skye asks.

"It's silly. I'm not trying to get involved with anything

46

distracting while I'm in this tough program." I pick at the loose threads on my pillowcase's embroidery. It's taken a few paychecks from my old ice cream parlor job, but I'm managing to redecorate my room with stuff I buy entirely from local and online small businesses. At this point—aside from the furniture—I can hardly pick out one thing my mom bought.

"Zora, you're human. You can't help what you're feeling. And you can't be about grant writing or the Walk Me Home program all the time."

I'm quiet, because I don't have an answer to her refrain about not being a workaholic. It's not like Skye doesn't go hard for what she wants, too.

"Oh, I didn't even ask you about your presentation," I remember.

"No, don't worry about it. It went fine. I'll tell you later. I'm going back to my show now."

"Wait, one last thing! I never heard the end of that story from two days ago—did Kyree really end up sleeping at the school overnight?"

"Yes, my aunt and uncle fixed him good. I don't think he'll try that stunt again anytime soon," she laughs.

I wake up the next morning knowing just what I should do, and it doesn't involve Halstead University, or Prince Owen (I didn't answer his first text, and he sent two more—both of which I avoided reading). I'm going to visit Anaya and the other kids from the Walk Me Home program again. They'll be so excited that I was able to visit twice in one week.

"Don't you have one class later today?" My mom pokes her head in my room before she heads to work. My stepdad is already solving IT emergencies at his job, and Zach is no doubt still asleep after his late-night shift for his EMT internship.

"It's more of a study hall," I explain. "The professor already gave us the syllabus and he expects us to keep pace on our own."

It's only half a lie. My community organizing class is more freestyle than the others, but we are still expected to attend the lectures. I still haven't made up my mind whether I'll go in. I just don't want to deal.

"You're back!" says Ms. Nelson when she sees me. She's carrying a box full of supplies to the shed tucked under the oak tree at the edge of the playground.

"Hi, Ms. Nelson."

I walk over and give her the hug she deserved when I saw her on Wednesday. If it weren't for Ms. Nelson's generosity, this summer camp would not have happened.

Ms. Nelson continues our conversation as if she saw me just a minute ago.

"Did I tell you I met a few of the students who go to Halstead U-ni-ver-si-ty," she overly enunciates each syllable again. "Yes, ma'am. A group came down last week to teach my grandson and other kids to swim."

I become fixated with the duct tape in her supply box and imagine sealing Ms. Nelson's lips with it. I'd rather talk about anything but Halstead U.

I take her supply box and she holds the shed door open as I enter.

"Right there is fine." Ms. Nelson points to a cleared-out wooden shelf. Once we're outside, she detains me again with her long story.

She leans back against the tall boulder next to the shed, a cozy perch for her extended rambling.

"Mm-hmm. Started a swim program for our youth last year all by themselves, they did. They got all types of national press for it, too. Our own Media Club produced a montage of all the news segments that aired coverage. It was on NBC, ABC, CBS, and I'm not just talking local news. Remember?"

I don't want to remember.

"But"—she pauses for a beat—"regardless of whether they started the swim program to be called heroes, or even just to see how our hair reacts to water, those generous kids still dedicated their time to help others less fortunate."

Her words are jabbing me in the ego. Halstead students aren't the only ones who can help this community. I still have the chance to do my part. Campus gossip isn't worth risking my mission.

"If you don't need any more help, I really should be going to class," I hear myself say. "I'll just pop in to say a quick hi to the kids."

I check the time on my phone. I can still make my noon class if I leave soon.

"Go, go!" Ms. Nelson puts up a threatening finger. "Don't you go up there and show those folks you operate on Black People Time. Stay prompt!" Her cowlick is trembling again. "And if you try jaywalking up *there* like you do down here, they'll *lock you up*. They are not gonna give you as many chances to mess up as they give their own. You get my meaning?"

"Yes, Ms. Nelson," I say over my shoulder. I stop into the main building to give a few hugs to the kids, and then I'm on my way.

On the train, I give myself a different kind of pep talk. The facts are, I had a wack first week. I'm used to planning, predicting events, and having more control. But hey, occasional chaos gonna chaos.

By the time I make it through an uneventful class and pack up my things to head off campus, I'm feeling relieved enough to cheer. I'm glad I didn't stay away from school. Nothing nutty happened. Plus, I didn't see a trace of—eye roll—the *prince*.

This is good.

While waiting on the Halstead U platform for the train, grateful for my drama-free day, my phone rings.

I don't recognize the number, but I'm in a good mood, so I answer anyway.

"Hello, is this Zora Emerson?"

The guy's voice isn't familiar, but he sounds like someone my age.

"Yes?"

"I'm Finn Burlington, a reporter with Halstead's journalism summer program, and I'd like to interview you for a story we're working on about your run-in with Prince Owen of Landerel."

That feeling when you think you're home free and trouble literally comes calling? Yeah, it pretty much sucks.

Chapter 6

"ZORA, ARE you there?" the caller's voice pipes into my ear. Actually, it's more onto my cheek, because that's how low my phone slides, thanks to a sudden onslaught of stress sweat and shock-induced weakened grip.

I close my mouth before a truck drives through it. After a deep inhale of suburban train station air, I recover the phone.

"Wha-what kind of story?" I don't care to hear the answer, which makes my question instantly ironic.

"The situation between you and Prince Owen," he says as if he's already tired of me playing dumb.

I swallow to keep my stomach from coming up with this morning's bagel. I've hardly had time to process this . . . non-thing between me and Owen and we're already a public discussion.

My silence prompts the reporter kid to expound, unwittingly digging his hole deeper.

"A journalism student from your Grant Writing class witnessed you being led into the campus police station because of some mix-up with Prince Owen's phone. We've deemed that newsworthy," he says.

"Oh," I realize aloud. "I didn't know anyone followed us."

I do a mental rewind to that humiliating moment and search for details I may have overlooked. Did I miss the fact that someone from class tailed us to the station?

Our conversation pauses then, because it would be decidedly un-Halstead of either one of us to shout over the screeching brakes of the arriving train. I've been a summer program student here long enough to know that Halstead Hopefuls work hard to out-Halstead the institution's actual full-time students.

I board the train in a daze and make a beeline to a seat. No one even dares outpace me to it. But I am vaguely aware of passengers stepping out of my path. And I hear an elderly woman complain to a fellow passenger, "What kind of *putz* doctor sends out a patient with dilated eyes?" Great. Now I have people confusing my dazed expression with vision impairment.

That's a new one. But I'll just have to lay that one down. I have more pressing issues keeping me awake in my daydream at the moment. I'm still coming up with no recollection of someone shadowing me to the station.

"Do journalism students generally stalk people around campus?" I ask the reporter on the phone. I decide to stay on the offensive.

The reporter lets out a sheepish chuckle, and then, "Let me

backtrack here. That is not the type of journalism I mean to project. I want to be factual, and I'm afraid I haven't been."

Somehow, I've frazzled the reporter without even meaning to. I guess he's taking my comment as a whistle blow to his journalistic integrity. I'm just trying to avoid his questions, but it's having a rattling effect on him.

"A journalism student in your class witnessed the campus police confirm your possession of Prince Owen's phone, so of course we deemed that newsworthy," he rephrases. I can hear him choose his words carefully, and he speaks with a hint of respect that was missing before.

What a relief. No one followed me after all.

"Oh, *now* that makes sense," I say, getting a feel for the upper hand and kind of enjoying it.

"Let me also say this story will not be posted or made public. The university is careful about the prince maintaining his privacy. What you tell me will go in a story we're preparing for in-class use only."

The farther the train pulls away from the Halstead campus, the less bent I am to play the Halstead Hopeful role. This is an interesting turn of events.

"What do you need to know?"

"We'd love your response to Prince Owen's quote. He was kind enough to give us a brief interview to set the record straight."

I cross my legs at the ankles, then quickly uncross them to fidget in my seat before crossing them again. The man in the oversized suit sitting next to me gets up and exits, so I slide over to his window seat for more privacy. I turn my back to everything and tuck in closer to the window. Thankfully, the reporter doesn't pick up on how frazzled I'm suddenly feeling.

"I'm listening," I say evenly.

"Quote, 'This was an innocent mix-up that unfortunately led to a humiliating event for Ms. Emerson. It was simply a case of what happens when two students are immersed in their studies and look-alike phones inadvertently get swapped. I had Ms. Emerson's phone, but I did not know her name or identity. I am sorry for the embarrassment that this no-fault occurrence has visited on Ms. Emerson, and I would do anything to have this lens of scrutiny look away from her. She was exceptionally graceful in cooperating with officials and assisting in this situation's resolution.' End quote."

I breathe normally and lean back in my seat for the first time.

Outside the window, there are more electric poles than trees, and more city buses than fancy coaches. We are now a world away from Halstead University, and it seems like layers of expectations are peeling away. Even the passengers shift from a cautious, reserved demeanor to a more relaxed, unrehearsed one. A couple in their twenties hold an animated conversation in Spanish, the conductor exits his hidden compartment to chat with a dude I recognize from my light-rail stop. A girl no older than Anaya smacks her gum as she speaks to her two moms, her little hands and wiry neck flowing to the rhythm of her storytelling. I feel safe and at home. I don't have to play a role for this Halstead audience of one.

"We're about to go through a tunnel. I will lose you, so I'll need to hang up now," I say.

"Do you have anything you'd like to add to the story?"

I don't owe this reporter anything, especially anything I'm uncomfortable doing. *It's half past woman o'clock!* is what my mom would say to me with a finger snap if she were here.

"No. But thank you for contacting me."

Cell service out.

"An innocent mix-up" Owen called it. "Graceful" he called me.

Later that evening, after faking my way through dinner with my mom, stepdad, and brother ("No, really, everything's going *just* fine!"), I lay my head on my pillow imagining these words spoken in Owen's Landerelian accent. No doubt he delivered it with his effortless charm and a casual-cool manner. I bet he had the reporter eating out of his hand in no time.

I'm glad Owen has spoken to the "press," because there is no way I will. The thought of being contacted by a student reporter for a response is wild, and kind of funny. *Me, the topic of a breaking news story?* My high school newspaper barely wants to interview me about registering senior citizens to vote, and now I have to face the fact that I may be the talk of the summer program. I hope not.

An hour later, I am still playing out the different scenarios of Owen's interview in my head when I rethink Owen's statement of apology. He's used to this kind of scrutiny, so a need for that sort of statement must come up all the time. I think of all those girls I saw him with in photos online. I bet he mumbles things like "no-fault occurrence" and "exceptionally graceful" in his sleep. Wherever he winds up for college, I'm sure he'll major in talking game. He probably *wasn't* actually focused on getting the attention off of me. I'm sure he's just doing his usual PR spin to try to save face. That's why I can't read his texts until I'm thinking clearly.

I'm still thinking about Owen, somewhere in the middle of a pros and cons analysis, when I finally drift off to sleep.

In the morning, though, the first thing I do is finally read his texts.

> *Hello again. I will take your silence to mean I should not call you. Very well. This is my attempt to text you a sincere apology and a promise. Please know I will correct any misconceptions surrounding the incident. Zora, I'm terribly sorry.*

There go the butterflies fluttering in my stomach again. *Ugh. What is it about this guy that's got me in my feelings?*

Next:

> *Hi, sorry to disturb you with another text message. You should be aware that a student reporter reached out to me, and I have spoken to him. I wanted to inform you in case he contacts you. I hope you're well.*

I can sense the regret stitched into his every text. Owen has it all covered—the sincerity, humility . . . Just about the only thing missing from his apologies is the "please, baby, please." But I suppose royalty don't get down like that. I wouldn't be surprised if he's already broken some type of protocol for getting way too close to "please, baby, please" than folks of his pedigree are allowed.

Since I'm already down the rabbit hole, I Google Owen some more.

Yup. He's always surrounded by girls, laughing and going to parties. He *does* seem like someone I should catch a fast train ride away from. A couple of compliments from him in the middle of a press statement—and some earnest texts—shouldn't change how I feel.

But this—the re-Googling—isn't a good sign. He's apologized. The student journalist is satisfied with his response. The whole thing is over. What more am I looking for? What am I hoping for? And how did I come to be in this position that I'm ghosting a prince?

I need to clear my head, and there is only one place I know of where I can do that. Saturday morning at my favorite bookstore cannot have come at a better time.

Ingrum's Books is a beloved bookstore decorated to look like an old library. There are those wooden cabinets with the tiny drawers, retro index cards remixed into store signage, and the bookshelves are even the skeletal, look-through ones. The bookstore sits in an outdoor shopping plaza across from a plaza with a fountain.

It's only about eleven miles from Appleton, but it takes me two buses to get there. The foot traffic is still light when I walk into the store. It's barely 10:00 a.m.

"Hey there," the friendly bookseller greets me in her familiar way.

"Good morning, Eliana." I smile back. "Please tell me the couch is still free."

"This time you beat him to it. He hasn't been in yet."

"It's my lucky day!"

"I'm happy for you," says Eliana, laughing.

"If anyone asks, I'm off duty today," I tell her.

It's my own fault when people confuse me for an employee here. I have the bad habit of inserting myself in other people's conversations, then showing them how to use the book request kiosk, pointing them to the nearest bathroom, or telling them when story time begins. Over the years, I've become friendly with the booksellers, too, which makes it even more confusing whenever folks find out I don't work here.

I'm just a few paces away from the very vacant sweet spot in the back reading nook (the one flooded with sunlight, and with outlets within arm's reach), but I find myself taking a detour instead. It means the bookish middle-aged man I have a friendly battle with for the reading nook may beat me to it today, but I don't care.

I hook a left and head toward a sign that lures me over. I've never been interested in perusing these shelves before. The travel section is not my usual go-to. Without admitting my objective to myself, I scan the spines of the books listed in alphabetical order by destination, until I land on "L" for "Landerel."

I choose the book with the most skimmable format and the most vivid photography.

Truth be told, these pages are structured for a child's understanding of geography, but that's what I appreciate about it. A few details stand out right away.

Landerel's Population: Eight million.

Man, that's like the size of New York City.

Landmass: Comparable to the State of Virginia.

I can totally picture that.

Language: English.

Spoken in the cutest accent.

Current Monarchy:

There it is. A picture of Owen's family.

It's a picture my mom would recognize now that she's on round-the-clock royal wedding watch. This is from the wedding of the eldest son, Lionel. He and his bejeweled wife are waving to the adoring masses from a festooned balcony, flanked by a crowd of well-dressed people. *The royal family in happier times*, the caption reads.

Did I miss something? I turn back several pages until I see it: images from a funeral. Throngs of mourners line the streets in pouring rain. This was nine years ago, before their Olympic-hosting moment on the international stage.

I flip back another page and I'm face-to-face with the deceased. It's a picture of a smiling teenage girl who looks like the female version of Owen. His ginger hair and defined jawline stand out on him as much as they do on this girl. The caption identifies her as Emily Whittelsey, the only daughter of Queen Mildred and Prince Consort Victor.

Owen's sister.

I continue reading and learn that she died at the age of fifteen, when Owen was just eight years old. Apparently, when she was younger, a royal biographer dubbed her the "redheaded stepchild." Sadly, the unfortunate moniker stuck. The royal spokesperson's act of holding the name up as a no-no had the opposite effect. The mean moniker found a home among the trolls for safekeeping. It looks like besides Owen, Emily was the only family member with that coloring. And she was considered chubby. The body shaming, the merciless trolling, the unflattering memes everywhere all threw her down a self-destructive path that ultimately led to her tragic death. Her body was found off a cliff in a mountain range along the southern coast of Landerel. It's still unclear whether she tumbled or jumped, but the high level of alcohol in her system pointed to an accidental death. Either way, it was a tragic, needless end to a short life.

I didn't expect to be moved like this. Not by a royal family. Here in an exclusive world that seems as far removed as possible from the average human experience, there is a sadness that humbles me. Emily is described as a "sensitive soul" who yearned to be loved and accepted. Identified as one constant source of Emily's happiness in life was her baby brother, Owen. It's tough to find a clear image of Owen. In any photos the two of them are in together, Owen's head is bowed in laughter next to his grinning sister despite the rest of the family having a more stoic look.

I go back to the "happier times" photo and pull the book closer to my face for the zoom-in effect. I think I see Owen. Behind a waving white-gloved hand, I can just make out the right side of his much younger face. The corner of his smile. Half an expression of joy. One twinkling eye.

"Yes, that is me right there," says a guy's voice behind me.

I snap the book shut and whip around to see Owen standing right there in the travel books aisle. He's holding a bouquet of bright, gorgeous flowers and extending it to me.

I'm so busted.

Chapter 7

MY ROYAL crush in the flesh.

"Hi, Zora," says Owen in a gentle tone. "I was hoping I would find you here. I remembered you said this is your favorite weekend-morning spot."

"Oh."

My breathing is shallow, like I've just climbed a flight of stairs. I still catch a heavenly whiff of the flowers and that alone makes this moment stink a lot less. As much as I want to act like I've forgotten Owen, I'm not going to convince him of this when I'm holding the Landerel travel guide in my hands. Owen's eyes dart down to the cover of the book I'm still clutching and the corner of his mouth curls up in restrained amusement.

Silence sits its baggage between us like a rude person hogging up two seats on the bus, and I don't know how to break it.

"These are for you," says Owen. The warm tone in his voice, the fragrant flowers . . . it's all not even close to what I expected when I came to this bookstore today.

He's wearing his vintage maroon baseball cap again. Aren't his countrymen fans of the game cricket? I guess the cap is his way of hiding his identity in public. I don't think Owen needs to worry about anyone outside of campus recognizing him. He's done a great job of staying hidden from the American spotlight, unlike his older brothers. I guess his family planned it that way.

I put back the book and accept the flowers. Not just because it's the most beautiful bouquet I've ever seen, but because I need something to do with my hands, other than hold on to the Landerel travel book.

Yes, every single stemmed perfection in this bouquet is living its best life. But thankfully, the flowers are exquisite without being over-the-top. It's a small, lightweight arrangement I can easily carry.

"Thank you," I say.

I finally turn my full attention to Owen. Being on the same side of a bookcase with him is nice. Really nice. He stands a few inches taller than me in a crisp button-up short-sleeve white shirt, khaki shorts, and tan loafers. Under the shadow of his cap, I can make out his flushed cheeks.

"I hope this isn't an intrusion on your private time. It's just that I want to properly apologize to you, face-to-face," he says. "I didn't get the chance the other day, and texting isn't the same."

"Okay," I say, looking into his hazel eyes.

He takes off his cap and holds it to his heart, just like a baseball player during the national anthem. I'm not sure if he is serious or not.

"Zora Emerson of New Jersey—"

"Appleton, New Jersey," I clarify teasingly.

"Zora Emerson of Appleton, New Jersey," he begins again. "I am solemnly sorry."

He sounds sincere. Maybe he really did mean everything he said in his texts. But is that a mischievous gleam in his eye?

"And if there's anything I can do to resolve matters any further . . ." he continues.

"No, I appreciate you speaking to that student reporter. That went a long way."

". . . or if there's anything I can do to answer your questions about Landerel or my family, I'll be happy to cover anything that book didn't address."

There it is. The real reason behind the twinkle in his eye.

"Oh, so we've skipped the humility and jumped straight into bragging rights. Wow, and in less time than a Landerelian sports car goes from zero to sixty," I call him out with a smirk on my face.

"No, I can assure you, you've got my humility," says Owen. He puts his cap back on. "Unanswered text messages have a particularly painful way of skewering the ego. But I'll take that. I'll say I even deserve that."

"That's better." I smile.

How is he so easy to talk to? I feel my hesitations get blurry in the face of his sincere demeanor.

"But," Owen says, his eyes twinkling again as he nods to the travel book, "I can be of service if you need to ascertain what features or even what blemishes I may or may not have on my face. Feel free to come in as close as you'd like to determine for yourself."

"Oh, so you saw me . . . zooming in."

"That I did." He takes a random book from the shelf, leafs through it, then holds his face within an inch of its open pages.

I shake my head and briefly cover my mouth to hide my grin.

"Okay, get it all out," I say. "But pack your toys because here come the Men in Black to get you."

Owen wipes the mischief off his face faster than you can say "God save the queen." He twists his neck this way and that way in search of the suits.

I can't hold in my laughter.

"I got you! The look on your face." I point at him like a child who's just tagged someone It.

He tries to regain his cool and stuffs one hand back in his front pocket.

"Well played, Zora."

Owen tips his cap without removing it. He is smiling with his whole face now, which makes him look all the more attractive. I hate that my heart is skipping like it's the hopscotch Olympics.

I take glimpses at him, to avoid all-out staring. Owen clearly doesn't believe in the same approach because I keep catching him staring at me. Like, now, he is staring a little too long.

"Let me guess. There are zero Black friends in your social circle," I joke, hoping to snap him out of it.

It's better than letting him believe I consider his fascination with my appearance kind of flattering. But he keeps looking at me like I'm calling out the lottery numbers he's got on his ticket.

"Pardon my rudeness. I mean no offense."

The warmth is back in his voice, which of course turns up the heat between us. Why does he do that? Could he know what that does to a girl who already thinks he's cute, easy to talk to, and fun to be around?

What does Owen think this thing between us is anyway? If it can even be called a *thing*. Picture me hanging out with the aristocracy, trying to figure out why they speak like their jaws are wired shut. And let's not begin to wonder what they'd think about me. Hanging out in Owen's world would be unreal. I have an awkward enough relationship with the Halstead University wannabes every day.

The hesitations start to creep back in, and Owen can read it on my face.

"What's the problem, something in my nose?" He uses his cap to cover his nose as he pretends to check for himself.

I'm not sure if Owen is back to teasing banter or not. Surely he jests, right? He can't be serious, so I'd be a fool to consider what I may or may not be feeling for him.

I'm too lost in my thoughts to react. Owen's smile fades a bit, and his eyes are more piercing now, like he wants to capture my full attention. He fidgets with his cap.

"Zora, if I may—"

Suddenly, two stately black cars pull up outside the bookstore. Looks like the official Men-in-Black-mobile. Owen apologizes to me one last time and rushes outside. He makes himself known to the car before anyone can step out.

I watch him say something to the driver. And then he turns around and rushes back into the bookstore and finds me.

"I'd like to show you something," he says. "Can you meet me Monday at the passageway outside Hurston Hall?"

In spite of it all, I know I won't give any other answer. "Yes." I smile.

"What time works for you?"

"Noon," I tell him without wiping the smile off my face.

"Brilliant." He smiles back. "See you then."

He rushes back outside and hops into the waiting black car, and the sleek fleet carries him away.

Chapter 8

THE SWEET perfume of the flowers Owen gave me yesterday (peonies, I learned when I looked them up online) is doing a great job keeping my Sunday blues away. My mom hasn't been in my room yet, but I overheard her wondering if the heavenly scent wafting into the hallway was coming from her unopened box of incense. "That's some powerful stuff," she said at the time.

"Are you daydreaming?" Skye looks like she's about to reach through the video chat screen and slap me awake. I'm on my bed, sharing space with more than a few crumpled paper balls and a notebook filled with pages of scribbled notes.

"Sorry, I was just wondering if there's a way you can beef up the part where you talk about your purpose," I tell her. Skye's just read her speech to me and I'm helping her smooth it out. Funny how we both have a major event to attend. Mine isn't a sure thing. I get an honorable mention but no guaranteed award—or money. Skye is being honored for her advanced work in robotics. She entered a contest months ago, and thanks to her high-scoring sophisticated design, she gets to show off her creation at a cool science center.

"I'm not changing that part again," Skye whines, and I watch her drop her head, which lands with a thud on her desk like a felled tree. The top of her headscarf fills the screen, and I find myself mesmerized by the blue-and-gold hieroglyphics print.

I'd like to stay on with her, because it's fun and it keeps my mind off Owen. I don't tell her about my urge to call him. Or about the fact that I am buzzing wondering what he wants to show me tomorrow.

Skye is still head down. We both should have finalized our acceptance speeches by yesterday. We have that specific summer goals schedule we put together months ago. It isn't too realistic, but it's still a good way to stay on task. Come fall, when we're elbow deep in college applications, we'll be too busy to organize every detail of our personal vs. school vs. career goals.

"Okay, it's time for a break." I let her off the hook.

She pops her head up whack-a-mole style, suddenly full of energy. I shake my head at her.

Since middle school, this is how it's been between me and Skye. We hold strategy meetings like we're on some workplace TV drama until one of us is too tired to go on. We used to compete against each other, up until some point in seventh grade, when we finally realized we were on the same team. It helped that we became interested in two very different fields. I think it was about the time we realized talking to each other about our dreams and plans somehow helped make them come true. Like workout buddies, we push each other, keep tabs on our progress, hold each other accountable. These strategy rituals have led to some pretty amazing results.

I hear the timer on the oven go off.

"The brownies are ready." I hop to my feet, laptop in hand. "Let's head to the kitchen."

"Who are you bribing or buttering up this time?" Skye asks.

Skye knows all my tricks. She's watched me buy or whip up sweet treats for my volunteers and would-be volunteers. Free food is the next best incentive to money. It's the quickest way to get people to sign up, donate, pitch in, whatever. I've learned so much about the power of baking. And even though people like Skye figure out the treats come with a catch, my strategy keeps on reeling them in.

"I'm not bribing anyone. At least not this time," I say. "Just making a treat for the kids at camp."

I carefully pull out the hot tray, leave it on the stovetop to cool down for a few minutes, and take a seat at the kitchen island to finish my chat with Skye.

"Aaay!" Zach walks in with a skip in his step. He's wearing his blue EMT uniform, all ready for his night shift. "Something smells good!"

"Don't touch—they're for the kids," I warn him. "Skye, don't you just love his timing?"

"Where's Skye?" Zach hovers over my brownies and doesn't seem interested in my answer.

"She's on video chat because she's in Atlanta for the summer."

That somehow captures Zach's interest. He makes his way to my laptop.

"A to the T to the L, whaddup, fam?"

A strange squeak-grunt combo is the only response heard, but we can't be sure it came from Skye because she's no longer on-screen.

"Yo, Skye, we can't see you," says Zach.

"This is *my* phone call and you come here talking about 'we,'" I chastise him. "Skye, you there?"

I almost get vertigo looking at the shaky footage of her ceiling. Is this call suddenly on mute?

Maybe she can't hear us.

"Did you drop the phone or something, fam?" asks Zach, chuckling.

"That's so strange." I'm starting to worry. I try one last time. "Skye, please answer."

"I'm right here!" She's back on the phone, but this time without her headscarf. And is that pale pink gloss popping on her lips?

"There she is." Zach leans his forearm on my shoulder and bends over for a closer look.

"Ouch!" I shrug his arm off.

He pulls up a stool and sits next to me. "Skye, I might be heading to Atlanta for a week this month. A medical resident at my job is heading to a Morehouse alumni event and he wants to introduce me to a few people there," he says.

"Oh, that sounds cool." Skye bats her eyelashes.

"Yeah, that sounds like it could lead to a good opportunity," I tell Zach.

"I mean, I'm just lucky these dudes want to let a little homie tag along," he says.

Skye keeps the fluttering eyelashes thing going. It kinda looks like she's nervous, but I can't call it. Something is definitely off.

Zach notices it, too. "Hey, Lady Skye, if you have something in your eye, make sure you flush that out with cool water." He's dropped his swag and is in medical mode. Show him an open sore, a cut wound, or even a toilet full of barf and Zach won't be able to look away. People tell him he'd be perfect in the ER, the place where stomach-churning gross scenes play on repeat.

"Last week on my morning run, a gnat flew right into my eye," he says.

"Oh yeah, that was wild. I remember how irritated your eye was for, like, days," I say.

"It was too tiny to get out for hours." He nods his head. "Hours."

I notice Skye has disappeared again.

Zach shouts louder in case she's within the vicinity of her phone.

"I'll let you go, but during my visit, if I have a chance to say hi, I'll get your contact info from Zora."

"Cool. All right." We hear Skye, but don't see her.

"Other than that, you good down there?" Zach asks as he hops off the stool and stretches his tattooed arms to the ceiling.

"Uh, yeah, no issues." Skye's voice is clear, though she's still hidden.

"Good." Zach nods. "Be easy, kid."

Once Zach leaves the area and heads out the front door, Skye is back in view.

"What was that all about?" I ask her.

"Stupid fake eyelash got stuck in my eye." She's still picking at her left eye.

"Since when do you wear false eyelashes? And why would you be putting them on on a random night? You going back out?"

Skye looks embarrassed.

"Is this the dress rehearsal for your event? Ooh, maybe I should play with a different look, too."

"It's Zach, okay? Geesh, woman, does a neon sign have to fall on top of your head?"

My *brother*?

"Zach? Wait. When did this happen?"

Ever since middle school, Skye and Zach have been indifferent to each other, at most. Like ships in the night, they passed by each other unnoticed playdate after playdate, sleepover after sleepover, study session after study session.

"Ignore me. I'll get over it."

"I'm sure you will, but I'm just curious where this is all coming from?" I ask.

"Ever since he went off to college and got ambition, it's been a good look on him," says Skye.

"Yeah, Ma never thought he'd get there. She was worried Daddy got his grips on him too good for there to be any hope."

"Coming through scoring high marks on college biology exams and whatnot." Skye shakes her head. "Messing me all up."

"This is wild. I wouldn't ever have guessed it." I lean in as close to the screen as possible before springing back. My animated movements land swaying hair strands in my wide-open mouth.

"That's pretty accurate." Skye is still annoyed by my cluelessness. "You sure wouldn't have."

"And imagine if he *does* transfer to U of A. You guys will overlap for two years on the same campus," I say. It's not something I'm hoping for or against, but the thought comes to mind.

"Let's move on and pretend I didn't just make a fool of myself," Skye says. "Can we change the subject?"

"Okay, but just know that Zach couldn't care less about false eyelashes. If you're gonna risk poking out your eyeball again, do it for yourself, not for Zach or any other guy."

I bat one of my eyelashes at warp speed, and Skye can't help but laugh. It's a beautiful sound that lets me know she'll survive this crush . . . and hopefully move on from it.

"Surprise me," I tell Daddy. "I'll stay out here and grab a table."

He enters Jefferson's Ice Cream and heads to the counter with the same spring in his step Zach had earlier tonight.

Daddy's been taking me out on ice cream dates since I was a little girl. It's our way of having alone time. He could be doing this just for old times' sake, or he could want something. I'm not sure if I can let down my guard yet.

Since he picked me up a half hour ago, we've just been having small talk about the breezy, cooler weather, like friendly neighbors on an apartment building elevator ride. Now I'm sitting at a tiny mosaic-top table watching the fireflies blink, enjoying the people watching from my sidewalk table, but wondering what it is Daddy wants to speak to me about.

"I got your favorite," he says when he returns with an ice cream sandwich.

"Thank you." I smile but don't tell him this hasn't been my favorite since I was in middle school.

"Consider this a mini celebration for your honor at Friday's Gala."

I always had the sense Daddy didn't care too much for my community service impulses. Years ago, he caught me donating the fancy leftover meals he brought us after his shift at the country club. He told me it wasn't a leftover, but a dish he'd made special for me and Zach. I felt horrible, yet confused by his anger.

"Aw, that's very sweet of you, Daddy." I pause and put my hand to my heart now. "I really appreciate that."

Of course if Ma were here, she'd be clenching her jaw and crossing her arms, thinking about how her countless daily thoughtful acts don't elicit half the outpouring of thanks from me and Zach. I still haven't figured out exactly why Zach and I do this. I think it has something to do with keeping the peace.

I take a tooth-tingling bite, and Daddy tells me about the grease fire his sous chef started in the restaurant kitchen at work today. No one can tell a story like my dad. When he's got the floor, he can hold court better than the NBA. I laugh at all his sound effects and vocal acrobatics.

"And then, WOO-HAH, the flames were taller than his high top fade—which, if you know Jayvon, is pretty tall. He's the dude we thought was six feet four until the day he came in with a haircut."

This is the most fun I've had with my dad in a while. Once my cackling has eased, I recommend an ointment Jayvon can use that worked for me the last time I got singed by the oven pulling out a batch of fresh-baked chocolate chip cookies.

Just like our earlier phone chat, this whole night is a pleasant surprise. We just kick it. It's so cool to sit in and have an easygoing conversation with him. That's why when he says what he says at the end of the night, I am completely thrown off guard.

"So, what time do I need to be ready for your grand Gala Friday?" he asks after he pulls up to my house. He's just turned down the music on his old-school hip-hop station, and the car idles like it's waiting on my answer, too.

I stare blankly at him because I honestly don't get it. I think this is a good time for Skye's neon sign to drop from the heavens and land on my head. We're double-parked, so I better think of something to say, quick.

"I'm assuming your parents are invited to attend with you?" he asks.

"Well, yeah, but no worries, Daddy." I try to sound as casual as possible. "You don't have to go out of your way. Mom is already coming."

"It's no trouble. That's my job! Listen, text me the info, and I'll meet you and your mom there!"

There you have it. The entire night's other shoe has finally dropped. And only after I gave up expecting it to. *Rookie mistake, Zora. Rookie mistake.*

Chapter 9

MONDAY MORNING can't go by fast enough. I check the time—on my phone, my laptop, the classroom walls—so often that the minutes crawl by. I promise myself that I'll get absorbed in all of the fascinating lectures and readings tomorrow. But today, I'll let myself have a little fun and daydream in anticipation of meeting up with Owen.

As promised, Owen is waiting for me outside the Hurston Hall passageway. He walks toward me when he sees me turn the corner.

"Hi." He smiles.

"Hi," I say with an uncontrollable smile. "What exactly is it that you want to show me?"

"My hideout spots," he says with a wink. "I showed up at yours on Saturday, so you deserve to see mine. It's only fair. You ready?"

I nod like he's just offered me the last piece of double chocolate cake. "Where do we start?"

Owen motions to the eastern part of the campus, and we start walking side by side in that direction. Across the green, we stay in tandem but do not touch. Owen's hands jammed into his front pockets seem like they're digging for hands to hold. My hands. But we keep a friendly distance apart.

"Thank you for humoring me with this today," he says between energetic strides. "And just so you know, there's no need to worry about my security troubling you ever again."

It seems like so long ago when the Men in Black made a guest appearance at my house.

"Oh, no?" I ask.

"I've since learned to trust my security chief, Colin, with a few secrets," says Owen. "But just a few."

There's a stubborn mischief in his tone that makes me smirk.

"You must've been a pain to track down when you were younger."

"Hide-and-seek games in a castle were epic," he says. "And I learned from the best. My sister taught me everything I know."

"She sounds like she was a fun person to be around," I say softly.

"The best."

I want to ask more about her, but I hold back.

He stops in front of the botany and zoology building.

"I've never been inside this building," I say, "but it's one of the first ones I noticed because it's the most modern."

"Wait until you see the inside."

We take two lefts off the stunningly sleek entryway and find a back hallway. It's brightly lit by artificial lighting and seemingly endless. It could double as a dream sequence setting from a fantasy movie. The pristine, soulless corridor and the bright orange doors lining each side look like a physical metaphor for life's challenging choices.

"These are the labs where graduate students work," Owen tells me. "I know most of the graduate hangouts because I live in the graduate residence on campus. It's more private and independent—a security team's ideal."

That makes sense.

"So, no interest in any, uh, cooler graduate hot spots?" I ask, looking around. "Why would you want to be in a building where poor helpless animals are probably tested?" I wonder aloud. "Do you hide out in one of the cages or something?"

"No, though I can't say that I haven't been desperate enough to consider it," he responds without hesitation.

"I can't imagine this place at night," I say with a shudder.

"Or the people who lurk here at odd hours." He winces.

Our voices become more layered with echoes the farther into the hallway we walk.

"We need to catch the elevator at the end of this hall, and then from there it's just three floors up," Owen says, pointing.

I'm so curious about what's waiting for us upstairs, but I don't dare ask about it, because I love surprises. My quiet, baby-seal hand claps let Owen know this, too. He's tickled and gives me a light shoulder bump. I pretend to stumble a few steps to the side.

I guess our silly fun has made our presence known; one of the hallway doors behind us creeps open and it sounds like the scariest thing. We must both get the same image of us suddenly strapped to some mad scientist's exam table, because we bolt. Owen grabs my hand, and we run the rest of the way down the hallway

"*Ohmygod*, my heart!" I sputter when we're safely inside the elevator. "Where have you *taken* me? So far, this whole building seems like the inside of some evil genius's mind."

"Where we're going will make up for it, hopefully." His eyes dance.

"It better," I say playfully as we step off the elevator and walk over to a set of doors.

"Aaah, you made it in time for lunch." An older dude with a badge marked "R.J." greets us when he answers Owen's knock on the door.

Owen steps aside and gestures for me to walk in first.

"After you, my lady," he says with a hand flourish and bow.

"Oh my goodness, look at this place!" I say. I take a slow 360-degree whirl. Under a glass ceiling is a green space that is lush and otherworldly. I feel like I've stepped into some kind of wonderland.

The plants remind me of the first people to arrive at a school dance. They're in groups segregated in clearly delineated areas. The wallflowers slumping to one side, the soaring heights of the sunlight-hogging plants with the best positioning, the yet-to-sprout plants budding together, some stretching above the others as if craning to peak at the fully blossomed wonders they aspire to become.

This is the green more valuable than money.

There's a reason people demand green spaces in cities all over the world. I'm glad to live in a city known for its oak trees and community parks. Nothing is more calming and welcoming than nature.

It's also why I feel a lot more chill now.

"I guess I wore the right dress for the occasion," I say, nodding down at the floral prints on my sundress.

"You definitely did," Owen replies.

If his tickled expression is any indication, I must have the most gleeful look of surprise on my face. The humidity that envelops this place has me checking on my hair. Of all the days to wear it down. It looked super cute when I stopped by the ladies' room on my way to meet Owen. But who knows how it looks now. Well, Owen knows, that's who.

"Are you okay?" He watches as I casually pat down one side of my head . . . yet again.

"The humidity does things to my hair," I say.

"It looks beautiful," Owen says.

My breath catches, and I cover my gasp with a soft chuckle.

It's sweet of him to say, but the minute I start seeing my hair expand into the sightlines of my peripheral vision, I'll know it's time to step out for a breather. A little extra puff is nothing to be afraid of when you have hair as seriously big as mine. But for vanity's sake, I grab a hair tie from my bag and make a quick topknot.

"How did you find this place?" I ask Owen.

"R.J., my neighbor in the graduate dorm, conducts research

here," Owen explains. "He invited me to swing by once, and I've been coming back regularly ever since."

"Swing by *once*, huh?" I tease. "Way to take advantage of an invite." I give Owen a thumbs-up.

"Indeed. I'm just glad he hasn't worked up the nerve to ask me to stop coming," Owen says loud enough for R.J. to hear.

"Don't worry, I'm taking as much advantage as he is of me." R.J. pushes a small wheelbarrow and parks it in the corner near us. "Owen here has a green thumb. Plus, I get to boss around someone with a fancy accent."

"You garden, too?" I ask Owen, impressed.

"I follow step-by-step orders until it leads to something that looks like gardening," says Owen. Even when he's being humble, he's flexing that charming personality of his.

"Let's see it," I say.

"That's our next stop. I have a little something started."

It's a bright terra-cotta pot housing a single resident. The sturdy stem reaching from the soil is already budding vibrant-colored leaves. I can't identify the plant.

"This is for you, Zora," Owen says. "Delphinium flowers— the mini-sized variety. They're known for their protective spirit and are associated with success and an inner light, a lot like you are."

I feel my cheeks get hot. "That's so sweet, Owen, thank you." I pick up the pot and cradle it in both my hands, marveling over the cobalt-blue and pale pink petals. "Plant selfie?" I ask.

"Why not?" Owen grabs his phone and positions himself next to me. He leans in closer and extends his arm and snaps our very first selfie. He clicks twice.

He stays standing close by me as we check out the pictures. In them, our heads are tilted toward each other and practically all our teeth are showing.

There's a stark contrast in our skin tones, but we both have the same sun-kissed look going on. The summer sun gives my skin a moisturized glow that brown skin loves, and for Owen, there's a freckled tan that doesn't darken his skin but reddens it in the areas most exposed to the sun, like his forehead and his cheekbones.

"We look good together," says Owen.

He's not wrong. Despite being two people from two different backgrounds, walks of life, and social statuses, our personalities go together near PB&J level. From the moment we started vibing at the library, that was clear. Just like certain talents we're all born with, it's difficult to explain why some things require so little effort.

But I'm not going to admit that to him just yet.

I shake my head and hide my smile.

"Shall I keep the plant here until it's a little further along?" I sit the pot back in its personalized nook on the shelf.

"Yes, and we can visit it anytime," he says.

"It really is so awesome in here," I say, scanning the shelved area.

"I've got one more thing to show you." Owen wears his

excitement in a much less wide-eyed way than I do. It's more in his sped-up speech, almost like he's rapping to a beat.

We stroll down a path leading to an outdoor garden.

"I can see why you love this place," I say. "It's so private, like a hidden oasis from the outside world."

"It's a special space, but it's not always this quiet," says Owen. "R.J. lets me stop in when it's closed to the research teams and other students. Come this way."

We arrive at a grassy nook where a picnic is set up. I touch my cheeks in surprise.

"Did you do this?" I ask, eyeing the smoothies, the tower of macarons, the blanket.

"Don't be too impressed. It's all store-brought."

"I don't care. I am impressed."

We sit and sip, and this feels like a real date. I force myself to make conversation even though I'm still so wowed by everything.

"So, what is it like to have a title?" I finally ask between bites of macarons.

"I don't know what it's like not to have one," Owen says thoughtfully. "I like to tell myself everyone has one. It's my way of feeling less of a standout, I guess."

"You know, you may be right about everyone having a title. Now that I think of it, I had one a few years ago," I say.

He looks at me earnestly. "Really? What was it?"

"For a time, the kids at my middle school nicknamed me Mayo."

"I'm sorry, what's that?" Owen leans in with one ear facing me. "Mayo as in mayonnaise?"

"Mayo as in little mayor. I know—not exactly clever, but my tormentor made up for that with his genius comedic timing. *Extra Mayo, pleeeaze!*" I repeat the taunt, and roll my eyes. I throw my head back and let out a breathy, "Ugh, I hated that. I don't think I was all that *extra* . . . most of the time."

"Your outrage is understandable." Owen dips his words in a thick sauce of faux concern.

"Picture being labeled *Mayo* just for suggesting that the class take a walking tour of Appleton," I say.

"I am in *no* way massively impressed with that nickname," he clarifies.

"It could've been worse. I slipped up one day and wore my number ten soccer jersey to lunch. That entire period I braced myself for it, but no one in the cafeteria made the connection."

"The 10th Condiment?" guesses Owen.

"See? *You* wouldn't have let that slide," I say, impressed.

"Missed opportunity." Owen shakes his head.

"Totally."

A sudden thought lights up his face. "Oooh, and what if your jersey number were five?"

"Cinco de Mayo!" we both shout at the same time in a race to beat each other to the punch line.

Like freshly braided hair, our laughter and the summer sounds of the garden we're in interweave neatly.

I try not to smile too hard. "So, what about you? For someone from such an uptight place, you come across more laid-back than I'd imagine."

"More than my family imagines, as well." Owen shrugs. "I guess I can't seem to shake that tiny inner voice telling me life is short."

I think of his late sister and feel pretty sure he's thinking of her, too.

"What are you studying at Halstead this summer?" I ask him.

"Creative writing," he says. *Cool.* He wipes away invisible crumbs on his lap. "Much to my mother's utter chagrin, I chose not to study family favorites like art history or geography."

"You gotta make your own path," I say. "So, what do you like writing about?"

"Mostly about what motivates people." He shrugs his shoulders again. "Especially the fascinating, everyday people I meet at home and abroad."

"You have a way with getting folks to open up to you, so I'm sure that skill comes in handy for a writer."

Owen and I lock eyes, and the memory of our library chat is the inside joke pulling up the corners of our lips. After a few seconds, I'm the first to look away.

"My life may interest the public, but I personally couldn't be more in awe of how extraordinary so-called ordinary people are," he says. "I guess that sounds a bit voyeuristic of me."

"No, I get it—we've all been guilty of people watching," I say. "It's human nature."

"Speaking of everyone having a story to tell . . ." He leans over and lightly shoulder bumps me again. A tingle goes down my arm. "Did the mayor-in-training ever manage to get her middle school to jump on board any of her ideas?"

"As a matter of fact, the school just celebrated its fifth year of walking tours!" I do a happy dance in my spot on the blanket. "And in a few weeks, at Appleton's annual Fam Fest, the *real* mayor will announce the city's expanded place-based learning program for all schools." Owen holds out his palm for a high five, and I meet it with mine. "High-fiving, too? Very American of you."

"When in Rome and all that," he says playfully.

"Just don't let me catch you line-dancing at a frat party. Then I'll know we got you."

"You are a cheeky one, you are," he says.

"What, like a chipmunk?"

Owen drops his head and grins.

"Talking of chipmunks, who is that darling little girl in your lock screen photo?" he asks me.

"Oh, that's Anaya from my Walk Me Home program." I smile, taking out my phone. Owen looks prepared to listen thoughtfully, so I fill him in. "In my city, small kids who live within two miles of school and don't qualify for school bus rides have to walk home alone. Either their caretakers work long hours and can't afford aftercare, or they have elderly guardians who aren't able to pick them up. Anaya is the first student I walked home two years ago, and because of the need, my program grew from there."

"That's fantastic, Zora," says Owen. "It sounds like you're quite close to these children."

"They crack me up, they're so fun. The program is all about making them feel heard, seen, and valued. We want them to know they're special, but in the end, they make *me* feel like a star." I shake my head in disbelief.

"I can relate to the feeling you get from helping the little ones. I did some community work abroad with students around that age, and it changed me."

When Owen tells me about his outreach in parts of Europe and Africa, there's an animated spark in his hazel eyes and he starts talking with his hands. We laugh and nibble on cookies and I love hearing about something Owen is passionate about.

Thanks to Skye's own Owen research online (in her attempt to prove to me that not all the news about Owen's reputation is negative), Skye could testify that he helped build schools, teach English, and plant trees. In one picture she sent me of Owen planting trees, she noted that Owen was looking "ruggedly *goodt*."

After we're done with the picnic, Owen perks up and says, "All right, one more stop."

"Another mystery destination?"

"If you're up for it."

"I'm game," I say with a smile.

He tells me he'll come back later to clean up the picnic things (royal busboy) and he leads me down a different path through the trees. I didn't realize quite how big the campus is. He turns to stop in front of me.

"Important question," he says. "Fairies or gnomes?"

I laugh at the randomness of everything. "Fairies all the way, without a doubt."

"Perfect. I present to you, this whisper bench."

A long, curved bench that looks like it's made from the same large slab of stone sits at the end of the path. If I'm not exaggerating, it can fit about twenty PATH train seats from one end to the other. The seat back is tall, and at one end of the bench is a carved decorative fairy and at the other end is a gnome.

"Is this the one where two people sitting at either corner can hear each other whisper?" I ask, remembering what I read about the bench on Halstead's website when I got into the program.

"Shall we test it out?" Owen asks, and I nod enthusiastically.

We sit at each end (I'm on the fairy side), and I wait for him to say something. I get as close to the nook as possible. When I don't hear anything after a few seconds, I look over to Owen. He shouts directly to me:

"Are you trying to read my lips?"

"I can't hear anything," I tell him.

"That's because I haven't said anything yet," he says.

"Well, hurry up!" I laugh.

"Be patient," he says.

"Fine," I say more to myself. I go back to tucking my ear into the nook, and I close my eyes to concentrate. And then I hear him speak, his words ricocheting off the cool, smooth stone directly into my ear.

"I like you."

And just like that, the fairies score another magical coup.

I look over at Owen where he's seated. He checks me out at the same time. It's like we're both trying to figure out how two people on opposite sides of the bench can click so well without even trying. So far apart, yet so connected.

I face the corner where the bench back meets the side wall and send my words into it.

"I like you, too," I say, well above a whisper.

The slow spread of Owen's smile tells me the message is received, loud and clear.

Owen's gait is confident and charismatic as he walks over to me from his corner of the whisper bench. I sit watching him, replaying the last few seconds of our exchange.

His "I like you" echoes in my mind.

What can he say to top that right now?

"Permission to 'Hold the Mayo'?" Owen asks the second he reaches me.

I crack up even though I don't want to ruin the moment.

"You had to go there, did you?" I tell him, but still take his extended hand and let him pull me to my feet.

My arms reach around the back of his neck as he wraps his around the small of my back. We rest our chins on each other's shoulders.

He smells like he bathed in the ocean. Not the ocean of fishermen battling punishing waves, but the ocean of tropical paradises that inspire body lotions and candles. There's a windswept wonderfulness to him.

Romantic hugs are so underrated. The friendly, congratulatory ones get all of the shine, but romantic hugs don't go viral. I could write a TED Talk about how nice it is being wrapped up in Owen's arms.

"I promise I'll let you go," he says. "On the count of three—one . . . two . . . three."

He lifts my feet off the ground, and I let out a happy shriek.

We both hear a laugh from down the pathway, and Owen sets my feet back on the ground. We look toward the sound, both of us clearly remembering that even though we feel like we're in our own little world, we're still outdoors and likely to be seen by someone.

As slowed-down as those intimate moments felt, time is speeding up again. We need to leave this sanctuary.

Just as we arrived, we walk out through campus in tandem, with a respectable distance apart. Not touching. But in my mind, we are still in that embrace. And from the look on Owen's face, I can tell the same is true for him.

Chapter 10

OWEN CALLS me the next morning.

"What time are you catching the train in?" he asks.

I'm in a bathrobe carrying an armful of hair products in bottles, jars, and various other containers. I've just come from the shower. "I'll probably leave here in about a half hour," I say.

"I can have you picked up if you'd like," he offers.

"Tempting," I say. "But, no thanks."

Skye would do a double take if she heard me say that, but that's just me. I don't want to set those kinds of expectations. I do, however, agree to meet Owen after my last class.

"There's something else I'd like to show you," he tells me before we hang up.

"You think it's the queen's collection of tiaras this time?" Skye asks me twenty minutes later. I'm holding the phone between my shoulder and my ear while I try to zip up my crowded bag. When it won't close, I dig in and pull out the bulky bag of unused hair products I've accumulated, coily hair product enthusiast that I am. No choice but to carry this bag separately.

"Tiaras?" I ask Skye.

"He probably wants to ask you to his brother's wedding!" She sounds exasperated by my ignorance.

"And why would I need a tiara when I'm not the bride?"

"You're confusing me!" she shouts like a whiny toddler, and we both crack up at our inside joke. We never let each other forget the chatty six-year-old girl in the Walk Me Home program who just had to be right about everything. Any time her flawed information was proven false, she would shout, "You're confusing me!"

"It's too early in the morning for all that cackling," Zach says from the hallway as I step out of my room. He's half-asleep, walking to the stairs like a zombie with only one eye open.

"I'm surprised you're even up," I tell him. "Didn't you work the late shift?"

"Is that Zach?" Skye's voice sounds like she's twirling her hair. I ignore her.

"I'm trying to go to bed an hour earlier each day," he says while managing to climb down each step slowly. I follow him, my bag of products swishing and clanking along the way. "Starting next week, my shift will be switching to mornings."

"Listen to him modifying his behavior and thinking ahead," Skye says to me. "Zach planning for success is messing me up in a major way, and I can't."

"Who's that on the phone? Ma?" Zach wants to know.

"No, it's Skye," I tell him.

Skye seems to hold her breath. It's so quiet on her end, I can almost hear her false eyelashes batting.

And then Zach does the strangest thing. When we get to the bottom of the stairs, he asks to speak to her.

"Hey, Skye, quick question for you," Zach says with Skye on speaker.

Silence.

"You there?" Zach looks at me like, *What's up with your girl?*

"I'm here." Skye's voice is echoey, like she's backed away a few yards from the phone.

She better not be taking off her headscarf and poking herself in the eye again. Zach clearly cannot see her, plus it's hard to gauge whether he would even notice the difference between a glammed-out Skye and Skye with a rolled-out-of-bed look. He does not deserve the effort that Skye puts into all her relationships, romantic or not. Maybe the responsible thing would be to start steering her away from this Zach crush.

"I was wondering if—" Zach pauses to yawn.

"Yes?" Skye sounds so hopeful, bless her heart.

"Does your uncle down there still run an Airbnb, and if so, what's his name?" Zach asks.

Skye's family is a colorful cast of characters. Being around her, you can't help but pick up a funny story about different members and what they're up to. Her Airbnb uncle is the one who always has box seat tickets to some concert or sporting event, is still clubbin' on the regular at fortysomething years old, and seems determined to be an eternal bachelor.

"I'm not sure, but I could find out for you," Skye says. Boy, she's sobered up quick.

"Thank you. Do you have my number? I'll have Zora text it to you," Zach says.

"I'm not your secretary," I snap at Zach. Mostly because I want to crack a smile on Skye's face at his expense.

"I'm sorry, Your Highness." Zach rolls his eyes. "Skye, may I please have your number? I'll text you from my phone so you have my info."

Skye gives him her number before she runs off the phone to get ready for her classes. I leave the house as soon as I've eaten the Taylor ham and egg on a roll my mom left me. It's going to be another long day focusing on classes rather than anticipating my meet-up with Owen, so I'll need all the brain food I can get.

On my way to the light-rail station, I take a detour two streets over to drop off the hair products at the Fredricksons' home. The family with four big-haired daughters are on a tight budget, so styling products are low on the parents' priority, but high on their girls'. They'll make better use of this stash than my mom and I have.

I intend to do the bag drop on their front porch like I'd discussed with the girls' mom. But Layla, the eleven-year-old who is most eager for these products, sees me and opens the door.

"Ohmygod, thank you, Zora!" Layla squeals. She gives me a

quick hug, grabs the bag, and practically leaps across the carpeted floor onto the reclining chair in the living room to examine its contents. I follow her a few paces and lean against the open doorway.

"Don't forget to save some for your sisters," I joke.

"Eeeee!" she says, holding the shea butter moisturizer. "I wanna use *this* one today!"

The amused smile wipes clean off my face when I see the morning show news report on the TV behind her.

"There's a prince on the loose in New Jersey," the stiff-haired anchorman reports to his coanchors and in-studio audience.

The over-acting cohost leans in and guffaws. "Really? What exit off the turnpike?"

"Our sources tell us that Prince Owen, younger brother of Landerel heartthrob Prince Gideon, can be found walking the hallowed halls of Halstead University taking summer classes," the anchorman reports. "The school would not comment on whether or not he is enrolled, but we can imagine the excitement surrounding him right now. Especially ahead of the much-anticipated royal wedding at the end of the summer."

"Welp, there you have it—a prince in *Joisey*," recaps the cohost with another guffaw. "You got a problem with that?"

A flood of thoughts comes rushing in, like *What does this mean? Will there be a media circus camping out at school today? Are things going to change drastically now?*

"Right, Zora?" I hear Layla break through. "Zora?"

I blink away the worry.

Layla looks at me, then back at the TV screen, trying to figure out what's got me so shook.

"I better head out now, but text me if you need me to help braid your sisters' hair." I turn and flee before Layla can ask any questions.

Chapter 11

WHEN I step on campus an hour later, I half expect the media to be hiding behind trees—or worse, sticking a microphone in my face. But, nothing.

At least, not until I walk into my Intro to Community Organizing classroom.

I'm the first one there, so I take a seat at the large conference table that anchors the space. Then a guy with dark hair walks in, and he sits down across from me. I know this is judgy, but he seems like one of those snobby socialite types you wouldn't expect to be interested in a community organizing class. I'm learning most of the kids in my classes are into big billionaire-level or corporate philanthropy.

There's a mildly exasperated look on this guy's face now, as if *he* were hoping to be the first to arrive.

Sorry, Charlie.

He looks like he wants to say something to me, but I plant my feet on the floor, sit up straight, fire up my laptop, cue up my notes, and ignore him.

Then It Girl—Kelsey—walks in and takes a seat next to the dark-haired guy. Awkward silence follows. Yesterday, on my date with Owen, I was tempted to ask him about Kelsey—how he knew her exactly, why she was with him at royal events. But I didn't want to spoil the moment by bringing her up, and I'm glad. Now I'm tempted to ask *her* about Owen, but I don't.

This is so not me.

If this were Appleton, there would be far less mystery and I'd know all my classmates by now. Usually one week into doing anything, anywhere, I have a decent handle on the backstory of the place. A week is enough time for me to build a working knowledge of my surroundings, and the easiest way I get this info is by connecting with folks on a casual level, chatting and asking questions.

"You're such a busybody," the kids at my high school joke. But out of the other side of their mouths, they usually go, "Where would we get our info without you, girl?"

Choppin' it up with folks is like scrolling through my Instagram feed. You get the highlights, a few low points, and a general sense of what's good in the hood. Without speaking to people, I'd never know enough to help myself or others with info you didn't think you needed. News about open part-time jobs, affordable guitar lessons, the tastiest Jamaican patties, DJs who can spin both hip-hop and Afrobeats music, the best Trinidadian roti, the quickest hair-braiding stylist, the closest West African seamstress, and, yes, of course, the dopest basement parties have all started with a casual conversation.

While I seriously doubt Kelsey knows the best hair product to keep my edges looking tight, she may know something else that could be of interest—aside from Prince Owen, of course. Like, maybe she's tapped into the podcasting scene here. It's supposed to be huge, and I'd love to know if there's a good one on community organizing.

My curiosity is pushing me out of my corner. There's so much to find out. For starters, who exactly *is* this girl?

"How's it going today?" I say, breaking free from that Halstead Hopeful persona and feeling more like myself.

Kelsey looks surprised. Her eyebrows move closer to each other for a split second.

"Fine," she answers tersely.

"That's cool," I say, as in *Don't worry, I won't talk to you anymore.*

Now *she's* the one avoiding eye contact. She taps her perfect fingernails several times on her cell phone. I study her. *Owen's not-girlfriend.* Owen hasn't said anything about her. I have to say something to her about him. Right? My cool threatens to abandon me like it just saw its ghostly reflection, but I just manage to grab its Casper-sheet hem and yank it back.

More kids swarm into the class then, talking and laughing and filling up the table.

"How is everything?" asks the guy across from me. I'm as

surprised by his greeting as Kelsey was of mine. "You know," he says sincerely. "After what happened last week."

"Thanks so much for asking, I'm fine," I reply, successfully resisting my urge to ask, Jersey-style, "You *tawkin'* to me?" Not the impression I am going for.

"I hope you know that if campus police had mistreated you or forcibly escorted you out, I was ready to film it."

"Thank you," I say. "I appreciate that."

He holds out his hand. "Matt Aquino."

"Zora Emerson." I shake his hand. "Nice to meet you."

I have to say, he doesn't seem as snobby as I'd assumed he was a few minutes ago. Maybe I do need to give some people more of a chance.

By now, Kelsey is whispering to the whale-logo guy who today is wearing a pale pink polo with the collars pointed up like the sails of a yacht he probably lunches on. They both glance at me before resuming their conversation. Hmm. Could he be the journalism student who got the ball rolling on my breaking news story? If so, did Kelsey help connect the reporter to Owen? Did anybody see me and Owen on our campus date yesterday?

I decide to return my focus to the guy across from me.

"Do you know anyone else in our class?" I ask Matt.

"One of them was in my campus tour group months ago, and I've gotten to know about half of them from running into them at the dorm. What about you?"

"I commute, so you're really one of the first people I've spoken to," I say.

"That's not really what I've heard," Whale Guy butts in.

"What do you mean?" I say, raising my eyebrow at him.

"Just that there's at least one person you've done more than speak to."

Before I can formulate a response to that, Matt jumps in, endearing him to me so much more.

"You should come by the dorm tonight for Taco Tuesday, Zora," he says. "We're ordering in and having dinner together. It was fun last week, so we decided to make it a thing."

I hesitate. "Maybe next time." The last thing I need is more of this speculation swirling around me. And anyway, I have plans with Owen for this evening—not that I'm going to bring that up in front of Kelsey and Whale Boy.

Matt is cheerily undeterred. "Absolutely, next time." He nods.

I give him a grateful nod back.

The professor's presence grabs everyone's full attention. We've all started to get used to being on alert for the questions he tosses at us every few minutes. His style of lecturing almost feels like going for a run with a person who likes to hold conversations at an eight-minute-mile pace. Not only do you have to keep up, but you need to maintain an understanding of what's being said.

I notice Kelsey texting a few times during class, and I wonder if she's reaching out to Owen. The minute he pops into my mind, it takes a little extra concentration not to revisit the thoughts of our amazing picnic, and hug, yesterday.

After class, Matt and I end up leaving at the same time. As we walk down the marble halls, I check for signs of Kelsey and Whale Boy, but thankfully they're nowhere to be seen. It's nice to have made a new semi-friend, and maybe at some point I'll take him up on Taco Tuesday.

After I part ways with Matt, I think about the fact that things seem like they might be on their way to becoming drama-free. Maybe the insanity of this Halstead U summer peaked last week. When you start off like I did, there's nowhere to go but boring. At least, that's what I'm hoping.

Chapter 12

"THERE'S THE perfect place in town to watch the sun go down," Owen says.

We meet at the end of the day, finally, at the Clock, an Instagram-famous landmark at the entrance to the campus. Next to the iron gates that bridge the entryway's brick walls is the non-functioning timepiece that students universally and simply call "the Clock." Only shadowy impressions of its original clock face remain.

So many Halstead Hopefuls take selfies with it or rock dignified poses around it that to see it in person is almost a letdown. It's physically of average scale and not at all larger-than-life, despite being a huge part of school lore. Still, there's usually a small crowd at its feet, waxing poetic about how the Clock has inspired their lives.

I am more than ready for a sunset moment with Owen. He hands me two bottles of water from the vending machine for the uphill hike he describes as "terribly steep" in some places, and leads me a few blocks off campus and up the winding streets of a quiet residential neighborhood.

It's a workout, so we collapse when we finally get to the short brick wall overlooking the Halstead campus and the towns beyond it. The brick wall borders the walking path and the grassy downhill drop.

I drink the last bit of water left in my bottle and take in the peaceful sight.

"How did you find this place?" I ask him.

"It's amazing what you're motivated to find when you're just yearning for one second when your every move is not being tracked," says Owen. "One evening, right after the whole phone debacle with us, I went over to the train station—thinking I might see you there," he adds with a small smile, his cheeks turning red. I roll my eyes and nudge him. "And from that elevated platform," he goes on, "I could see this lookout spot in the distance. I didn't stop walking until I could find it."

"You weren't being followed by your security team that night?"

"No." Owen's voice lowers. "They gave me some space."

We sit in silence next to each other, our shoulders touching. For a few minutes, we just take in the world below. The pre-sunset hues soften the Gothic heights of the library where we met. It gives the elevated stone bridge carrying crisscross trains a dreamy glow. We can see the clear space of the quad, the dense pockets of trees scattered here and there, the greenhouse we visited yesterday, and, beyond that, lit windows in cozy homes. Farther out are the white and red streaks of car lights on the Garden State Parkway. It's mesmerizing.

"Quick question." I break the silence. "Fairies or gnomes?"

Owen stretches an arm behind me and leans it on the brick wall.

"Gnomes for sure. Didn't you hear R.J. talk about my green thumb?"

"Fair enough," I say. I realize I'm starting to use some of Owen's phrasing. *How'd that happen?*

"Don't think I didn't notice your choice of words," he says smugly.

I laugh. "Hey, if you can mimic the Jersey accent, I can at least pick up a saying or two along the way," I tell him.

"Fair enough," he answers.

Owen is looking at me, and he is so close, I can hear him breathing. My cheeks get all tingly.

"Beautiful view," I say when I shouldn't have said a thing. This moment is so perfect.

"Yes, beautiful," he says softly.

I turn my head to meet his stare. Our lips are inches apart, yet he's still approaching me. I close my eyes and prepare to feel his kiss, when a dog barks right behind us.

Owen and I are startled out of our moment. We twist around to see two college-age girls walking a tiny yapping dog.

"It's such a great view, isn't it?" says the girl not holding the leash.

We nod politely and give half smiles.

"No one from Halstead knows about it because it used to be

private property until last year, when they knocked down the old house that used to be here," she continues.

"I want to brag about this, but then I wouldn't want this place overrun with annoying Halstead students. No offense," says the dog walker. "But I go to Rutgers."

"No, none taken," Owen and I answer at the same time.

Rutgers is on my short list of schools I'll be applying to in the fall. It's on Skye's list, too.

"Hey, nice accent," the non–dog walker says to Owen. "Where are you from?"

"Uh—" Owen seems to lose his cool worrying his cover is blown.

"Thanks, I'm from Appleton, up in Essex County," I crack.

The dog walker's friend thinks I'm being a wise guy, and she gets a little attitude over it.

"I was *talking* to him," she says.

Owen takes my hand in his.

"We better get going," he tells me.

"Wait, it's a Landerel accent, isn't it?" asks the dog walker. She seems like the brighter one, by far. "Oh my *gawd*. Are you that Halstead prince they mentioned on the news?"

"It is him!" agrees her friend. "Can we take a selfie with you, Prince Landerel?"

"I'm sorry, but I really shouldn't," says Owen. He and I stand up and start backing away from the girls. He's still holding my hand.

The attitude girl is already cuing up her phone for the picture.

"Please? It'll only take a second," she pleads. "If not, no one will believe we actually met you."

I appeal to the dog walker. "Once this gets posted, your private lookout spot will be a thing of the past. So many people will start coming here, pitching a tent, waiting for a sighting . . . and I agree with you, it should stay a hidden gem for the neighbors in this community."

Instead of answering me, the dog walker turns to her friend, who is giving me a superpower glare Daddy would be impressed by.

She thinks about this so long. When she speaks, she looks like she's recovering from a cold-drink brain freeze. "I got it—I'll just take a zoomed-in pic and no one will know."

"That's all right, there's no need to make a fuss," says Owen, still backing us away even though the girls keep following. "It was nice meeting you both."

The dog walker already has her friends on video chat. She's pointing the camera to us to give them a closer look.

"See?" she cries. " It's really him!"

"Who's that girl with him?" says a voice on speaker.

"She said she's from Appleton."

Owen and I are so busted, and need to get out of here before more of their friends show up. I definitely feel fight-or-flight impulses kicking in. When things turn from chill to thrill this quickly, you can't help but feel a rush of adrenaline.

Owen and I turn our faces away from both phones as we walk down to the end of the block.

"Perfect timing on getting your security team to give you more space," I wisecrack, in an attempt to lighten the mood. But Owen seems focused on an escape plan. He's on his phone with his security team now, giving them our exact location.

"I'm terribly sorry about this," he says after hanging up.

"It's not anyone's fault," I tell him.

You'd think things would blow over now that we've been tailed a block away from the lookout spot, but no.

"What? No picture?" A loud guy has joined the two girls who spotted Owen. He's clearly amused by the selfie standoff going on. "How can you turn down the fans, bro? They make or break you, dude!"

"Does that guy think you drop albums or something?" I whisper to him.

"Just don't look back at them," Owen says, in his damage-control mode.

"Okay, this has officially crossed over into a *scene*."

Owen shakes his head. "I took you off campus without proper security presence, and I shouldn't have exposed you to this." He answers his ringing phone. "Yes, I think I see you now," he tells the caller. *Whew.* Sounds like our ride is finally here.

That's when I catch a glimpse of what's going on half a block behind us.

It looks like a mini party in front of a house. The two girls and the dog, the loudmouth guy, and about five of their friends are together now. One of them starts filming when he sees me looking back, and I show him the back of my head.

I hear the girl I recognize as the dog walker second-guess herself. She says, "Maybe it's not even him."

"Yeah, like, no offense, but why would he be hanging with someone like *her*," someone responds. "Did you say she's from Appleton?"

"Ew," says a third person loud enough for me to hear.

Owen tries to get my attention. He squeezes my hand that he's holding. "Zora," he repeats. "You go in first when they pull up."

"Okay, sure," I say. I can't hide that I'm a bit deflated. No matter what you tell yourself, words offend. But the extra something behind those words—the belittling, the attempt to make me feel unworthy—that's the part that is harder to shake.

The sleek black town car has just pulled up. The Man in Black in the passenger seat jumps out and holds the door open while eagle eyeing the small crowd up the hill. I climb in first, and I slide over to make room for Owen.

If they were doubting whether or not Owen was Owen, it's confirmed now. Not everyone can make a distress call and then have a Secret Service–like response a few minutes later.

"Thank you for coming so quickly," Owen tells the driver, who I assume is the security chief, Colin, he told me about.

There's a whiff of tension in the car, but Colin keeps his I-told-you-so to himself, or perhaps he's only putting it on hold until a more appropriate time.

"Are you okay?" Owen asks me.

"Fine, I'm fine," I say. From the look on his face, he isn't convinced. He doesn't let go of my hand, and I squeeze it in an attempt to ease his mind. But the truth is, I still haven't shaken off the shade from Owen's fan club. And thinking of them as his fan club is a sign of the shade's contamination of my mood.

"Can we take you home?" Owen asks.

I shake my head. "No, thank you. The train will be much quicker right now. And I have an audiobook to finish," I add, which is a sort of lame excuse.

"Okay," Owen says with a sigh. He asks Colin to drive us to the train station, and the rest of the drive is silent.

Owen walks me to the platform and waits for the train with me. This time, Colin isn't far behind, and I'm okay with that. Owen found a spare baseball cap in the car, so he's wearing it now. Just like when we walk together on campus, we don't touch, but the way we stroll side by side makes it seem like there's an invisible thread linking us to each other.

I'm not doing a great job acting okay with everything because Owen still looks concerned.

"I didn't mean for our evening out to end this way," he tells me.

"That's not what's bothering me, exactly," I say.

I scan the distance for the lookout area we've just come from.

"Something I said?" he asks.

"Something I heard from those people," I say.

"What is it?"

"They wondered what you were doing hanging out with someone like me." I look at my toes. They're painted orange, my go-to polish color for the summer.

"Argh! They're blowing my cover," he says teasingly. "I've been selfishly hoping you don't notice."

I take the bait and ask. "Notice what?"

"Zora, of the two of us, you're the one who's truly regal," he says.

And right on cue, here's my iron horse and carriage coming to take me back to my kingdom, where I belong.

Owen is still standing on the platform as the train pulls away.

Chapter 13

"YOU AND Owen have been spending a lot of time together," Ma singsongs into my room the next morning. I'm in front of my flimsy closet-door mirror, putting on two different lip shades in search of the perfect blend of plum.

"What are you still doing home at eight forty-five on a Wednesday morning?" I ask her through the reflection. She's poking around my dresser, smelling my lotion bottles. Like me, my mother is already showered and dressed in a comfy sundress. I'm not used to seeing her so casual on a workday. Her locs are all down, in a free-flowing style, instead of pulled back in a bun like she normally wears to work.

"Today's my office's summer picnic, remember?" she says.

"Already?" I recall Ma asking me to save the date, but I had to decline because of classes.

"This will be the first one you and your brother will miss." Ma pouts. When she gets nostalgic over how fast we're growing, there are often tears. She doesn't go for the telenovela lip tremble or makeup-smeared cry. But the cracked voice followed by the abruptly muted conversation is enough to make me feel sad. Less sad since she met John, though. The best thing to do is give her the silver lining, stat.

"At least John can go, I hope?" I say.

"Yes, he's taken the morning off and is downstairs on a work call right now."

She snatches the brush out of my hand when I don't stop to look at her.

"How can I help you?" I give her my full attention. She looks happy to have it.

"So, what's the scoop? First you used to come straight home. Now it's all campus sightseeing with Owen."

When I decided to keep Ma in the loop, I didn't think she would be like a living, breathing Alexa, keeping track of my calendar and talking to me about it like she's been programmed to.

"We just like hanging out with each other, that's all," I tell her.

"And my name is Steve Urkel." Ma grins.

"I'm going to the center before class," I say. "And this line of questioning isn't going to help me get there any sooner."

I leave her to snoop alone in my room, but when I get to the top of the stairs, I have to stop short or I'd fall over the rolling suitcase sitting on the top step.

"Whose bag is this?" I yell to anyone within earshot, which is everyone.

"Your brother is heading to Atlanta this weekend, and he's being dramatic about packing for a week's stay." Ma pokes her head out of my room.

"He doesn't even leave until tomorrow! And if he keeps this here, the only trip that's gonna happen is one of us tripping over it."

My threat works. Zach sleepwalks his way out of his room, grabs his bag, and proceeds to carry it downstairs. Grumpy mumbling aside, I must say, my brother seems fully committed to this new acting civilized mode. The old Zach would've kicked the luggage down the stairs.

"Enjoy the picnic, Ma and John!" I shout before heading out the door.

I'd promised my program kids that I'd eat breakfast with them today. If I wasn't careful, I'd be late by at least ten minutes, which is an eternity to grade-school kids.

"How you doing this morning, Mr. Stanley?" I greet my next-door neighbor. It's good to see him sipping coffee on his front stoop, because it means I'm still on the early side. You can set your clock to Mr. Stanley's daily routines. He's retired military.

"I'm still making roll call, I can't complain." The man bellows every time he speaks. He'd be great in a stage play.

"That's okay, I'll complain enough for the both of us," I say with a smile.

Mr. Stanley's explosive laughter clears the nearby tree of skittish birds.

"I ain't worried about you one bit, Miss Zora," he says. "You'll always land on your feet."

Like the smell of Mr. Stanley's fresh-brewed coffee, his words swirl and linger. I wait for it to drift on a summer breeze, so I'm not reminded that lately my self-confidence isn't as strong as it used to be. I wonder if Halstead did that. *Maybe I've just been faking it all this time.*

I'm rounding the halal meat store, when my phone starts blowing up with texts from Skye.

Has he kissed you yet? she writes without so much as a morning greeting.

No is my succinct answer.

Why not?

It's a question I've been pondering a little lately. Okay, a lot lately. I take a deep breath and catch a whiff of car exhaust. Remembering our moment at the lookout point, I can't help but think about that failed opportunity. The beautiful view, the romantic sunset . . .

I don't know. Maybe there's something about royal protocol? I text back.

It's possible.

I hear the Landerelian royal family is supposed to be super conservative, texts Skye.

Then pause.

Maybe you should make the first move, Skye writes.

I will not, I respond.

Okay, but if dude never finds the nerve to kiss you, you'll kick yourself for not setting things in motion.

I'll take that chance. And then I wonder another thing: *Has Zach reached out to you?*

Did he tell you he did? is her rapid reply.

No, that's why I'm asking you.

He did.

Do you know he'll be down there this weekend? I text.

Yes. But he may not have time to see me.

If he does, I'd consider that a major hint.

My phone rings right away, and I pick up.

"You think so?" Skye asks as soon as I answer.

"I do, yes," I tell her. It's still so weird hearing Skye get worked up over Zach. I wish I never brought it up. But I feel like I need to monitor the situation.

"I'm not going to even read too much into things at this point," Skye is saying. "And I'm not going to let myself look forward to seeing him, because he may not come."

"I think that's a healthy way of looking at this," I say. "My brother can be a heartbreaker, because he's just so clueless sometimes."

"Don't worry about me. Just keep enjoying the sights with Owen," says Skye.

"I am having so much fun hanging out with him," I admit. "And it really isn't an issue that he hasn't kissed me yet." And I mean it. I like taking things slow. I feel like we're still just starting to get to know each other.

119

"I'm a little jealous because geeking out over new places is the type of thing you and I do together," Skye says with a laugh. "And funny enough, if you count our air-kiss greetings, even *we* kiss more than you and Owen do."

"Good-bye for now, Skye," I singsong like my mother does. Skye chuckles and hangs up.

I walk into the center just as I put my phone away. And after dropping my bag in the usual vacant locker and tracking the kids to the reading room, I'm ready to devote all my attention to them.

This time they group hug me so hard, we all nearly tumble to the floor in laughter. No sooner have I physically untangled us all do I have to work through a tangle of verbal updates. I answer each child at first, until I just can't keep up.

"Zoorra, Zoorra, I read the whole entire book you borrowed me! Page one, page two, page three—" Prentice reports without taking a breath.

"I'm proud of you, Prentice!" I smile.

Dante can't stop jumping up and down to get my attention. "My mom said we get to keep the cat so it can get rid of the mice!"

"Congratulations!" I say. "On the cat, not the mice."

Then, from the raspy voice behind me: "Me, my mom, my brother, and my sister are going to the Mets game Friday."

At the same time small, sticky fingers are poking my side. "I thought my auntie would name my new baby cousin T'Challa, but his name is Will."

While Prentice continues: " —page eight, page nine, page—"

"Okay, okay, guys!" I try and calm them down. "Sounds like so much has happened in just a week. I'm happy for all of you, but remember, we need to practice for the festival." I may sound like the older, more responsible one, but really it's an act. It's either this or come up with an excuse to Ms. Nelson why the kids don't have their routine together.

The kids have decided to recite a poem together for the Fam Fest, which is coming up in a few weeks. After breakfast, one group heads to the playground and the other stays with me. They each say a line or two, and as of now, no one has any recollection as to who speaks what line. I have my work cut out for me.

I give it one last push before leaving, in case I can lock in a good head start for next week's rehearsals. As the kids chorus out their good-byes to me, I think of the Gala coming up fast. I can't believe it's in two days. I'm not nervous for me. I'm just stressing because of all the good I could do for these kids if I win. I may have some backup plans in the works, but nothing that could get the program $15,000 so fast.

But the few extra minutes are the reason I am not the first to arrive to class. In fact, I am the last. At this point, the only seat available is right next to Kelsey. She has to remove her things from my chair.

"Thanks," I say under my breath as I sit. She doesn't even say *You're welcome.*

She looks for a place to put her belongings—a designer handbag and . . . a cap? A maroon baseball cap. I can't imagine her wearing that to class. I take a second look at the cap. Is that Owen's? It looks like the exact cap Owen had on when he met me at Ingrum's Books.

I try to look away from it, but I guess I don't succeed, because now Kelsey is aware of my eye problem. She glances at me and then starts petting the cap like it's a purring kitten.

It's a message. Directed at me. And it's coming in loud and clear.

Chapter 14

"WHAT IS this place?" Owen asks me. We're in the musty basement of the Humanities Center, where I texted Owen to meet me
after class. It's not the most romantic spot, but it's cool. I want to
prove that I can take him off the beaten path, too.

"The Halstead archives—photos from yesteryear mainly." I've
visited the archives once before, my first day at Halstead, but didn't
have time for a true perusal.

"This is amazing," he says appreciatively.

You could probably take two bookcases from the castle library
and stack them on top of each other and they would not be taller
than these archive cases.

"May I offer any assistance?" A thin elderly man wearing a lanyard appears from a back room and addresses us.

"No, thank you," I say. As he turns to leave, I have second
thoughts. "Actually—are there any early history photos of African
American students at Halstead?" I'm just taking a chance, and I
keep my expectations low.

We follow the man as he shuffles his way down one aisle after another until he hooks a right by a reference desk.

"Early African American documentation can be found here, in chronological order from the founding of the university in 1833," he says, gesturing to a blue binder.

"Thank you!" I say.

It doesn't take long for me to find it. I have nothing in mind, and do not follow any logical search method. Gut and pure nosiness lead me to the binder labeled "The Clock."

There it is—the Clock with an actual clock face. Everything looks the same as it does now, with the exception of the fancy wrought-iron roman numerals. And standing underneath the clock holding a sign reading "A Time for Change" are four African American students—three guys and one girl.

"This is incredible," Owen whispers.

"Excuse me while I zoom in for this close-up," I tell him before I draw the photo closer to my face.

"It's a privilege to witness your zoom-in again, Zora, thank you," says Owen with a smile.

I hold the image within inches of my face, because I want to take in every last bit of info. I want to mentally scan and imprint this photo in my mind. The look on the four attractive faces—chiseled by angles, but softened by rounded curves—their style of dress and the sign they hold. Especially the sign. It's white with black lettering in all caps. Each hand touches one part of it. They share the weight of the sign's message.

The photo, like most of the photos in the archives, is in a clear, protective sheath. Touching it directly is not allowed, no matter how much I suddenly want to run my fingers over it. I flip to the back of the photo and I'm excited to see handwritten notes there. The year of the photo is recorded. The names of the students. Their graduation date. I am floored. This photo was taken in 1886—during the Reconstruction era!

"This is exceptional." Owen says what I cannot. I'm too choked up to speak just yet. "Are you all right?" he asks, and rests a comforting hand on my back.

I take a steadying breath. "It's just, seeing this means so much to me. To come face-to-face with young trailblazing African Americans who grew up in the aftermath of slavery? It's this shining real-world example of our resilience and determination as a people. And it's right here at my fingertips. I feel like I found a pot of gold."

Owen rubs my back and nods slowly. "Imagine how seeing this will make your program kids feel," he says.

Thinking about it this way gets me excited. I pull out my phone and take a pic of the photo at every angle; then I leave the archives room walking on air.

Owen and I emerge from the building into the summer humidity. It's nice of him to walk me back to the library, where I plan on studying for a few hours.

"Zora, I had hoped to ask you out for dinner, but plans have changed."

Oh. I wonder if those plans have anything to do with Kelsey.

"In light of the recent news report, and because of what happened at the lookout the other day, my security team advised that we don't go anyplace public for now."

"I understand," I say, hiding my disappointment. Still, I'm grateful we can hang out on campus. We enter the library, and Owen sits with me at a study cubicle. He pulls up a chair while I start unpacking my bag.

"I'll leave you to your studies, but if it's not too uncomfortable, I'd like to invite you to dinner at my place."

Oh!

"Is this all some elaborate scheme to get me to come over?" I ask with a teasing smile.

Owen fights to hide his own smile. "We won't be alone. Colin will be in the next room. I don't want you to feel obligated or uncomfortable. In fact, I would understand if you'd rather not—"

Owen is clearly nervous he's overstepping, but it's all good.

"No, you're fine," I chuckle. "Thanks for the invite, it sounds nice. When were you thinking?"

"I know you mentioned you have a special event to go to Friday, and I have some boring function to attend due to royal duties." He makes a face. "I was thinking Saturday?"

The Gala is on Friday—I've been trying not to think about it. Now Saturday will get the butterflies going, too. "That works for me," I say, hoping I don't sound too agreeable. Only when Owen exhales a puff of air does it occur to me that while waiting for my response, he had been holding his breath.

"Can I pick you up?" he asks. "Will you be home?"

"Yes. I was just planning on spending the day in to catch up on some much-needed studying."

"Why, has something been distracting you lately?" he asks, back to his relaxed playfulness.

"I wouldn't say some*thing*, it's more like some*one*," I tease him.

He smirks but at the same time seems to smile at me with his eyes. I look back at him, remembering how very close he came to kissing me the other day.

"What is it?" he asks, obviously catching a wordless message in my expression. My face is always telling on me. I wish it would stop being so transparent.

"Oh, nothing," we both say at the same time, only Owen says it in a high-pitched voice and with an American accent.

I crack up and throw a balled-up scrap of paper at him. Too bad he ducks just in time for it to blow past his face.

Chapter 15

"IT WAS just here not a second ago, and now it's disappeared!" I exclaim.

I want to cry. When did my dresser top get so cluttered? And why is my nail polish already chipping?

Gala night has arrived. And my just-in-case speech is nowhere to be found.

"Calm down, we'll find it. It couldn't have just walked away," says my mom. She's all dressed up in a flattering black cocktail dress and rummaging through the mess on my bed, shaking out my damp towel, looking under the two backup dresses I've laid out. I can tell she's getting worked up—her forehead is glistening. She grabs the piece of paper sitting on my bed and starts fanning herself.

"That's it! My speech!" I point to her makeshift fan. "You found it."

"This?" She stops fanning and hands it to me before plopping herself on my bed to put on the shoes she walked in carrying.

The speech goes in my hidden side pocket. Dresses with pockets are the dopest kinds. This one is in a cool violet shade. It's got a fitted boatneck, sleeveless design, and it flairs a bit at the hip before tapering at the hem above the knee.

"Everything's going to go great tonight. Your dad will behave and you'll enjoy the evening, whether or not you get the top prize," Ma is saying.

I nod and take one last look in my flimsy closet door mirror.

I smooth down the skirt of my dress. I check my right pocket one more time for my speech and make sure my touch-up lipstick is in the left pocket. Okay.

"Good to go, Zora?" says John from the doorway. Sensing the frantic mood is neutralizing, he's reemerged. As the newest member of the family, John fades to the background when we crave space and shows up when we're in most need of help. He'd been retracing my steps around the house, in search of the now-found piece of speech paper.

"Yeah, I think so," I say. My worries about Daddy's behavior keep bubbling up and threatening to spill out in tears.

"Your mom is right. It'll all go well tonight." He smiles at Ma. "Babe, make sure you take a pic of our girl when she's standing up there accepting her award."

There's pride in John's voice, and it makes my heart smile. It also makes me feel guilty about complaining about my dad. Here I am with two father figures willing to stand with me, and that's something cool to focus on to calm my nerves.

Ma gets us into New York City in good time. Besides a little traffic at the Holland Tunnel toll, we manage to beat the Friday-night rush hour before it starts. I hope my dad makes it before the roads get super congested with clubgoers and barhoppers looking to party in the city.

The crowd is still thin when we arrive at the dimly lit grand ballroom. Despite the grandness of the space, the cathedral ceilings, and the textured, ornate drapery hanging on the walls, the setup doesn't feel false or over-the-top. The classical music sets the tone you'd expect of an event giving away tens of thousands of dollars to organizations. The back of the space is dotted with tall, slender cocktail tables and is perfect for mingling. There's even a small dance floor in the back center. The front area near the stage is for dining. Some of the waitstaff in crisp black and white are carrying shiny silver trays through a maze of round dining tables, while others are smoothing down the white tablecloths and arranging cutlery and dishes. A man in a black suit is onstage at the podium, plugging in wires. A few elegantly dressed people are seated at different tables, absorbed in murmured conversations.

"Let's go find out where we're sitting," says Ma.

There are seating assignments, and a helpful waiter escorts us to table 8. I immediately take my phone out of my pocket and text my dad.

We're here. Come to table 8.

"Did you let him know where we're sitting?" Ma asks. Her face looks strained. In all of my concern over myself, I haven't thought about how Daddy's presence would affect her. My parents split up almost a decade ago, and throughout that time, I can count on one hand how many times I've seen them chill together. Even at Zach's high school graduation, they sat apart. We weren't sure if they'd take pictures together, but for Zach's sake they did. I know people whose parents aren't together, but they still do the occasional thing as a family. Not mine. My parents are not friends.

When we were younger, Ma was very careful not to bad-mouth Daddy in front of me and Zach. She wouldn't even let us do it. But now that we're older, she doesn't go out of her way to mask what she thinks of him—if not verbally, physically. Like now. Her shoulders are practically level with her ears, and she's obviously texting one of her sisters for moral support, because she has her phone nearby with its screen faced up, which is highly unusual for my mom, the queen of enforcing screen-free zones at dinner tables.

"Are you okay?" I ask her.

She looks away from her phone and gives me the eye contact she's famous for. "Sure, baby. I'm excited for you."

"No, I mean, with Daddy coming tonight."

She forces a smile and reaches out to place her hand on mine.

"Don't you worry. I'm telling you, it'll be a great night. I can feel it in my bones."

"I'm just glad to be spending this night with you both—especially you, Ma." I grab ahold of one of her fingers and give it a loving squeeze.

"Aw, thank you, Zora," she whispers, and exhales a bit. "Hey, let's get some comfort food going. You wanna go grab us an appetizer so we can have something to munch on while we people watch?"

"Good idea." I sniff away the sentimental moment before I get teary eyed. "I'll see what they have floating around."

I stand up, smooth down my dress, and head to the cocktail area of the ballroom. There are a lot more people there now, chatting with drinks in hand. A few of them look around my age, and I figure they must be the other honorees from surrounding area schools.

There's a clear path to the buffet table, where chafing dishes are lined up and ready to be mined. Halfway down my runway, I'm drawn to the sight of one guy's wavy ginger hair. From the back, he reminds me of Owen. My grandma always warned me to be careful about staring too long at someone or they'll sense you doing it. Sure enough, the guy must feel my eyes on him because he turns to face me just as I'm walking by.

It *is* Owen.

My Owen is here?

I almost run up and throw my arms around him, until I see who is by his side. Kelsey is standing with him.

"Zora!"

"Owen!" I say at the same time.

We beam at each other.

Kelsey turns around and gives me a look of recognition. She's taller than me by a few inches, but that's not the only reason she's looking down on me.

"Zora, this is Kelsey Reston," Owen says cordially. "Kelsey, meet Zora Emerson."

"We've met," I say. "In class. How do you know each other?"

"I've known Kelsey a long time," he says. "We went to school together back home. She's the daughter of the American ambassador to Landerel."

Oh.

I turn my attention back to Owen. "I didn't expect—"

Kelsey cuts me off. "Zora, do you mind taking a photo of me and Owen?"

"Uh, sure," I hear myself say. Kelsey hands me the phone from her exquisite wrist bag, and takes Owen's arm. This is totally no more awkward than that time I did an entire class presentation with a piece of spinach stuck in my front teeth.

As I center them in the screen's vertical view, I have to admit, Owen and Kelsey look good as a couple. Kelsey in her jewel-toned minidress and Owen in black-tie classic.

"Thank you." Kelsey takes back her phone, and she doesn't move from Owen's side.

I turn my attention to him. "I didn't expect to see you here." I manage to get out what I tried to say before.

"I know. I saw your name in the program when I arrived and thought, this is mad!"

"I'm in the program? Great, now I'm going to have to stop my mom from collecting every program she finds tonight," I say to try to loosen things up.

"She's here?" Owen asks. "I'd love to meet her at some point, but I take it tonight's not the best time." I nod at him, feeling a tingly warmth from his thoughtfulness.

"You found out why I'm here, but I still don't know what brings you here," I say.

Kelsey has finished examining her picture with Owen and silently observes our back-and-forth. She cuts in to speak for Owen. "This event is sponsored by the royal family of Landerel. This is part of their philanthropy, helping young leaders of limited means."

Something in the way she said that offends me. I slo-mo replay it in my mind, and there's nothing but factual statements in her words. But man, it stings. Was it the delivery? Or the messenger?

"Yeah, well, not everyone was born with a silver spoon in their mouth," I clap back cheerfully.

Nasty nice, Skye calls it.

Kelsey looks at Owen, then back at me. "I meant no harm."

"What makes you think I'm injured?" I shake off my annoyance and paint a polite smile on my face. I won't give her the satisfaction of letting her know she got under my skin. "You stated a fact, and then I stated a fact."

Owen takes a sip of his drink. But I get the sense he's somewhat pleased with my handling of Kelsey. I catch a twinkle in his eye, and it makes me smirk. If he could dab or throw me a high five right now, he would.

"There's my baby girl!" My dad cuts through the crowd and wraps his arms around me with what feels like his full weight. I take a stumble backward.

Now it's Kelsey who has the smirk on her face. Owen just looks perplexed.

"Oh, hi," I say in a feeble voice.

Daddy looks handsome dressed in a smart navy suit. But unlike the majority of the men here wearing dark, solid tones, Daddy wears pinstripes like he plays for the Yankees. If the ballroom lighting were just a tad dimmer, the stripes would be tough to make out. But they aren't. And he doesn't stop there. Instead of a classic color shirt, Daddy's is pink, and his tie is shiny violet with embossed patterns. "Fresh to death" is what he would call himself right now. I'm sure that was the last thing he said in the mirror before leaving home.

"That traffic was a beast. I'm glad I left home early." Daddy pulls back from his embrace a little and holds on to my arms. "Did I miss anything?"

"No, no," I say. I want to give him my full attention since he seems so relieved and amazed that he made it here on time, but it's hard. I'm hyper-aware of Owen's and Kelsey's presence over his shoulder. The good thing is Daddy's back is to them since he basically bulldozed his way into our circle, so he isn't aware that he's interrupted a group discussion. I'll take advantage of this. My plan is to escort him away from here before he can embarrass me with one of his longwinded, outlandish stories.

"Ooo-wee, look at this place!" He marvels at the tall ceilings. It's a surprise he can see anything at all with his shades still on. The combination of the suit, sunglasses, and Bluetooth earpiece makes him look like FBI—well, a very bright, fly FBI agent. It's no wonder a few people are craning their necks to get a good look at me. They must think I'm some VIP worthy of Secret Service protection. That would actually be Owen.

"It is beautiful," I say. "Let me give you a quick walk-through before we get to our table." Daddy holds out his arm, which I gladly take.

"Uh, Zora, I'm sure Owen here is interested in meeting your . . . father, is it?" says Kelsey for the nasty-nice championship win.

Daddy turns and notices the small audience for the first time.

"Who do we have here?" he asks in his jovial way.

"Daddy, this is Owen and his friend Kelsey."

"So, Kelsey, I know that you're Owen's friend," Daddy starts. "But, Owen, I didn't get your connection to my daughter."

I can feel my face getting hot.

"Owen and I—"

"Zora and I—"

We both start at once.

Now Daddy's sunglasses come off, and his eyeballs ping-pong back and forth suspiciously between Owen and me. I've seen that face before. He's picking up on a scent.

"Zora, Owen can speak for himself," he says.

"How do you do, Mr. Emerson?" Owen manages to find his courage. My dad shakes his hand firmly and slowly. Owen's Adam's apple bounces as he swallows. "To answer your question, I met Zora at the Halstead University library, and we've stayed in touch ever since," he says.

Daddy nods and finally lets go of Owen's hand.

"Stayed in *touch*, you say?" my dad asks.

"In—in close contact, sir," Owen stammers a bit.

"Close?"

"In contact. We've remained in contact." Owen's bobbing Adam's apple is all the satisfaction my dad needs. He's sticking it to the rich, and he's enjoying every moment.

I don't think Kelsey's ever witnessed someone schooling a prince of Landerel before. Her eyes are popping out of her head, but she dares not utter a nasty-nice word to my dad.

"Shall we grab you a drink before we get started on the tour?" I tug on Daddy's arm.

"Is that an open bar?"

"I'm pretty sure." I can't bring myself to look at Owen. "Let's go find out."

At the bar, Daddy shares jokes with the bartender, who is also a Black man of a certain age.

"Thanks, brother," Daddy tells him as we step away. "You be easy."

I don't mention Owen, nor does Daddy ask any other questions about him. But he seems to be keeping the matter on his radar.

"You look beautiful," he says. "And see how connected we are, Zora? My tie matches your beautiful dress. If this music had any type of *flava*, we'd turn this into a daddy-daughter dance."

That makes me smile.

"Aw, thank you, Daddy. I noticed our matching colors. And you don't look too bad yourself!"

"You know I had to come correct, fresh to death," Daddy says.

I shake my head and laugh, which helps break some of the tension I've been feeling tonight. We're still chuckling when we get to our table. Ma tucks in her pout when she sees the two of us joking around. She looks like she's been fighting boredom while I've been away. More people have joined the table, but no one is sitting close enough to her for a chat. Her cell phone screen has just faded to black, which means her sisters have been filling her head with their usual gripes about my father "not knowing how to act" or "always showing his ass."

We take the two empty seats next to Ma, but of course, I position myself in between my parents.

"Hello, Yvette." My dad puts down his drink and pivots slightly toward my mother in greeting.

"Kenney." My mom nods her head and begins fidgeting with her phone.

"And how are your sisters doing?" Daddy goes there immediately.

"Everyone's fine." Ma clears her throat.

I need to teach my mom how to be fluent in nasty nice.

"Cheers to our exceptional children," Daddy bellows to everyone at the table, holding up his glass.

My mother seems to hold her breath for a minute, and then when everyone (but her) raises their glasses and shares a few jokes with Daddy, she begins nibbling the finger foods I brought her.

Ma often says I get my familiar way with people from "the one and only Kenney." But I disagree. As important and special as Daddy can make a person feel when he befriends them, he also has a knack for burning bridges. The minute a friendship turns sour—which his often do—he'll feud with that person as if their bond never existed.

On the other hand, Ma's friendships are long-lasting and cherished. The only person I've ever seen her have a falling-out with is my dad. You can tell she's not comfortable with things being so strained between them, but she prefers it this way. "Staying friends with Kenney would be exhausting," I overheard her tell one of her sisters once.

As everyone gets settled at the table, I glance over my shoulder at the rest of the seated crowd. I spot Owen at a far-off table near the stage, and he shoots me a wink that makes my stomach flip.

Then I spot Kelsey next to him, telling him something, and I turn away.

"Looks like we're finally getting started," Daddy addresses his new fan club at our table.

An hour into the program, after we have been served our main dish and are eating dessert, the Gala president takes the stage to spotlight the high school student nominees.

I feel a burst of nervousness and I stop eating the fancy chocolate pudding cup. I twist my hands in my lap.

"Best of luck to all of the honorees," Daddy says to the two other families at our table. With his next breath, he turns to me and whispers, "But we all know the winner tonight will be my daughter."

I shake my head at him, then try to listen as the president drones about the award and the prize and all the good we've done as students. She introduces each nominee with a short description of our programs. Then, she finally announces, "The Goodie award with a fifteen-thousand-dollar grant is being awarded tonight to Appleton High School rising senior Zora Emerson."

I instantly seek my mom's hand, and there it is, already reaching for mine. "Amen, amen, amen," she leans over and whispers in my ear.

Daddy is already on his feet clapping, but I tug him back to his seat because the Gala president's presentation is not yet over. She begins reading my bio and about why the committee chose to award the grant to me. It feels totally surreal. Ma holds my hand, and Daddy records the presentation on his phone, the sensor on his earpiece flashing green every few seconds like he's my personal documentarian.

"Zora's proposal for expanding her Walk Me Home program and providing affordable aftercare for her community moved the committee," the president says, and I feel like I only can take in half of her words. "Her incredible grasp of the community's needs was reflected in her excellent proposal's detailed budget, projected growth, and five-point plan. Ladies and gentlemen, let's welcome Zora to the stage."

I hug my parents and then walk on wobbly legs to the stage podium.

From that height, I can appreciate how large the crowd is. It doesn't take me long to spot Owen. I can't make out the expression on his face, but I see Kelsey watching me with mingled admiration and skepticism. I look back at my parents, who are now seated next to each other. Daddy is in my seat, and they're both leaning toward me, their elbows on the table, their faces glistening with emotion.

"Thank you to the committee, the sponsors, the teachers, and the Gala president for this tremendous honor," I start, one shaky hand on the edge of the podium. I take a deep breath. "Our program's purpose is more than providing a babysitting solution to parents in Appleton, New Jersey. It's about joining hands with the families to safeguard children from one of society's greatest ills: apathy. This program models the idea that in the absence of your parents or guardian, your community is your family. You never walk alone. Thank you."

It's not until I am seated again that I realize my speech that I went bananas looking for is still folded up in my pocket, untouched. It's an amazing feeling of accomplishment that I want to last forever.

Chapter 16

THERE'S NO sign of Owen or Kelsey when I'm asked to stay behind for official pictures and a word with the Gala committee chair. Sounds like a big deal. When she introduces herself to me and Ma, she comes off less grandiose than her title. She's kind enough to pull us aside somewhere quiet in the service staff room.

Fortunately, Daddy is talking sports with his new bartender friend, so we're able to chat uninterrupted for a few minutes.

"I'm sorry to keep you so late, but this is an emergency," she says. "After a careful review, the committee and I have decided to rescind your grant honor."

"Wait, what? Why?" asks Ma.

I feel queasy. Am I hearing this right?

"It's nothing you have done, Zora. You are a stellar student and an exciting community leader. We were just concerned about— well, there's a conflict of interest."

"I don't understand," I say.

"It's about your previous connections with the prince of Landerel," she says.

Owen? My confused silence speaks volumes.

"The award's biggest sponsor is the royal family of Landerel."

"I—I didn't know," I say.

One time, I smacked into the fancy glass door of a coffeehouse, and the crowd inside witnessed it. I didn't have the option of just not entering that coffeehouse, because it was my first day at work there. Multiply that humiliating feeling by one hundred, and you get this moment.

I think of the kids who I made promises to. I think about Ms. Nelson and all the people gathered at the center for the livestreaming of this event.

"Here they are." It's Daddy's bartender friend leading him to us.

"Thanks, brother." Daddy gives him dap before the bartender leaves.

His casual expression changes when he reads the room.

"What's going on?"

"They're rescinding our baby's award," says Ma. Hearing the heartbreak in her voice snaps me back to crisis resolution mode. I don't want her worrying about me.

"No, someone's going to have to explain to me why this is happening." Daddy's voice rises as his anger brews.

"We realize that chances are Zora didn't know about the prince's affiliations," the chairwoman is saying, "but because of the

144

optics, our co-chairperson and attorney have advised us to step away from our decision and offer it to our runner-up."

Dad looks at me and walks away a few paces for some breathing room. I know this move, because it's something I do when the pressure's on. The fact that he's got a lot of catching up to do makes things worse. When he met "my friend Owen," he didn't realize Owen was this prince who's being referred to here.

Ma silently rubs my back. I try to swallow the lump in my throat.

"Zora, I know you worked hard for this," the chairwoman is saying earnestly. "We respect your privacy and that of the prince, so we will report that the committee miscalculated our point system. But we have good news for you. Independent of our organization, a New Jersey–based corporate sponsor in attendance tonight was inspired by your story and wants to donate five thousand dollars to your endeavor. They will get in touch with you soon."

She apologizes again and assures us they will not speak to the press, but will release an official statement explaining the error in calculation and announcing the new winner.

The only person with links to the award ceremony and to school besides Owen is Kelsey. But I brush aside any temptation to make her the villain. That would be too easy and too cliché.

Daddy walks back over once the official has left.

"You mean that that boy you introduced me to out there who could barely look me in my eye or give me a straight answer? That's your prince?"

"Kenney, this isn't the time," Ma interrupts him.

"Owen and I have been hanging out as friends," I say.

"Oh, so while he's sitting on his crown jewels, he's also blocking you from your dream opportunity? How is that right?"

"Kenney, this isn't helping."

"According to you, Yvette, the way I do things never helps matters, huh?"

"Can we not do this now? Here?" I ask, exhausted.

"Fine, it's over and done with." Daddy holds up his hands. "But I'll just say this: I don't care how much this prince is worth, he's not worth the trouble he's causing you."

Now it's my turn to walk away and get some air.

Chapter 17

IN ONE moment, I'm sweetly slumbering in that space between realms, enveloped in stillness, suspended in time. In the next, I'm yanked awake as if by a squirt of nasal spray, smelling-salt edition. My eyes snap open and search my bedroom ceiling. My frozen body has yet to catch up to the frantic thought loop in my brain. I'm no forest ranger, but dang if there isn't a late-morning brightness to the sun poking through the blinds. *Oh no. Have I overslept? Did I miss my class?* My arm frees itself from my bedsheet cocoon and swats at the side table before pulling back my phone. *Whew.* It's only 7:05 a.m. And it's Saturday.

Relief.

No, *DREAD!*

The sight of my phone brings it all miserably back to me. My lock screen is lit with text notifications.

Congratulations, Zora! You do Appleton proud. That's from Ms. Nelson.

So much better than the speech you wrote. Except for the part where you forgot to thank me! ☺ That's from Skye.

I'm impressed. You accomplished the impossible—getting Ma & Dad to sit together. From Zach.

The only person I text back is Skye.

They rescinded the prize money because of my link to Owen. His family is a major sponsor. I hit *send*.

It's still early, but she'll see the message when she gets up.

No crisis can make me cry, sis. No crisis can make me cry, sis. With my eyes sealed tight, I repeat the goofy catchphrase Skye and I made up until I feel the bounce-back courage rise up my spine.

I take a deep breath, get on my feet, grab a notepad and pen from my backpack, and pace the room while I crunch the numbers.

I figure at minimum I need $10,000, which is at least six months of teachers' pay and provisions for a two-hour aftercare program. That just covers the bare necessities, but it's doable.

Let's see, I've raised $1,000 in donations and personal savings. If this corporate sponsor really comes through with $5,000, we have enough to stay the course. That should give parents around three and a half months of aftercare. That's long enough of a heads-up for them to make alternate plans.

My Grant Writing class professor thinks I'm a shoo-in for at least another $3,000 in federal grants. But I won't know for sure until the very end of the summer. If I get that, we'll cover close to five months of aftercare.

Time to crack open my plan B. It's simple . . . kinda. I just need a lot more participants at the fundraising events I've already got planned for the Appleton Fam Fest in one week. The main one is the scavenger hunt. It's the five-year anniversary of place-based learning at Appleton schools, so I'm hoping an Appleton-centric scavenger hunt will be popular. More participants equals more pledge money from businesses. Most of the game stops are at local shops, and they're happy about all the social media shout-outs they'll be getting from each hunter.

I don't brush my teeth, shower, or answer any texts until I've hammered out the details. I post the Fam Fest announcement online and invite people to sign up for the scavenger hunt, silent auction for local artwork, kid-choreographed parent dance-off, double Dutch contest, and—hoping for the next moneymaking idea—I add "plus more fun surprises." Maybe I could do something unexpected and rent a dunk tank. I don't care if I'm the one who has to be the dunkee, I'll do it. I'm desperate. Working on the details helps keep my mind off of the disappointment.

My phone buzzes. It's a text from Owen.

Good morning. How are you feeling?? 🎉

My heart races. What? Is he trying to be ironic? Why would he ask me that after such a huge roller coaster of a night?

He texts again.

I know we already have plans for tonight, but are you free to meet up this morning? Ingrum's Books?

I think about everything Daddy said about Owen and wonder

if Owen has been playing me. *Game recognize game.* If he is, I have no one to blame but myself. I was warned from day one.

But it still doesn't mean I shouldn't walk right up to Owen when I see him and say my piece. Just like the other ideas sparking up this morning, that idea feels right. I think I'll do just that.

Give me about two hours, I text Owen.

Chapter 18

"WE KISSED."

I'm totally distracted, because I can't get the right lipstick blend going. I've got to head out if I want to meet up with Owen on time. It isn't until I'm wiping a tissue across my bottom lip that Skye's words play back in my mind. I look from the colorful tissue to the phone that's resting on my bathroom sink.

"For the hundredth time, Skye, Owen and I never kissed."

"Girl, please, I've got no time to wait on y'all." Skye sounds like she's given up on the idea of a royal lip lock. "I'm talking about me . . . and Zach."

I pick up my phone to gape at the video chat screen. Skye's hand is on her mouth and her eyes are squeezed shut. "Can't believe I just said that!" she shrieks more to herself than to me.

"Can't believe I've just *heard* that!"

She drops her hand. "Um, that came out mad salty. Aren't you happy for me?"

"It's not that exactly." I sit on the edge of my tub and try to soften the edge in my voice. "Are you sure about this?"

Zach? With Skye? It's like the feeling you get running into someone out of context. My worlds are colliding and it's surprisingly uncomfortable.

"Actually? I guess. I still can't make sense of it myself," she says breathlessly. Skye lies back, sinking into a furry couch pillow. "The moment we saw each other at Piedmont Park, there was this connection. It's hard to explain. It was almost like, why ignore something that feels so easy?"

Listening to the emotion in Skye's words, imagining the feelings she and my brother are experiencing . . . I can't believe it. Is this really Zach she's talking about? It's all too much.

Skye's face settles, and I wonder if she's frozen. This bathroom doesn't get the best reception.

"Are—are you okay?" she asks me with concern. I missed my window for reacting like a supportive friend, so anything I say beyond this point may sound forced. I might as well go for honesty.

"I just don't think Zach deserves you." There, I said it.

"What do you mean?" Skye sits up.

Um, where do I begin? Zach is the same kid who for years cared nothing about school, or about keeping peace in our house. He would rage out at home at me or my mom, steal if he had to— sometimes right out of Ma's purse. And the lying. Ugh. That was the worst. He would sometimes lie when it wouldn't even make sense to lie. But Skye knows a lot of this. I jog her memory.

"He spent most of my life causing my mom all types of grief," I say. "He's been disrespectful to her, and I just can't forget all the hurt he put her through."

Skye frowns. "He's turned his life around since those days. Can't you see that?"

"I do see it, and I'm proud of him for it. But I just don't think he's earned a prize like you."

"Zora, nobody's perfect." Skye's voice softens. "And everything he's doing now to make better decisions is a daily apology to your mom."

"I don't see it that way. Everything he's doing now seems to be just benefiting him."

She shakes her head. "Your mom has forgiven Zach. Why can't you?"

"I'm working on it." I look away from the screen to avoid Skye's piercing eye contact.

"Are you? Is that why you're heading out now to tell off Owen? It looks like you're on a one-person mission to punish people who maybe take the messier way and don't have their life mapped and figured out like you do."

"I have every right to be mad at Owen. He's the reason Walk Me Home is going to be scrambling."

"Sure, you do. And Zach, too. But when you stay angry for this long, I have to wonder if it's really Zach and Owen that you're mad at."

"I'm not mad at myself, if that's what you're trying to say."

"That's not who I meant. I'm talking about your dad."

My throat tightens. "You know what? I'm running late. I gotta go."

Owen and I arrive at the same time. I see him outside of Ingrum's, and we take a seat at the fountain wall across the plaza.

Owen's wearing a striped rugby shirt that's making him look good enough to tackle. I shake off those thoughts, immediately.

"I just heard," he says, his voice low and concerned.

"Oh, so you didn't have any idea this was going to be a conflict?" I ask stonily.

"What I said was true—I didn't even know you were one of the honorees until I saw the evening's program," he says, turning to me. "Zora, I'm so sorry. I can't imagine what a terrible blow this must be. Everything you had planned for Walk Me Home . . ." He reaches his hand out, but I don't take it.

"It'll be fine," I sigh. I know it's not *really* his fault I lost the money. But this wouldn't have happened if we didn't have this connection. "I'm working on finding another way. But for now, I just think it's better we cool things off." I start talking as quickly as I can, to get it all out. "I don't want to come over for dinner tonight. It's too upsetting otherwise." This summer could've gone as I'd planned had I just walked away from Owen to begin with.

Owen is silent for a moment. Then when he speaks again, his voice is even lower. He sounds more upset than I would have expected.

"Zora, can we take a moment and just calmly talk things out?" he asks me.

I shake my head, avoiding looking at him. "Are you trying to say I'm not being calm about this? You know, I was warned to stay away from you," I say. "I should've listened."

"What do you mean?" he asks.

"I picked up a call when I had your phone, thinking it was you. It was a girl who was pissed off to hear me on the other end."

Owen sighs and rests his elbows on his knees.

"Was it from a New York number?"

"Yes."

"That's a girl my mother arranged as my date for my brother's wedding. She's a socialite, so of course she's someone my mother approves of."

"And I'm someone you know your mom won't approve of. Is that why you've been spending so much time with me?"

"What? No, Zora."

"Just like your skydiving and playboy reputation, you do things that'll piss her off. For all I know you're just this thrill seeker, this adrenaline junkie who is obviously now out for a different kind of thrill. Jersey girl and a Black one at that! Well, hmmm, no, I don't think so."

"Where is this coming from?" Owen plays the confused role pretty well.

"It doesn't matter," I say. "At this point, I would just rather walk away while we still kinda have a friendship."

And walk away is what I do next.

Chapter 19

AS I wait for the train on a hot platform Monday morning, my mental mantra loops like the hook from a hip-hop track (pun intended). I silently rap my made-up lyrics to the chugga-chugga rhythm of the moving train.

That's my decision. / Aaay! / I stand by it all day. / Yea!
/ I'm about that mission. / What! / Can't keep me away.
/ Leggo!

The more I silent rap, the more it sinks in. *My* decision.

"Have you decided what you'll do this summer?" my high school civics teacher, Mr. Gaines, asked me earlier this year after class. It was Mr. Gaines who first told me about the competitive college summer programs, and reading about all the classes they offered blew my mind. Who knew there were classes about community outreach? Suddenly it felt like I could come up with a solid game plan. If I could start Walk Me Home with the little I knew about organizing, I could do a lot more if I had a deeper understanding of the subject.

"Yup, I'm going to apply to Halstead U," I told Mr. Gaines. "I don't know if I'll get in, and I don't even know how I'll pay for it, but I'll go through the application process and see how far I get."

A surprise acceptance letter and a generous scholarship offer later, I'm a card-carrying Halstead summer student like, *Heck yeah!*

But if only things could be going as smoothly as I'd planned.

I squeeze onto the crowded train. It's standing room only. I end up standing in front of the train door, and the door's glass panel shows me my reflection. I can partially make out the deep-in-thought stare of my eyes. When Daddy is beefing with some bodega cashier over his grief of the week (for you name it—favoring meat eaters, not ordering enough coconut water, whatever), he asks me to accompany him to the bodega so that I can *stare* at the cashier. "A few seconds of those intense eyes digging into his soul and he won't skip a morning prayer ever again," says Daddy. Thus far, I've always been conveniently too busy to go to any bodega, mechanic shop, pizzeria, or barbershop with my father.

I study the reflection of my silhouette closer when I notice that my two cornrows look like a crown on top of my head. The smaller braid starts at my temple and reaches behind my ear to the back of my neck, where it tucks under the larger, bumpy braid that stretches from my side part and snakes above my forehead before wrapping around my head. My large teardrop earrings and brass bracelet catch the sunlight and my white earplugs run down my torso like a blood-pumping, life-supplying artery.

> *That's my decision. / Aaay! / I stand by it all day. / Yea! / I'm about that mission. / What! / Can't keep me away. / Leggo!*

I need to get back on my grind.

"Next stop, Halstead University campus," the conductor's voice echoes.

Passengers rouse to life. The crinkling of fast-food bags and zipping of backpacks and purses ring out. Murmuring and laughter waft onto the outdoor platform as the doors release about a dozen passengers, including me.

I walk into class feeling like a boss in command of the place. My internal hip-hop mantra is on loop, full blast, and I step in time to its beat with goddess-in-charge strides across the room.

Matt is already sitting in the corner, and even though he sits close to Kelsey's usual seat, I head over to the empty chair next to him.

"Hey." He smiles. "How was your weekend?"

"Well," I say. "Let's just say I'm pretty determined to make this week better."

"I hear you. That's sort of the idea of our program, right? Imagining a better world?"

I pause, in awe. Matt just might be as cheesy as I am, and it's a beautiful thing. "That's exactly right," I say.

"I think you'd really like my other friends in the dorms. Tomorrow is already Taco Tuesday time. Wanna join us?"

Kelsey drops into her seat, looking every bit as polished as her nails. She glances over at me.

"Yes," I say to Matt with my biggest smile. "I'd love to join y'all."

After classes, I hit the library again, and I can't help but think of Owen when I'm here. But my game face and my headphones are on, so I stay focused. I got behind on my audiobook last week (Skye would be shocked if I told her, so I haven't), so I make some strides in catching back up. Plus, I put in some extra work on my grants, along with writing down some new Fam Fest ideas. Thinking of the Fam Fest puts me in a good mood. Every year, Skye and I have the best time there. It's so much fun sampling the food trucks, watching Appleton High's band do their thing, and, of course, people watching. It won't be the same without Skye there this year.

On my way out of the library, I dart behind a stack when I see Owen at a table. Really? I may be on a mission to crush it this week, but that doesn't mean I'm not distracted by the sight of him.

I peer through the books even though I know I should leave. He's with Kelsey, and their books are completely abandoned beside them. They're both leaning over Owen's phone, their heads very close together. Kelsey giggles.

I'm not jealous. *I'm not*, I assure myself. They've just known each other forever, and even if Kelsey is interested, it's not like Owen ever said anything about her. I think of his whispered "I like you," and our hug, and our almost kiss . . . and then I think of the people following us at sunset, the rescinded money . . .

I have no claim on Owen. I decided that this weekend. He and Kelsey can whisper about anything they want.

Kelsey looks up, and I turn away quickly, even though I don't think she saw me. Without a look back, I head for the aisle of books I need. And then I am on a train back to Appleton, where I belong.

> *That's my decision. / Aaay! / I stand by it all day. / Yea!*
> */ I'm about that mission. / What! / Can't keep me away.*
> */ Leggo!*

Chapter 20

IT'S TACO Tuesday, and I'm in da house. Grosvenor House to be precise. The coed dorm is one of the newer residences on campus. Matt meets me at the security check-in at 7:00 p.m. sharp. He looks a lot more relaxed away from class. He's ditched his button-up for a cool graphic tee repping his home state of California. He's wearing flip-flops, plus his dark hair is floppier than it was yesterday. As we take the elevator to the gathering, Matt gives me a rundown of who I'll be meeting tonight.

"Abby goes to St. Ignatius with me, so we're pretty tight. Perez is my roommate, and he's cool, too. Amir is a Halstead college student who's also our RA. The only person I'd say is not the friendliest is Kelsey. But I don't think she can make it tonight."

That's a relief.

The party is in a common area that looks like what Ms. DeStefano, my Appleton High librarian, would call a makerspace. There are two comfy egg chairs flanking a couch on each side of the room. Ms. D brought the same kind of egg chairs into our school and arranged them in a similar way. At first, no one knew what to make of this and used them as a hidden spot to sneak in a nap or phone call and enjoy some contraband snacks. But soon people figured out sitting in those chairs is the quickest way to get into a focused zone when you need to cram for a test or get absorbed in a book. On any given school day, there's usually a race to claim those seats before anyone else.

Cushioned ottomans alongside coffee tables make for lots of foot resting and taco building. About five people are already there, plastic cups in hand. Hip-hop music is coming from a tiny boxy speaker.

"Everybody, this is Zora," Matt calls out.

"Hi." I give a general greeting. A guy who looks like he could pass for a college student waves back from across the room. He must be Amir, the RA.

"Hi, I'm Abby." A cheerful girl wearing paint-splatter-print eye frames and a matte red lip shade is the first to walk over. She cranks my hand in an excitable greeting like she's half expecting the maneuver to jack me a few inches above the ground. She must be Matt's friend who hails from Southern California, like him.

"So, Matt tells me you commute in every day?" Abby asks as she escorts me to the drinks table. Unlike Kelsey and her snobby friends, her tone isn't filled with bewilderment *or* mockery; she's just matter-of-fact.

"Yup." I nod. "New Jersey Transit is no Hogwarts Express, but it's magical in its own dysfunctional way."

Before I can follow up with a self-deprecating eye roll at my own corny joke, Abby breaks out a loud giggle-snort, and then keeps cool and carries on as if snorting is as mundane and every-day as sneezing or coughing.

"No way, it's super cool that you take the train. I think I met one other person who doesn't dorm, but he drives in. What's your commute like?"

The food and beverages are all here, and I remind myself that I have to make sure to contribute to whoever bought everything. I grab a sweaty bottle of cold water and a napkin.

"If you asked me a week ago, I would have told you it's not bad, but I secretly wish I didn't have to do it," I tell her. "But now I feel like I don't know what I would do without that time on the train to catch up on reading. Plus, I kinda like stepping off campus at the end of the day."

"Yeah, it can get pretty intense here," she admits. "I'm so far from home. Plus, I'm so unfamiliar with everything around here—and this area of the country for that matter—so I haven't ventured out much farther than the Clock."

"Have you checked out Viv and Wally's?" I ask. "It's a world-famous Jersey diner not far from here."

"No," says Abby. "You see? I'm so in need of help."

"Well, anytime you're feeling adventurous, I'm happy to take you sightseeing to any part of Jersey you want to check out."

"The Jersey Shore, please! I've heard so much about it." Abby does a happy hop, and I watch her glasses resettle on the bridge of her nose.

"And they say reality TV can't be a gateway to culture." I purse my lips.

"And by culture, you mean dance clubs, right?" she asks. For the second time, she casually giggle-snorts. I'm starting to wonder if she has a deviated septum or something. Either way, I like how she's committed to normalizing snorting. Like, why does society get to decide what's an acceptable bodily sound and what isn't? I'm on Abby's side, all the way.

"Don't forget tacky boardwalk shops," I tell her, not missing a beat. It's as if I hear bursts of snorts every waking hour, and it doesn't give me pause.

"Boardwalks, too? Okay, now I have to go because that sounds like the life I miss." Abby grabs a can of LaCroix and walks to the other side of the room to sit next to Matt on the couch. "You should come to the beach with me and Zora, and get a taste of home," she tells him.

"Here, we say 'down the shore,'" I say.

"I beg to differ," a guy on the other couch shouts from across the room. "Only a Benny from North Jersey has to come 'down' to hit the beach. We South Jerseyans are already here."

"Who's Benny?" Abby is confused.

"It stands for the northern places we travel from—Bayonne, Elizabeth, Newark, and New York," I explain.

"Yeah, Bennies eat subs and we eat hoagies," the guy continues. "They call pork rolls Taylor ham, and it makes no sense."

"Did someone spike your drink, Pork Roll?" I ask him.

"Whoa, Taylor Ham's got attitude. I like it."

"Ignore him. That's just Dominic Russo messing with you," says Abby. "How about it, Matt, ready for some homesickness cure?"

"I'm feeling pretty at home here, thank you very much." Matt gestures to his dorm room, located right off the common area. "But cool, count me in for some seaside sightseeing by the seashore, Sally."

"Speaking of feeling at home, I'm loving how open everyone is with their cheesy jokes here," I say. "I think I've found my people." And it's true; I'm surprised at how comfortable I'm feeling now.

Abby holds up her LaCroix can in a toast, nailing that viral-meme pose. "Cheers, friend, and welcome to your village."

A guy wearing a Puerto Rican flag shirt and carrying a laptop strolls out of Matt's room. He plops down on the couch, stretches his legs out on the ottoman, and opens up his laptop.

"You must be Perez," I greet him. "I'm Zora. I take community organizing with Matt."

"Ugh, another save-the-world person," Perez jokes.

"In the flesh." I smile.

"Hey, I think I recognize you now," Perez says. "Do you hang out with that prince on campus?"

I freeze. He didn't just go there.

"Perez, really?" Matt looks disappointed in his roommate's etiquette.

"Are you talking about the prince again?" asks Abby.

"I'm just asking Zora about her friendship with him." He

holds up his hands in self-defense. He looks at me. "Is 'friendship' the right word?"

"You work for the school paper?" I tease.

"No, I'm a future MBA. I don't count words, I count money," he jokes.

"Oh, okay. I can already see why you're going for an MBA—you mind other folks' business pretty well." I can hardly get the words out before I start laughing.

"Burn!" shouts Matt.

Laughter breaks out from the other couch, too, and I think for a second that they're laughing at my corny joke. I glance over and Dominic and another girl are sitting there cracking up at something they're watching on a cell phone. Matt goes over to investigate.

"You guys have got to see this video," Matt calls us over. "It's a Taco Tuesday challenge."

The video shows people making the craziest faces as they try not to drink milk to douse out the fire hot sauce flavors in their tacos. As serious as I expected this crowd of future leaders to be, all it takes is laughing at that video to get them to challenge each other to their own Taco Tuesday fun.

"You are to find one mystery ingredient from your dorm fridge or drawer or wherever and add it to a taco. The person with the most delicious add-ons will win tonight's challenge," says Dominic, after sharing the video with everyone.

"Amir, cover your ears," says Matt to the guy I correctly

assumed is the RA. "I don't want you to come across any info you may have to report."

"Hey, as long as you guys don't expect me to participate, we won't have a problem," says Amir.

"I don't live here, so I get to sit this one out, too, right?" I ask. The small crowd boos and whines. I'm holding my belly with laughter and try to talk over all the jeers and *nos*. "I'm perfectly happy to film this for YouTube if you need a cameraperson. No charge."

"Wait, Taylor Ham, how about you get to be our impartial judge and taste tester?" says Dominic.

"Um, Pork Roll, I would love to accept that position, but I'm going with another offer," I counter. "If you all really insist, this bag is my home on the go." I pat my backpack. "I must have some kind of snack left in here."

"You can't use toothpaste or crap like that," Dominic answers like some street game show host. "Only edible, non-medicated food and foodstuffs."

"Bet! I got this. I'm in," I tell him.

As gross as this challenge sounds, it turns out to be the most fun I've had with Halstead Hopefuls (not counting Owen, of course). I guess as hard as we work, we can play just as hard. Here I am beating my chest and talking a good game, in the same way I do back in Appleton when I'm losing at a game of spades against Zach. I don't even know what, if any, ingredients I have in my backpack, but when the stopwatch goes off, I manage to find a half-eaten pack of sour cream and onion chips, an unopened packet of vending machine oatmeal raisin cookies, and three individually wrapped chocolate caramel nuggets I was saving for the kids at camp. I get to crumbling everything down and sprinkling bits of each over a veggie taco.

The whole time I can't help but think Owen would love this gathering. I wonder what type of snacks he would bring to the table. You can usually tell a lot about a person by what they snack on. This group is so laid-back. They pull out Cheetos, nachos, and every other cheese snack you can think of.

Kelsey doesn't seem like the type to enjoy this kind of stuff, and I can't claim to be upset she doesn't show up. Matt says the only reason she gets invited is because she's Abby's roommate and Abby doesn't feel comfortable excluding her.

Everyone's in such a cool mood, and it's only Tuesday. It's a much chiller vibe than the one I've been on lately. I guess that's the power of tacos, rituals, and food with mystery ingredients.

The concoctions aren't all disgusting. They are all relatively edible. I only have to race to the nearest trash can and spit out my food once. Technically, it's more like the nearest *available* trash can. Just my luck, the closest receptacle is, ahem, occupied when I need it. And I learn the uncomfortable way that the second-closest one is located next to the stairwell door down the hall and around the corner. With an equally-grossed-out Abby leading the way, I make it just in time to spit out the food with class. We cough, laugh, and (on Abby's part) snort out the contents. There's the sound of the stairwell doorknob twisting, but we don't see who's swinging the door open until we're upright and consider the figure standing frozen in front of the exit.

"You girls in need of medical assistance?" It's Uncle-Officer, the campus policeman who escorted me out of class. He has a crinkled-up and questioning look on his face.

"Good afternoon," I say for some reason. It's a knee-jerk response possibly thanks to my painfully awkward way of over-compensating.

"We're fine now, thank you, Officer Kirkwood!" Abby is sunny and friendly and shows zero signs of embarrassment. I feel Uncle-Officer's silent once-over as Abby and I walk back to our chill zone. Uncle-Officer follows. Like a driver spotting flashing lights in her rearview and assuming the worst, I almost pull over before realizing that Uncle-Officer isn't here to ticket me. He moves past me and Abby and heads in the opposite direction once we reach the main hallway.

"His son is Amir Kirkwood, our dorm monitor." Abby sets my paranoia over being tailed by campus police at ease.

In fact, Amir is clutch as a contest official—even though the "surprise" was entirely on his part.

"Guys, this isn't exactly how I envisioned my night ending, but okay." Amir grins, his voice booming. Not able to convince Amir to taste test anything, we invite him to confirm all ingredients are aboveboard. As a rising sophomore in Halstead's chemistry program, there's no better person to fill this hastily created role.

In the end, Perez wins for mixing crumbled Fritos and tuna

salad into what he called a *fritotu* taco. No one knows it's Perez's creation until Dominic looks at the slip of paper under his winning taco's plastic plate.

Perez even makes an acceptance speech that is low-key classy.

"I feel like all the hours and hours of crappy videos and challenges I've watched have come together," he announces to the common room. "Everything led up to this moment cramming for this taco challenge, which I easily aced. I'm glad all that viewing made a difference here today."

And what a difference hanging with this crew definitely makes for me today, I think on my walk from Grosvenor House to the train station later. I gently assure myself that I'm back to my usual, down with the whole crowd. I remind myself that even though it feels like it, today is not Friday. So it's back to listening to my audiobook as I take in Halstead's summer-evening vibe.

A couple of mornings later, I'm back on campus earlier than usual. I'm still plugged into my audiobook, but there's a huge weight off my shoulders. I hadn't even realized just how heavy the stress I'd been carrying around was until I don't feel its presence. It's strange what you can get used to if you're not careful. We're trained to think it's normal to feel tense half of the time, but a crisp, harmless snort borne from a gleeful moment is like a flag on the play in this game of life.

I'm still thinking about this as I cut through campus en route to my first class. The quad is still dewy and the temp is cooler. Everything is still in the embrace of quiet, in between moments of birdsong. But I'm not alone. The oscillating breeze and gentler sun has bikers and runners out in strong numbers.

Outside a narrow passageway between two old buildings is where I see him. I've just hooked a right turn when I spot Owen, and he's walking in my direction.

This is it. The first time Owen is unavoidable since I left him behind at the bookstore on Saturday. Now I get to put my Dope Dress Test into effect, and I'm hoping it proves me right.

My Dope Dress Test is a theory that's only ever been exercised at the mall immediately after I eye the cutest dress I instantly want. I ask myself: Is this a passing fancy or love at first sight? Well, the first step is to find a full-length mirror, hold the dress against my body, and note how absolutely cute and perfect it looks. Next, I check out the dress from an arm's length away to examine if there are any flaws I haven't spotted. I calculate the sale price over and over again, and think about how I can cover the cost. The last step is to drape the dress over my arm and carry it around as I pick up the items that I truly need. I remember the reason I am shopping and prioritize those items.

Once I'm ready to buy whatever it is I've originally come to the mall to purchase, I'm usually totally fine with putting back the super-cute dress. Just like that. Nine and a half times out of ten, I am no longer obsessed. I don't even feel like I'm denying myself. Turns out, the mere act of touching, examining, having the dress wholly in my possession for those moments is satisfying enough. I don't actually have to buy it at that point, because I've had my fill of it on some emotional level.

I'm counting on the fact that my interest in Owen has been acknowledged and considered, and so it will lead me to my usual Dope Dress Test results. I figure with a few days of not speaking or meeting up, we'll both see things logically and with a lot more clarity. If I'm right, this could be the start of not a romantic relationship, but a cool friendship. Maybe I can get him to come with me to a future Taco Tuesday party. I just know he'd crack me up with his ability to do silly things without breaking character.

I'm practically laughing at the thought already when I pull out my earplugs to holler at him.

"Hey, this is a first," I say when we stop and stand face-to-face in greeting. "I never run into you on campus." *Outside of the library*, I admit internally.

"Wow, Zora." His jaw clenches, and he keeps one hand clutching the shoulder strap of his leather rucksack. "That's the first time you've noticed me along your route," he says.

I frown when I recognize what he's saying. I'm looking into Owen's eyes, but I hear the playback of our very first conversation at the library. Still anonymous, Owen had talked about the "beautiful," "self-possessed" girl on campus he was into.

Me?

The girl who is always plugged in to her headphones and doesn't ever notice he's alive. The only girl on campus he wishes he could ask to his brother's wedding.

It's me.

"Have a good day, Zora." He holds my gaze as he takes a step toward me, then looks ahead in the middle distance as he turns in the direction he's heading. In surprised silence, I watch him walk away.

My belly butterflies fly around all in a tizzy, but oddly, I don't mind. Even though I failed the Dope Dress Test, this feels like a win.

Chapter 21

CUTE COUPLE! *Two of the dopest people on the* 🌍 . ♥

I finish my comment on the airport selfie that Skye posted of her and Zach. I'd stared at the photo for a while before deciding what to write.

It's true, they look good together. And happy. How could I stand in the way of that?

She FaceTimes me right away. "Hey, girl. Hey."

I wave at her. "I was just about to call you," I say. "I have some good news."

She beams. "Owen back in the picture?"

I shake my head. "No. Even though he's back on my mind." I don't mention our campus run-in from Thursday. I still need to think about that on my own. "My news is . . . I miss you." I whine and fake cry. Skye cracks up. "But seriously, Skye," I go on. "I'm really happy for you. I mean, like, if I totally ignore my discomfort and agony, I can see you and Zach being a great idea. You are two of the most tenacious people I know."

"Awww, thank you. I think," she says. "Then I guess you wouldn't mind if I do this." She pauses and lets out a loud *"Squeeeee!"*

I block one of my ears and laugh at her nuttiness. I've never seen her so gaga over a guy. It makes me smile.

"I'm sorry I'm going to miss Fam Fest this year," says Skye. "Big day for you. Let's see what you're wearing."

I walk over to my flimsy mirror and angle the phone to it.

"Off-the-shoulder jumpsuit, nice!" she says. Skye and I share a taste in fashion. I'm a little less afraid of bright colors, but both our closets are a mix of festival looks and preppy staples. "Your hair worn half-down like that looks cute, too."

"Thanks," I say, feeling suddenly nervous about today.

"Ready to make some money moves?" she asks.

I nod, tamping down my nerves. "Leggo!"

"It smells like hot glue and glitter paint out here." Zach comes out to the back porch, where I'm sitting on a bench, busy packing my personal art project into a black duffel bag.

"No, it doesn't, there's a nice cross breeze going on," I say. It's surprisingly good having Zach back home. Of course, I asked him about Skye when he arrived late last night. The smile on his face told me all I needed to know. He's genuinely into her. "Still buzzing off your Atlanta trip?" I ask.

"A little bit." Zach drops his guard with a goofy grin.

I give him a tight smile. He takes a seat next to me.

"I know this isn't easy for you to accept, and I understand why," he says. "I mean, sometimes I don't think much of myself, either. And that's word," he adds. "But then I look at Ma, at you, and I realize that through all of my ugly, God has been showing me beauty. And if that level of love can pull me from the darkness I was in, well, then that's a battle victory. Now I want to join the fight. Every day, I hope to fight for my family, for myself, and for the patients I meet at work. It's my thank-you to you and Ma for never giving up on me. It's my way of saying sorry." I see my brother swallow down the emotion bubbling up. "Zora, every day I pray my darkness didn't take away your light."

Something inside me releases, and I start to weep. Zach puts an arm around me and I rest my head on his shoulder for a few seconds. I feel his kiss on the top of my head.

"Were you out here most of the night?" Zach looks at the mountain of scrap paper and other office and art supplies around me. "I said I could help, but you didn't accept my offer."

"I was almost done when you asked." I wipe my nose and lift my head off his shoulder. "Perfect timing as usual."

"You wanna talk about perfect timing—if we don't leave now, we'll miss out on the good parking," he says. "You ready to head out?"

I nod and get to my feet. Zach throws my duffel bag on his shoulder and leads the way out the front door.

Ma and John are already in the car waiting for us. I know it makes Ma happy that there's one summer event we're all in attendance for—Appleton's annual Fam Fest.

We score one of the last parking spots but have a bit of a walk to the main stage of the festival, located at City Hall Plaza. On our way there, there's lots to see. A good three blocks on Main Street have been blocked off to traffic. Vendors line those streets selling artwork, books, clothes, accessories, and more. Some vendors simply advertise their businesses or announce that they offer services like home nurse's aid or piano lessons. Plus, there's a backpack and supplies drop-off for back-to-school donations. Our noses lead us to a grassy area with sizzling grills, food trucks, bouncy castles, and even a dance floor with a DJ.

"There's so much going on," says Zach as he dodges a carnival-style dancer on stilts.

It looks like a record number of people came out, and so many of them are joining the fundraising events. *Did my extra invites really work last minute?* I wonder, thinking about my posts online the morning after the Gala.

Zach goes to drop a cardboard box off at Skye's parents' booth promoting their capoeira school. Ma and John outpace us and grab a good spot in front of the City Hall Plaza stage. Appleton High's marching band is performing. I can see from here that the band is fully suited, despite the humid eighty-degree weather. The flag team is dancing with all the precision they would for homecoming. Everyone is giving their all. There is pride in every move.

I go and check on the dunk tank rental. I'm so proud I pulled it together so late, and even got Zach to agree to be the dunkee. His shift starts after the mayoral dedication. When I get there, I'm shocked to see a person swimming in the tank. There's already a long line formed.

What in the world—?

"R.J.?" I shriek and laugh at the same time.

Standing at the head of the line, collecting everyone's fee, is Owen's grad school friend R.J.

"How did—?"

"Your boy made a few calls to the Appleton Chamber of Commerce, and the rest is history," R.J. says with a grin.

My boy?

I turn toward the dunk tank. The person pulling himself out of the tank, ready to be dunked again is . . .

"Owen?" I say. He looks unrecognizable in a skydiver jumpsuit, helmet, and goggles. The sign next to the tank reads: ZORA EMERSON WOULD BE *THRILLED* TO SEE THIS SKYDIVER TAKE A TANK DIVE. HELP MAKE HER DAY TODAY.

I cover my now gaping mouth. I don't know whether to crack up or stand in line!

"Now you understand why I had to be here and see this for myself," R.J. says, shaking his head.

I make eye contact with Owen. "This is nuts, but I love it!" I shout to him. He laughs and waves at me.

I see Layla Fredrickson, her sisters, and her parents in line.

"This is our third try," says Ms. Fredrickson. "We'll get him for you, Zora."

Owen barely has time to give me the thumbs-up before he goes down again. I clap and laugh from the gut at the nuttiness of it all.

"Thank you," I mouth to Owen with my hand on my heart.

He nods at me. And then—*splash!* He goes down again.

I'm all ready with my short speech. I've been asked to say a few quick words about the place-based learning program I helped to start. But during my speech, I have a special surprise for the program kids. It's in the duffel bag in front of me.

I wait by the stage, ready to go, alongside my mom and John.

"There she is." It's my neighbor, Mr. Stanley, in full military uniform with his wife, Ms. June.

"I'm glad to see you here today, dear heart," says Ms. June. "I hope today's fundraisers make up for the grant you were robbed of."

"Thank you, Ms. June," I say.

"What's the last text you got from Dad?" Zach asks when he joins us. "He said he'd be here, but I can't find him."

I check my phone. "Uh . . . two days ago he texted me a raised fist emoji with an article: 'Trace Your Lineage to African Royalty.'"

"They've started!" John hushes us and we turn our attention to the stage ceremony in play.

The school superintendent is at the mic. "Appleton students have been transformed by place-based learning. Five years ago, a middle school student simply wanted to take an educational tour of her hometown. She wanted to know more about Appleton's storied past, and she knew that not only teachers, but her neighbors, could teach this to her."

I can hear Ms. June, Mr. Stanley, and others call out, "Mmm-hmm," "Sure can," "Yes, ma'am."

The superintendent continues. "So this student asked if she could invite to school Ms. Earley, a family friend, to share her knowledge with her classmates. Well, Ms. Earley became our first place-based-learning speaker. Since then, there have been many more witnesses to Appleton history sharing firsthand accounts of the 1968 riots, the civil rights movement, our transportation system, and more. I see a few of them out here." Mr. Stanley waves. "This program grew from guest speakers and history lessons to walking tours, outdoor science experiments, and even architecture drawing classes. And that curious student who started us down this road is here today to celebrate five years of this wonderful program. Ladies and gentlemen, Zora Emerson."

My family whoops, and hollers out their applause. As I make my way onto the stage, I can't help but feel a sense of pride for my city, for this program, for myself. Sure, a part of me feels like this is a do-over for the Gala, but a bigger part is excited to receive this honor so close to home. I spot Ms. Nelson smiling at me from the crowd. No livestreaming, no fancy black-tie attire, no bigwigs. Just me and the community I love sharing a special moment. By the time I get up there and shake the superintendent's hand, Appleton's superstar mayor, Aina Oyeyemi, is at the mic.

"Zora Emerson, we wish to bestow on you a special honor," Mayor Oyeyemi says. "To do this, we've borrowed from ancestral traditions. Here today is the Kofsua Dance and Drumming School."

The drummers and dancers I'd seen waiting in the wings walk onto the stage in a parade of vibrant head-to-toe African kente, beautiful beaded accessories, pulsating beats, and joyful movements. One dancer guides me to the center of their drumming circle, and I'm instructed to mimic her dance moves. We laugh as I catch on. I have so much fun waving my arms, swaying my hips, and rocking my head backward and forward that I keep up the dancing longer than they do. The crowd cheers when the music and dancing ends.

Reverend Wilson takes the stage with a mic in hand and prays a blessing over me, which I'm sure Ma appreciates.

Finally, Mayor Aina asks me to join her at the mic. "Zora, for all you have done and continue to do for our community, you are hereby crowned Hometown Princess." She places a tiara on my head. I'm feeling so much, but don't know what to say. My vision blurs, but I still make out my mom, crying, with John's arms around her.

"And for your support of local businesses, Appleton's Small Business Owners raised enough funds through community donations and fundraising efforts to help reach your aftercare program goals. By the way, you may recognize the gentleman holding the check. He got his employer to match the donation, for a total amount of five thousand dollars!"

The oversized check comes floating out onstage. The person's identity is hidden, but I'd know those velour track pants anywhere. Daddy's face pokes out with a warm smile. I run up and give him a hug. This is incredible!

I've got to hold it together to make this speech. "This is beautiful beyond words," I begin. My voice is cracking. "Thank you so much! I wanted to come here today to give the program kids a similar distinction and you guys beat me to it," I say.

My duffel bag is already on the stage and unzipped, and I pull out last night's art project—sparkly gold crowns made from poster paper, glue gun, and lots of imagination. I call to the stage any children from the program, and crown them all.

"You come from greatness and we will do all to support you to achieve your greatest," I tell them each.

The children stay onstage with their crowns on and recite the poem they've been rehearsing, "I, Too, Sing America," by Langston Hughes.

As I stand to the side listening, I look out into the crowd, where Ma, John, and Zach are beaming. Dad is there now, waving at me. And I find Owen, too, standing near the edge of the audience—soaked, and beaming. He really showed up today. Our eyes catch for a moment. Then the kids finish and the Kofsua school members applaud with more drumming.

When I step offstage, well-wishers swarm around me and offer positive words, warm hugs, and sweet smiles. I see a dried-off Owen waving good-bye to me from a short distance, and then he and R.J. slip out unnoticed. I'm grateful. And giddy. In fact, the rest of the festival, I feel like I'm walking on air.

Chapter 22

"YOU BEAT him to the spot!" My bookseller buddy Eliana greets me with a mischievous grin from behind the counter.

Oh good! I really need that cozy reading nook today. I'm feeling brave enough to text Owen again but haven't actually done it yet. You can't get more comfy and encouraging than that reading nook. The two-seater faux leather couch is the perfect kind of used and worn.

"But you're going to want to head to the YA fantasy section first because the book you've been asking about is here, but there's only one copy!" Eliana sounds even more persuasive than usual. "I didn't get a chance to grab it for you, and can't leave my post now, but I wrote down where you can find it."

"Okay," I say tentatively.

She hands me a piece of scrap paper with her chicken scratch on it. I'm happy the book is in, but were it not for Eliana literally nudging me to the YA fantasy section, grabbing it would not be my number one priority.

"And don't worry about your reading nook. I have it blocked off for cleaning, so consider it reserved just for you."

"Thanks," I say.

Because she's watching, I take a few steps in the direction she's sending me. When I think the coast is clear, I turn around, but she's still staring. I give her a wave and give up faking my way to the nook and head to grab my fantasy novel. It's the series-ending book and I *am* a little excited it's here.

I read the note: "Lowest shelf, alphabetical, Rusnack."

Careful not to scrape my legs against the carpet and get them ashy, I take a seat on the floor to locate the "R" author names. It's a good thing I decided against wearing my mini summer dress. I'm rocking my fave denim shorts—loose-fit and distressed with a rolled-up hem—so there's no danger of exposing myself.

That's when I see it. But oddly, there's a cell phone pressed against my book. *Who left their phone there?*

"I don't know about you, but I need another confessional." The voice is coming from the other side of the bookshelf, as if the person is seated on the floor, too.

"Owen?"

"Ah-ah-ah," he says. "No recording devices may remain on your person during this conversation. You know what to do."

I cover my face with my hand and shake my head when I see him make room for my phone.

"Okay, see it now?" I ask when my phone is in place, next to his.

"Thank you," he says.

Eliana is in sight. She peeks her head down the aisle and, through gestures, asks if I'm okay. She's making sure she didn't aid and abet a creep. I give her the thumbs-up.

"Did you orchestrate this with Eliana?" I ask.

"I have to give her most of the credit. She knew your favorite bookshelf category." He pronounces "category" in three syllables. "I had originally gone over to the travel section expecting to see you zoom-in reading."

"How many times do I have to tell you there was a teeny-tiny caption on the page and I wanted so desperately to read it?" I say.

"That's right. Pardon, I keep letting actual facts cloud the details."

We're both facing the bookcase now. I can see the hunter-green cap he's wearing. I'm sure he can see my piled-on coily bangs.

"Congratulations on the festival yesterday," he says. "And it sounded like you met your fundraising goals?"

"It definitely made a splash," I say, even though I know it's corny. "Thanks in part to you."

"No, it was all you. The dunking was a gesture."

"Thank you." I decide to take the compliment. "That took humility."

"It was the least I could do, Zora, after the award fiasco."

"I was upset, but . . . I know there's nothing you could have done about that."

"Oh, really?" I hear him scoot closer. "Well, maybe now I can give you my news in person, instead of over text."

"What's the news?" I ask.

He speaks with a hushed, tender voice. "Remember the beautiful girl on campus who I wished would notice me? Well, a few days ago, she actually did."

My face warms up and my heart races. Just to make double sure we're speaking of the same person, I ask, "Really? Tell me what happened."

"I'm sure *you* can imagine," he plays along. "Instead of breezing right by, she finally saw me, halted her speed walking, pulled out her earbuds, and said hello."

"And where exactly did this happen?" Just to make triple sure.

"Right outside the Hurston Hall passageway," he says.

"When?" Quadruple.

"Let me see, it was . . . Thursday." He sounds like he's smiling.

"Oh, well, I'm happy for you." I touch my warm cheeks. "What is it that you said you saw in her again?"

"When I see her, she reminds me that some things in life aren't too good to be true," he says.

I catch my breath.

"That's beautiful," I whisper.

"That's the truth." He sounds relieved to have said it.

For a moment, we sit in the comforting echo of his sentiment.

The tenderness of his feelings and the bravery in saying something so personal are tugging us in each direction until we're rocking back and forth in a cradle of sweet sincerity.

I want to run over and give him a hug, but I tread carefully instead. "So, now that she's noticed you, what's your next step?" I ask.

"Well, that's why I've come here to talk to you. I was hoping you could offer some advice."

"That depends. What does she think about you?"

"At first I thought, I probably look nothing like the type of guy she goes for," he says. "But now, I don't know, I get the sense she thinks I'm a good-looking bloke. Plus, she seems to like hanging out with me."

His swagger gets me hyped. It's unexpectedly cool, like my chemistry teacher's killer drumming skills. If Owen weren't a royal, sometimes I'd think he were from the Landerelian equivalent of Appleton. And with that thought, I remind myself that at the end of the day, Owen is still a royal. *Hello, reality.*

"What about you being a prince and all that comes with that, like your jumpy Secret Service agents?" I ask.

"That I unfortunately can't change," he says. "But I'd be as transparent as possible with my security chief so there are no surprises from them, and so that they are more sensitive to her privacy and personal space."

"So, no more Men in Black banging down my front door?" I ask, abandoning all pretense of talking about "her."

"I promise, Zora." He raises his head above the books and I see his hazel eyes peer through. I sit on my legs to elevate my eye level to meet his.

"Permission to come over to your side of the aisle?" he asks, his eyes unblinking.

"Permission granted," I say.

In a few heart-pounding moments, he is walking toward me wearing a cute grin. I stay where I am, sitting on my legs, and he joins me on the floor.

Hoping to extend these seconds of bliss, we both sit there facing each other.

"Good to see you again," he says warmly, which is just what I wanted to say to *him*. An electric current runs through my arms, and I look down and smooth my hair.

"Nice to see you, too." Owen is wearing a crisp white V-neck tee, slim fit but relaxed jeans, and white sneakers. He takes off his cap and hooks it on one raised knee. His other leg threads underneath.

"Has your dad asked you to stay away from me?" he asks.

"No," I laugh. "Not yet."

"I was relieved he didn't spot me at the festival," he says. "By the way, any chance you're the type who the more your parents hate a person the more you like them?"

"Not always, sorry." I get comfy and sit on my bottom with my back to the bookcase. He does the same.

He fakes an injury to his heart.

"That's okay, I'll find another way to win you over," he says.

"Oh, were we talking about *me* all this time?" I ask playfully.

"You have to know how I feel about you," he says. "I'm pitiful around you."

My heart races at his words. "No, I wouldn't say pitiful," I say. "Although, you came pretty close when my dad started interrogating you."

We both crack up at the memory.

"Fair enough," he says. "Fair enough. But you should've seen your face when Kelsey asked you to take a photo of us."

"Oh, that?" I ask. I roll my eyes and shrug my shoulders. "I was just surprised, because I didn't take her for an Android phone type."

Owen is smiling at me now. I try not to smile back at him, but I'm failing.

"Okay, Zora. But just so you know, Kelsey and I are not dating. And we never did date. We're old friends and I have no interest in being any more than that with her. And the other girls I've been photographed with these past few years? They're my sister Emily's friends. They've taken me under their wings because they know how much I meant to Emily."

"I'm glad to hear that," I say, feeling a rush of relief.

"And I can't promise you that I won't get . . . attention from the media. But I will do everything I can not to let it get in our way."

I nod, grateful. "What's that you got there?" I ask, and I gesture to the book he walked over with. Owen grabs the book on the floor behind him and hands it to me.

"*Black Women in History,*" I read the title.

He smiles sheepishly. "Yeah, I figure, with all the Landerelian study and *close-up* look at me, I can learn something about you."

"I haven't—" I pause, but continue looking at the artsy images of the four women on the cover.

"You haven't what?" Owen asks.

"I started to say I haven't been to space or led an army. But I guess through these women, I kind of have, or at least feel like now I can."

I pass the book back to Owen with a nod of approval.

"And just so you know," I tell him. "That brief and not-so-close-up look at you was more for study than for pleasure."

"If you say so." He grins.

We have a fun time chatting, teasing each other, catching up. He admits to me it felt like a long week without really talking to each other, which gets my stomach twisting, in a good way. When Eliana pokes her head around again to check on me, I give her the thumbs-up. I also mouth to her that she can free up the reading nook (for my bookstore nemesis or whoever may want it). She beams at me and gives me the thumbs-up back. Then she gives Owen a meaningful glance and gives me *another* thumbs-up, this one clearly conveying her approval of Owen, specifically, his looks.

Wondering what I'm smiling about, Owen turns to Eliana, who by then is pretending to straighten books.

When he looks back at me, I give him my best innocent lamb look and shrug my shoulders.

"Okay, Zora Emerson." He gets back to the matter at hand. "What say you? Should we give us a try?"

"Sure," I answer, my heart pounding. "Let's give us a try."

Owen beams and I'm sure I do, too. But we don't make a move, because by now, there's a crowd of people milling around. He nods and wipes his hand over his mouth as if to stop it from smiling too hard.

"I like the sound of that," he says.

Chapter 23

"I STILL can't believe we raised so much money at Fam Fest!" I exclaim, leaning back against my headboard with my phone in one hand.

"Well, you worked your butt off with those fundraisers, so I'm not surprised," Skye says on speakerphone. "You need to just write the book on fundraising . . . *Skkrrrr-skrrrr.*" She suddenly makes a high-pitch screech to mimic a car braking. It's like going from playing elegant word piano to banging her elbows on the keys. There's a good chance everyone downstairs heard her, too. I have a feeling what this is about.

"Okay," she continues. "I know we have a rule about not making guys the center of our worlds, but dang, girl, we're not talking about just some average Joe. The prince of Landerel is your bae."

Skye is still talking when I see a text come through. It's from Owen!

Panic pulls me to my feet in no time.

His text reads: *I got a bit distracted this morning and forgot that I have something else to ask you. Might you be available to continue our conversation?*

I respond: *Sure, I'm free to chat now if you are.*

Brilliant. Are you home?

Yes.

I'm near Appleton and can pick you up if you'd like to go somewhere to talk. I can be over in 10 minutes if you send me your address.

I'm about to have dinner with my family. How about you just come over and we talk here? I type out my address and hit *send* before I can hesitate.

Owen responds almost instantly. *I'll be right there.*

"Ohmygodohmygod," I interrupt Skye. "Owen! He's coming right now! To Appleton! And I just invited him to my house."

"Now? What are you wearing?"

My closet door mirror never lies. And right now it's giving me the side-eye. Or rather, I'm giving my outfit the side-eye.

"Christmas pj bottoms and a coffee-stained tee."

"A dress! One and done. Go! Throw on a dress or romper, slap some shea butter on them legs, and top-knot that hair," Skye commands.

I know just what to throw on. I had already picked out tomorrow's outfit. Hoping to psych myself into kicking off the week strong and confident, I had set aside my favorite summer dress: a pretty mustard button-up with a ruffled hem. It's perfect, and at least I know I look good in it. Something about the way the mustard plays off my brown skin. Plus, it's the perfect mid-thigh length and has the right halter cut to show off my shoulders.

"No crisis can make me cry, sis!" Skye and I squeal at the same time before I hang up and jump into action. I barely have my big head through my dress's neckline opening when it hits me.

My family!

I grab my phone and race down the short hallway. I skip the last four steps and land downstairs with a thud.

"What in the Bell Biv DeVoe?" my mother calls out, startled.

I intercept Ma and John in the hallway before they can make it to the stairs to investigate. They look like middle-aged superheroes responding to a distress call—Ma in her workout gear, a pencil speared through her wavy auburn locs, and John holding his glasses like a Black Clark Kent mid–wardrobe change.

"I don't have much time to explain everything, but Owen is on his way over to see me in about five minutes." I pause to take a breath.

"Coming here? To our house? To see you? Here? Now?" My mom is short-circuiting. Fast. "I need to get dressed!"

In a hopscotch-esque move, she is halfway up the stairs, but then she freezes.

"The kitchen is a mess. All my paperwork."

Ma skips back down the last four steps.

"Yo, prince or no prince, you're both losing it and it's not a good look." Zach emerges from the kitchen, obviously having heard all the details. He brushes past us on his way to the front door, where he peers out the side window panels. "Tell that dude good luck finding a spot for his motorcade. Alternate side parking rules go in effect tomorrow, and folks are already claiming their spots," he says before dismissively reporting back to the family room couch.

Suddenly, my mom is a blur, speed-tidying from the dining table to the kitchen counter and to the adjoining family room, where the couch pillows are haphazardly placed.

"Yvette, he's not coming here for a house tour, he's coming to speak to Zora." John's glasses are back on his face, and he is as measured as you'd expect him to be. But his words only frazzle my mom further.

"What? Zora, you're not going to introduce him to the family?"

"I can, but please don't embarrass me."

Ding.

Our one-note doorbell still hasn't been fixed.

I don't even get the chance to top-knot my hair or lotion my legs. But somehow my mom manages to get the kitchen and family room in solid shape. And at some point, she also found the time to throw on a cute, lightweight sweater. She looks good.

"He's your guest—*you* answer the door." Zach sucks his teeth and lounges deeper into the couch.

I roll my eyes at Zach and stand there raking my tight coils with my fingers, gathering them up into a presentable updo. Thankfully, Ma hands me the stretchy hair tie she has around her wrist. The bell doesn't ring again. Maybe Owen had the good sense to leave.

John is enjoying this, I can tell. He leans back against the wall with his arms crossed over his chest.

"You want me to answer the door?" Ma offers.

"No, I'll do it," I say. "It's no biggie. I'll just chill with him for a bit, then he'll be on his way."

"No biggie." Ma shrugs her shoulders. "But you are brilliant and you look beautiful."

"Thanks, Ma."

She gives me a hug. "He's just a human being, baby. If you prick him, he bleeds, okay? Remember that."

"Yeah, and if you punch him he bruises, I promise you that," says Zach.

John shakes his head, still smiling to himself.

I ignore Zach's shade and make my way down the hallway to let Owen in.

Chapter 24

THERE HE is. Waiting patiently on the front stoop with another breathtaking floral arrangement in hand—this one is in an elegant square vase. He's standing a polite distance from the door—a few paces back. When Owen sees it's me, a slow smile spreads across his face. He seems focused on maintaining eye contact, but I suspect he's looking me up and down at the same time. It's a stealth skill I learned about from Zach. He once told me about the art of checking a person out without making it obvious, and I didn't understand it until now.

"I was hoping we could continue our conversation," says Owen.

We stare silently at each other for a moment. I can't believe Owen is standing here on my front stoop in Appleton. The early evening sun floods a spotlight on my handsome street. Bass thumping from a distant car's stereo is the neighborhood's heartbeat. Reverberating shouts and echoing calls from disciplining mothers, playing children, and chatty friends are the birdsongs. Pops of orange, yellow, and lilac from our sidewalk garden are like tiny pom-poms cheering with pride. The urban garden we planted with our block association months ago has come a long way.

"These are for your mother," says Owen, referring to the vase he's cradling.

"They're beautiful." I smile. Then, "Does your security know you're here? I don't want Appleton police racing over, sirens blaring."

"Yes, they are aware. No sirens, I promise."

"Are they still here, though?" I ask, and look up and down my block. "Oh, wait a minute."

That's when I see a guy who looks like he's come from central casting pedaling down the block. He sticks out like a sore thumb around here. No one in this area wears a full-on biking getup like that. This guy looks like he's ready for the Tour de France but is instead trapped in a Tour de Jersey. And with an ergonomic helmet like that, you'd expect him to ride a little faster. Instead, he is keeping his eyes on everything but the road.

"That's not exactly incognito for this neighborhood," I tell Owen.

"Noted." He frowns.

I chuckle at the embarrassed look on his face.

Lucky for Owen, the embarrassment scale is about to tip from him to me.

"Zora, are you all right out here?" It's my mother, poking her head in the screened front window, and her nose into my business. "Aren't you going to invite your guest in?"

"We'll be in shortly," I singsong to her in the hopes she stops spying.

By the time Owen and I step inside, I'm hoping everyone is close enough to back to normal as possible. Sunday afternoon usually finds everyone in my house gathered in the kitchen/family room area, and today is no different.

But when Owen and I walk into the room, almost nothing is as I expect it to be. Ma and John are both at the kitchen island chopping vegetables. Fresh veggies, not the frozen kind stuffing the shelves of our freezer that one of us usually plops in boiling water a few minutes before we sit to eat dinner. And for some reason the TV is piping jazz music from some streaming radio channel. Huh?

My mom walks over to greet him.

"I'm Yvette Sherman, Zora's mother. And this is my husband, John Sherman," she says warmly.

"It is indeed a pleasure to meet you, Mr. and Mrs. Sherman," says Owen. He sounds sincere.

My mom gives a small squeal when Owen hands her the vase.

"Owen, it's good to have you over." John is close behind with a firm handshake.

"I know you're used to castles and summer cottages the size of our governor's mansion," my mom says. I can tell that inside Ma is doing the electric slide, but her excitement is only escaping in tiny bursts of giddy giggles, which, though awkward, is at least not embarrassing.

The only person in his usual spot and acting one hundred percent himself is Zach. He doesn't even get up from his position on the couch. He just calls out to us, and oddly, I appreciate him for it.

"Ay yo, Zora, is this dude really a bona fide prince?"

"Zachariah Kofi Emerson, we do not comport ourselves like that in this house."

Did my mother just say *comport*? Oh yeah, it's going to be an interesting visit.

And as if my dad's antennas are sensing something's up, he calls my cell phone. I can just picture him standing here in all his velour tracksuit glory saying, "You're in Appleton now, and the only person ruling this house"—signature pause for effect—"is Jesus." Never mind that he's not a religious man. Daddy uses whatever tool at his disposal to clap back.

I send Daddy's call to voicemail and pray to the Prince of Peace he doesn't try Zach's phone next, because Zach will surely pick up at a time like this, just to spice up the day.

"Please, have a seat, make yourself at home." My mom gestures to one of the rustic bar stools on the opposite side of the granite island separating the kitchen and living room area.

Owen sits up with perfect posture and folds his hands on the counter for a quick breath before placing them on his lap instead. I grab the seat next to him and wait for somebody to start feeding peanuts to the elephant in the room.

It would help if Owen would stick with one mood. He looks at me and smiles like a kid with a kite on a windy day; then, in the next moment, he clears his throat and looks parent-pleasing serious.

Ma and John stand across from us, chopping away. It's doubtful if in one sitting we'll consume the quickly rising mound of colorful veggies they're building. Ma is, of course, the one to break the silence.

"Owen, up until a couple of weeks ago, I wouldn't have recognized you if I walked right by you," she says. "It's a wonder your family has done such a great job keeping you from the international press until you came of age. I sure hope it wasn't a kept-under-lock-and-key situation," she chuckles nervously. "Castles *are* known to have dungeons."

Owen clears his throat again, uncomfortably. I give her the wide-eyed reprimand, like, *Really, Ma?* She instantly looks sorry about her choice of words.

"But you look great!" she continues. "Not at all like you've been kept somewhere out of the sun . . . that much. Handsome young man."

I look pleadingly at John to *please* make her stop.

"So, my wife tells me your older brother is getting married soon?"

"Yes, sir. Gideon is to wed end of this summer."

"I have been so excited ever since I heard his wife-to-be is a woman of color," Mom dives in, fully recovered. "She was born in Landerel to a European mother and an African father," she explains to me and John.

"That's correct, yes." Owen smiles. "I didn't think most Americans followed Landerelian royal family news."

"Oh, when there's a sista joining the royal family, you best *believe* my friends and I gain interest," my mom replies. "We are so proud to see a brown princess."

"That's interesting." Zach rises from his video game coma, which I suspect was just a cover to appear unruffled by a princely house visit. He walks over to the kitchen counter, grabs a chopped carrot, and crunches it loudly. "Your brother is marrying a biracial sista, and here you come asking around for *my* sister. Trying to one-up your big bro, are you?"

"Zach!" my mother and I shout at the same time, except Ma says "Zachariah" again like she's on an American reboot of *Downton Abbey*.

Zach has been commended by his EMT crew for keeping a cool head under pressure and calming panicked scenes with his disarming charm and intimate way with people. But he is in full "one and only Kenney" mode tonight. All he's missing is the outdated velour tracksuit and chunky Bluetooth earpiece. It's like Daddy is remoting in through Zach's brain.

"I'm just asking a question. I'm allowed. If I can't be myself in my home with my family, where can I truly speak what's on my mind? Feel me, Owen?"

"If you're asking me about the lack of pretense among family, I'm afraid I am the wrong person to back you up there."

Owen's joke doesn't land. Way too soon to try and pal around with Zach. Owen tries again.

"Notwithstanding, your sentiments are clear and I understand completely. And I will happily answer your question. I did not look at things this way, but now that you mention it, I can see why you're suspicious. I wish my brother nothing but the best in life, and I don't see his happiness as something to begrudge, or, as you say, one-up."

"There, Zach, are you satisfied?" I ask.

"It's not about my satisfaction," Zach replies. "It's about my curiosity. Like, for example, how did you two even meet?"

Instead of calling off Zach, the family attack dog, my mom and stepdad seem to lean in closer.

I tell them about our library confessional and the accidentally swapped cell phones, but that's it.

"You see, remember when I was worried you wouldn't find a friend on campus? I told you God listens to a mother's prayer." Ma points a crisp slice of bell pepper at me.

"All right, how about we all take a seat at the table?" says John, his palms rubbing in anticipation. "Dinner's ready. Owen, we'll set a place for you."

This is when I'm expecting Owen to politely decline and apologize for not being able to stay. Instead he enthusiastically says, "That's very kind of you. Thank you!"

I can only assume that (1) Owen wants to spend time with me at any cost, or (2) his security detail must not be getting paid by the hour. *Flat rate is my guess.* Still, Owen takes out his cell and makes a call to update whomever about his slightly extended stay.

"Colin?" I guess after he hangs up.

"I know he comes off intense, but he's reasonable and supports my need for personal space," says Owen while my family is distracted with a side squabble about proper utensil placement.

"That's good," I say.

"No, *this* is good," Owen says low enough for only me to hear. From his subtle head nod to the general atmosphere, I take it he's talking about this visit, this moment, this thing budding between us. My heart skips a beat.

Thank goodness everyone relaxes by the time we dig into John's tasty crab cakes and sweet potato mash, which is served with an overflowing salad, a refreshing veggie smoothie (just made!), and as much veggie appetizer and dip to go around. It isn't long before Ma continues her line of questions.

"There's so much I'm dying to know!" Ma leans toward Owen. "Your brother Gideon is like this real-life Prince Charming that the ladies love, and he absolutely blew everyone away with his choice of fiancée."

"Sadie is a very special person," says Owen, nodding. "I've never seen my brother so happy."

"And I can never forget his fiancée's name is Sadie, because she is the spitting image of the singer Sade." Ma has stars in her eyes. The rest of us have only heard her come to this name-twinning conclusion about a dozen times before, but we don't show it. "Will she get a title?" Ma asks Owen.

"I suspect she'll be given the title of Duchess, like my sister-in-law, Rose."

"I used to be a *Dutchess*, you know," says Ma. Everyone pauses chewing and stares at her. "Really! That was the name of my double Dutch squad in junior high."

"And she can still jump today," John says with pride. "Can't you, babe?"

Ma's face leans into John's hand brushing her cheek.

"It's gotta be cool having security looking out for you," says Zach with zero conversation-segue game. "Like say, for example, some dudes try and jump you, do the security guys intervene?"

"Yes, they would." Owen puts a little extra bass in his voice.

Is this about to be a pissing contest?

Ma and John are busy clearing the table and piling the dishes in the sink. Zach and I will load the dishwasher later.

"What if it's just one person stepping to you?" Zach presses. "Do they let you handle it?" He narrows his eyes and takes ahold of the toothpick in his mouth. "Like, a man-to-man situation. I would think you could take care of that yourself, no?"

Goodness gracious. "We'll be hanging out back if anyone needs us." I get up from the table and motion to Owen to join me.

"No disrespect—just asking." Zach chuckles and leans back in his chair, mischief creasing the corners of his eyes.

"Mmm-hmm." I throw him shade on our way out.

The screened porch overlooking our small backyard is a lot more peaceful than the family room area, which faces the street. And it's private, thanks to a leafy covering that neighbors can't peek through during this time of the year. Owen and I sit a few inches apart on the cushioned wicker couch.

"Your family is amazing," says Owen.

"Sorry about my brother's third degree." I roll my eyes.

"He's just doing his job."

"That's one way to put it," I say. We're silent in time to appreciate the whirring buzz of cicadas in surround sound like a Doppler effect. "So, how do you like Appleton?"

"I like it," he answers without hesitation. "It's a massive departure from the Halstead campus, and there's this strong sense of community here that's palpable. I felt it at the festival."

"Our mayor is a super-smart woman who's inspiring people to move back here after college to build up businesses and organizations," I say, happy to talk about one of my favorite subjects.

Owen gives a soft chuckle and pivots to face me. "You could power this whole town with your enthusiasm right now."

"It's just exciting to me," I say in a calmer tone, careful not to get carried away again.

"In Landerel, we strictly reserve that kind of emotion for football matches."

"Oh, the entire world knows about your soccer games." I widen my eyes and shake my head.

After our laughter dies down and we rub our splitting sides, Owen gets quiet. He turns serious, too.

"This is why I like hanging out with you so much," he says. "I feel like I can be myself with you, and the things we do and say all come so easy."

"Yeah," I say in a quiet voice. "It was easy for me to lump everyone at Halstead into one lily-white package of privilege, maybe wrapped in a satin ribbon of bigotry. And, don't get me wrong, I still do for the most part. But, it must be some kind of cosmic joke that I clicked with probably the one person who could out-privilege everyone."

"Cosmic joke or no, please hold all laughter for what I'm about to ask you." Owen looks like he's been called to the principal's office.

"Okay."

"As you know, my brother Gideon is getting married in a few weeks. According to my family tradition, one must be accompanied by a special date when they're a member of the wedding party, as I am." He takes a breath. "From the first time I saw you, I've been trying to work up the nerve to ask you. And since our conversation this morning, I'm wondering if you might be interested. Zora Emerson, it would be an honor and a joy if you would be my date to my brother's wedding. Will you accompany me?"

My eyes stretch wide, and my heart is trying to jump out of my chest. And my thoughts are racing.

"You don't have to answer now," he says.

"I'd—um, I'd love to hear more about it," I manage to get out.

"How do you feel about dancing?" he asks.

"Dancing in public doesn't make me nervous," I say. I think about all the times Skye and I have drawn a crowd dancing at cookouts, weddings, house parties.

"How about dancing a waltz to classical music?"

"Oh, I see what you mean."

Owen explains the details, and I can barely utter a word in response. I'm shocked by the idea of going to a royal wedding. In Landerel. Before I get overwhelmed by how I might pull off such a huge trip, Owen says his family would handle and make all the travel arrangements, down to where I'd be staying. They would even arrange for a dance instructor and stylist to get me prepared for the day.

Um, am I really hearing this? It sounds like I'd essentially be princess for a day. But I don't know if I can accept or not. Saying yes to this invitation would put me on the world stage in a way that I don't know if I want to be.

Owen stands up and holds out his hand to me. I take it and stand up so we're face-to-face. He looks down at my hand he's still holding.

"Zora, if you feel uncomfortable with any of this, I would understand if you decide not to accompany me."

I blink a few times as reality slowly seeps in.

"Thank you for saying that," I say. "And thank you for the wedding invitation."

Owen bows his head and kisses my hand. I wonder if I can pass that off to Skye as our first kiss. She would probably just roll her eyes.

"It is you I should be thanking, my lady," says Owen, the memory imprint of his kiss still on my hand.

"Well, then, you're welcome," I say.

I curtsy and flick my wrist with a flourish.

"Am I welcome, really?" Owen's hazel eyes are dancing again.

"Indeed you are, sir."

"Welcome . . . to kiss you?"

"Indeed you are, sir," I whisper. Owen closes the distance between us and bows his head closer.

It's a kiss that starts with one soft, sweet peck, quickly followed by another. We look at each other and smile before taking a deeper dive with a tender kiss that lingers. We stay holding hands the whole time. A few seconds later, we pull back slowly.

"Well, uh—" says a clearly flustered Owen. A poor attempt to win back his chill. I'm not in any better shape. I wordlessly touch my cheeks to feel if they're as warm as I sense they are.

Yup, that definitely counts as a first kiss.

Chapter 25

I FIND Owen as soon as my classes end on Monday. I haven't given him a solid yes or no answer on the wedding yet, but I've invited him to a live podcast taping this afternoon.

"Tell me about this podcast you love so much," Owen says as we walk over. The taping is being held at a lecture hall right on campus.

"Well, the podcast is about innovative young people," I explain. "They interview a different innovative young person every episode, but it's always a surprise to the audience."

"That sounds awesome," Owen says, taking my hand. When we arrive, Owen comments that it's a cool theater where no seat is a bad seat.

I don't tell Owen, but I notice two guys down our row take an interest in us. The younger one looks like he's got a lot to say about me, or maybe to me. Could it be because we're an interracial couple? Could it be because he's recognized Owen? I'm not sure.

At one point, I catch the older guy he's sitting with staring right at me.

All of my paranoia completely disappears when the show starts and the special guest is announced. It's Appleton's mayor, Aina Oyeyemi!

Owen does his best to keep me from jumping out of my seat. I cheer louder than anyone there. Like, *ohmygawd*, what are the chances? Owen is excited, too. He's still on a mission to learn all he can about my interests. He been telling me all about the amazing Black women in the book he picked up, and he's started watching a documentary about New Jersey politics. Meanwhile, I've promised to read one of his favorite novels.

Mayor Aina's conversation style is sparkling, motivating, informative, provocative. I can't keep my crush on her to myself; I practically run to the mic during the Q&A session.

"Hi! My name is Zora Emerson. I don't know if you recognize me, but you introduced me at the Appleton Fam Fest. I just want to say I am so proud you're my mayor," I say in one nervous rush.

"Zora, don't underestimate yourself. Of course I recognize you," she says. "You are the perfect example of what I'm trying to do—engage the youth to take charge of their communities. I'm so proud to represent a community with young people like you working for its future."

I'm floating on air. How incredible to get a shout-out from someone as accomplished and dope as Mayor Aina.

They keep the floor open for one last question, and the guy

who I noticed was looking at me before the show steps up to the mic.

"Mayor, what a pleasure to have you on our campus. My name is Finn Burlington, and I—"

I freeze and panic in the calmest manner possible. His name rings a bell so loudly in my ear, it drowns out the rest of his words. He's the student reporter who called me for an interview after the campus police incident.

Owen looks at me. "Are you okay?" he mouths.

I take out my phone and text Owen a message about my suspicions. When he looks at his phone, his jaw tightens, but he remains silent. I see him send a quick text to Colin, alerting him that we won't be sticking around after this event.

Once the taping is over, throngs of well-wishers crowd the mayor, including the student reporter. It's the perfect distraction. He doesn't look like he'll be leaving anytime soon. He probably has to interview her for a story. We're in the clear.

Owen and I head away from the crowd; his security is meeting us at the rear exit. It's amazing how hiding from his security has made Owen an expert on secret passageways for practically every building on campus.

Once we turn a corner, the corridor leading to the unassuming exit is quiet, empty, and private. Owen takes my hand and pulls me in for a hug.

"Are you okay?" he asks.

"I am now." This is no time to flirt, but it's difficult not to with Owen this close.

He pulls me in closer for a quick, wonderful kiss.

We break apart when we hear footsteps behind us, though Owen keeps hold of my hand. I can sense he's in his protective mode again. We continue heading down the corridor.

"Prince Owen!"

We turn and see the same nosy older man from the podcast taping. His student reporter friend isn't with him.

"That was some kiss," the older man says. "Is this your girlfriend?"

He's wearing a lanyard identifying him as "Press." As if that gives him license to ask us personal questions. We continue walking to the exit, faster now. But he stays on our heels.

"And you, Zora Emerson of Appleton, is it? Will you be attending this summer's royal nuptials?"

I almost do a double take. My name in the mouth of a nosy stranger who has God-knows-what intentions? It's so not a good feeling.

As soon as we're outside, the black town car drives up. Colin jumps out of the passenger seat when he sees we're being followed. He gets into Men in Black mode and ushers us toward the back seat.

"Not to worry, I didn't snap a pic of their kiss." The reporter backs away, but only physically. As we climb into the car, I can hear him say, "We respect your privacy as students, but the public will be excited to hear that the prince has fallen for a Jersey girl."

Inside the safety of the car, Owen hugs me again.

"Zora, I am so sorry about this," he says. "I don't mean to frighten you, but you need to be prepared for the media storm coming."

"We'll take her right home," says Colin. "Hopefully we can beat them there."

"Them who?" I turn to Owen, feeling apprehensive.

"That reporter and who knows who else will be calling their affiliates right now—they may try to camp out where they think you're heading."

This cannot be happening. I call my mom and tell her what's going on.

"Try and calm down, honey. There's no one here. Just get home safely, and we'll deal with this together," she says.

I let my mother's advice ease my fretting. But it gets tougher to manage when we get caught in traffic.

When we finally get off the Parkway exit in Appleton, the neighborhood looks as it always does. People stand at bus stops like nothing has changed. The basketball courts are buzzing with kids in pickup games. An ice cream truck is pulled over dishing out refreshing treats to outstretched little arms.

But when we turn onto my street, the mood is different. I try to remember if anyone on my block is having a cookout, because it's poppin' with more activity than normal. At first, there's just a trickle of people hanging around, but the closer we get to my house, it's clear something is up. There was this same vibe when someone got hit by a car outside the Jamaican store earlier this summer.

That's when I see it. There's a news van parked and a small crowd of reporters outside my house. One person is carrying a large shoulder camera.

This can't be happening. I take a deep breath and turn to Owen, who is watching me warily. He looks ready, prepared to face everyone. I try to prepare myself, too. After all, I spoke to the mayor today. I spoke at the Gala, and at the Fam Fest, in front of all of Appleton. I can handle a few reporters. I nod at Owen.

Skye calls me just then, but I send the call to voicemail. My dad calls next, and I do the same.

We pull to a stop, and the reporters start buzzing outside our car. Colin turns to us from the front seat. "Zora, ask your mother to prepare to open the door. Owen, you stay here while I walk Zora inside."

"No, I'm going in with her," says Owen with an edge. He looks at me. "It's my fault you're in this situation, and I want to explain things in person to your mother."

My mother. I'll call her again. When I pull out my phone, I see she's already texted me:

> *I'm keeping watch at the door. I'll see you when you pull up. Just come straight in.*

"She's at the door," I tell Colin.

"Okay, here we go. Wait for me to open your door, and then stick close by me," says Colin.

It's a good thing Owen has to step out before I do. The car door swings open, and we cover our heads and rush like it's raining outside. The reporters shout all at once.

"Zora, sources tell us you are dating Prince Owen of Landerel. Do you have any comment?"

"Congratulations, you make a cute couple!"

"Zora! Zora! Zora!"

Since when did I get so popular with people over age twelve? I can barely get followers on social media, and somehow my name is ringing out in these streets?

I can hardly see where I'm going. Owen has his arm around me like I'm the celeb people are trying to get a glimpse of. We look at our feet as we walk to give the snapping cameras the least revealing and photogenic photos. Colin is in front of us, making a path for us to follow. Somehow he seems to be protecting us from the front *and* rear. I don't know how the man does it, but he does not mess around.

As we climb my front stoop, I notice for the first time that there's a figure standing at the top of the stairs. Whoever it is has an imposing enough vibe that the media haven't been able to get that close to the house.

It all happens in a flash, but as soon as we hit the top step, my mom waves us in the front door. The figure on the front stoop—my dad—comes in, too.

My mother grabs me into her arms. Owen, Colin, and Daddy huddle next to us there in the entryway.

"Are you all right?" asks Ma.

"I'm fine," I say, catching my breath. "Just a little shocked at how quickly things escalated." I lean against the console table Ma's always fussing over, but she gives me a pass. Owen is at my side gently rubbing my arm, and Colin is holding a hushed phone conversation, no doubt strategizing next moves. I take a peek at my dad to see if his ears are leaking hot lava. He's pacing the entry hallway like it's a fashion runway for this season's velour tracksuit collection.

"There's more dysfunction out there than at your mama's family reunions," Daddy says to Ma.

Having Daddy around my mother on a good day is bad enough. Having him around at a tense time is another thing entirely. Ma needs to try out her yoga calming tricks because she already looks ready to drop-kick Daddy in his solar plexus chakra.

Lights start flashing outside. Now the police have shown up. What a nightmare.

"I never meant for this to happen," says Owen. "But because I knew there was a great chance that it would, I should not have gotten you involved." He looks full of regret. Even the fire in his ginger hair seems dimmer.

Daddy slow claps. "Two points for Halstead homeboy for getting a clue!" My dad is fuming.

"Daddy, please," I tell him. Then I look at Owen. "Don't blame yourself. This is my decision now, too."

"Baby, you don't need this." Daddy shakes his head

emphatically. "Prince boy will turn this street into a three-ring circus. We have enough clowns who live here as it is."

"Kenney, you're not helping matters by making Owen the villain here," says Ma. I happen to know that this has always been one of Ma's concerns with my dad. He's known for treating every disagreement like a battle royale.

"Yvette, you know those people outside are not going to mess with a prince, because he's got people protecting him."

"Ma, Daddy," I break in. "I know a media stakeout in the neighborhood isn't ideal. But I knew what I was signing up for. Owen, there's a plan, right?" I turn to him, and he looks surprised but answers in his official, royal voice.

"Sir, madam, I can talk to the media and give them the interview they want so they can stay away from Zora," he offers.

"An interview confirming our daughter is the mystery girlfriend?" Dad says. "No, thank you."

"That won't be necessary, Prince Owen," says Colin. He's off his call, and I'm eager to hear what he's learned. "With your permission, we'd like to provide car service for Ms. Emerson to and from school."

"Yes, okay," says Ma, who looks worried. She peers out the window. "Looks like the police are pushing back the media a few more feet." Ma sighs in relief.

Owen looks at me. "I'd prefer to stay a while longer . . . but I think I'm the one drawing the attention."

I nod slowly. "You're right. I think once they get their shot of you walking out of here, there won't be anything else to stick around for."

Daddy studies the two of us. I can't believe how long he's gone without a wisecrack. "Well, look at you two. On damage control without me." He puts out his hand, and Owen meets it with a warm handshake. I smile at Daddy, pleased at his silent olive branch.

"I hate to leave you with all this going on," Owen tells me. "But I appreciate all your patience." More quietly, he says, "I'll call you tonight, Zora." His one last hug is extra tight, and I can feel his apology and thanks all wrapped up in it.

Colin addresses my parents with business cards in hand. "To safeguard your privacy and avoid any sound bites being used against you, it's best to avoid the press for now," he says. He hands them the cards. "I've arranged for a communications expert to work with you. They are on call and available to help at any hour."

My parents wordlessly take the cards.

Even though we do have a back exit, this time the only option is for Owen to leave out the front door.

We stand out of sight but peek through the window. Unlike when I was being escorted inside, the press stays at a respectable distance. I'm the hook that's baiting their big catch—a Prince Owen story. Everyone knows the press has an agreement with the university, thanks to Her Majesty the Queen (aka, Owen's influential mom). And then there's me. I'm fair game. And if they're talking about me, they're talking about the prince—at least indirectly.

When we all head to the family room to check out the local news, that much is clear.

"They think they're slick," Daddy says in a huff.

Stories are being framed in a way that absolves the media of being in any privacy violation. The news stories, the headlines, and the tweets all have this approach.

"How did a girl from Appleton snag a real-life Prince Charming? Well, rumor has it this Jersey girl will be attending the royal nuptials and dancing in the traditional ceremony at the royal reception," says a grinning on-the-street reporter. Good ole Mr. Stanley can be seen scowling in the background.

"This is the most exciting thing to happen to us in a long time!" shouts a girl on the street. The graphic under her identifies her as "Appleton Resident."

That's when it hits me—my kids from Walk Me Home. What will they think of this? At first, I worry about their reactions, but then I imagine them catching a glimpse of me at the royal wedding. Seeing just how far around the globe someone from right here in Appleton can go could be inspiring.

"That's it." Daddy storms away from the TV, past the kitchen, and makes for the entryway hallway. "I'm going to shut them down so hard."

"Daddy, no!" I jump up from my kitchen counter seat and try and cut him off at the door. I love my dad, but he flies off the handle, especially when he's fuming. He talks to the press, and I might as well never leave my house again. His tirade will no doubt go viral.

"Zora's right!" Ma hangs up on her call with John and speed-walks behind Daddy. "We shouldn't talk to them without a strategy."

Daddy has a head start, plus he's fueled by rage, so he swings open the front door before we can get to it.

I prepare to be mortified, but instead I'm relieved. The press has cleared. No one representing any news media organization is out there.

I spin to face my parents in victory. "Owen and I, we've got this," I say.

Chapter 26

"ZORA, SWEETHEART, you'll be late if you don't get up now," says Ma. She's sitting on my bed, trying to pry apart my bedsheet cocoon. I just groan in response.

I can't remember when I finally fell asleep. After fielding worried calls from Zach and Skye, I did some reading, but couldn't concentrate. My phone call with Owen just before bed must've done the trick.

I get dressed in something neutral so I don't stand out.

The bell rings. Ma and John answer it. It's one of the Men in Black—the one who's usually behind the wheel.

"Remember, they'll take you home whenever you're ready. You don't have to stay all day if you don't feel comfortable," says Ma.

"I'll be fine, Ma." I turn to my security escort, shake his hand, and ask his name.

"Call me Elliot," he says with the Landerelian accent I'm becoming so accustomed to.

"Thank you, Elliot," I tell him.

The morning is muggy and quiet. Nothing seems out of the ordinary, even though I know differently. Everything has changed overnight. Now the very security and black cars I once scoffed at are shuttling *me* around. Mr. Stanley is not having breakfast on his front stoop, and I wonder if it's because he'd rather avoid me thanks to the company I keep.

Elliot opens the rear door, and I climb in.

"Good morning, beautiful."

Owen is seated inside.

"What are you doing here?" I ask, surprised. "Back at the scene of the crime already?"

"My girlfriend lives here," says Owen. We search each other's eyes for a moment. "If . . . she'll have me," he says.

Colin is in the front passenger seat, and Elliot walks around the car and gets behind the wheel.

"I'm happy to see you." I smile, sliding over close to indicate I don't mind the girlfriend thing. And I'm not too worried that news of Owen and me will be swirling around campus today.

"I don't want to make things worse," Owen says, "but if I can make things a little better for you in any way possible, I'll do it."

His arm around me, my head on his shoulder. That's how we ride to school. I wish the ride were longer, but soon we pull up behind the building of my first class.

I run into Matt in the stairwell. Once I see him, I realize I forgot to answer the text he sent last night.

"Zora, are you all right?" he asks. "Abby and I were worried about you."

"Taco Tuesday better have lots of comfort food," I say. "Because things just got real, my friend."

"Done—you've earned it," he says. His smile fades. "Just so you know, I'm here if you ever need anything."

"Thank you."

"We're meeting in the piano lounge today for a change of pace," he says.

"Sounds good," I say. "Pun intended."

Everyone in class tries to act like there is no elephant in the room. Kelsey even offers a greeting, which I know is hard for her. Goodness, smiling looks painful for her.

That's okay, because there are lots of elephants way larger and stompier than mine roaming in this place. It's very "one and only Kenney" of me, but anyone wanting to discuss my personal life will have to first answer more pressing questions about what exactly they find unusual about Owen dating me.

The more righteous I feel, the less intimidated I am by all this superficial attention. So, a Landerelian prince is into me and has invited me to the royal wedding. If anyone has a problem with that, they can kick rocks. I'm coming for anyone who comes for me.

Taco Tuesday is the break I need from a straight three hours of studying. And this time, Owen is coming with me. He meets me at the library so we can walk over to the dorm together.

There's a sense we're no longer anonymous on campus. Though no one outright gawks at us, we catch more glances than usual. Even more surprising are the subtle greetings here and there—eye contact, head nods, and even a faint wave. The worst is when passersby pause in conversation as we stroll by. But nothing uncomfortable happens, especially not to the level of last night.

Perez is at the piano when we walk in. He is stupid talented and makes the piano sound like a full band. Dude can play any song we can think of by ear, as long as he's familiar with it. Abby fills out the sound with some highlighter drumming. Uncle-Officer's son Amir is also here.

Kelsey also shows up. It happens to be the first time Owen is attending. Coincidence much?

"I saw you walk in, so I had to stop by and see you," Kelsey tells Owen.

I leave her to chat with Owen. She always seems to have something pressing she needs to talk to him about. I've come to settle on the fact that this is just her personality. That and her painted-on underwhelmed expression. And who can blame her? It must be hard to impress someone who rubs shoulders with royalty and has traveled the world.

Owen nods politely at what Kelsey has to say, while I catch up with Abby. She's on a break from drumming.

"You and Owen look great together," she tells me. "Just so you know, the chemistry between you guys is giving me life right now."

"Aw, Abby," I say. "Thank you. It's not at all what I expected when I came to Halstead, but I'm having fun getting to know him."

"Drums, please!" Perez gives a shout for his bandmate.

"This next track is dedicated to you guys," says Abby. I crack up watching her exaggerated highlighter thrumming.

"Hey, Taylor Ham!" Dominic greets me.

"Whaddup, Pork Roll!" I yell back.

Dominic has caught Abby's bug, and he hits the floor with some zany moves.

"You've got nothing on these fly Filipino moves." Matt challenges him with some video game victory dance.

Kelsey makes an exit right after somebody dims the lights and the room gets a club vibe going. Perez and Abby up the beats, and Dom starts a rap freestyle that gets everybody out of their chairs.

Owen is tapping his feet to the beat.

"You know this song?" I tease.

"The amazing Onyx Santiago. I have all her albums."

I am floored. I stand up, sit down, and then stand up and sit down again. You would think I am at a Catholic church service.

I've never seen Owen laugh so hard.

"You refuse to give me any credit, but that's okay," he says. "At least I have haters. Not everyone can say that they do."

I pull Owen to his feet, and drag him to the makeshift dance floor.

"Come on with it, then. How can you be this shy about dancing when we have a whole routine to perform in public?" I ask.

"We?" He smiles.

"Owen, I would be happy to be your date for your brother's wedding," I declare. "That's what girlfriends are for."

Owen's eyes widen, and he lifts me off the floor. He lowers my feet with a quick kiss.

"Let's hear it for the undercover couple!" Matt raises his cup. "You guys are safe to emote with abandon here."

We pull apart, laughing, and we start to do a two-step to the music.

By the end of the night, we're singing together off-key as we climb into my ride home.

"Thanks for pushing me to hang out with your new friends," Owen says. "I usually shy away from these type of scenes, but I had a proper good time."

"Good," I say. "And don't worry—I won't expect it to be this fun at the wedding."

"Smart thinking," he says. "But I promise to show you a fun time sometime during your stay in Landerel. There are so many cool places to check out."

"I can't wait."

"But, Zora, be prepared for round two with the media," says Owen. "I was naive to think they would back off, and I see they'll continue latching onto you as a way in."

"I'll be ready," I say.

I guess it's my turn to be naive.

Chapter 27

I AM *so* not ready.

Yes, my mom's been consulting with the royal communications people and a friend of a friend of John's who runs a public relations agency in New York. With their help, she released a smartly crafted statement requesting privacy. It worked. In a way. Even though there have been no more crowds outside our home, the gossiping disguised as reporting keeps me looking over my shoulder.

Skye makes it her mission to monitor Instagram and Twitter for chatter. She says she wants to see it first so she can warn me, and then she texts me emojis as signals. There's the comforting visual of a thumbs-up emoji for low-chatter days and a red stop sign for the days I best not for any reason check social media.

But sometimes I can't help but sneak a peek.

First come the unconfirmed reports of my attending the wedding: *Is she or isn't she?* This type of story is more about explaining the traditions of Landerel. Beyond what Owen tells me, I learn that the wedding dance tradition is a presentation of Owen to society as the next unmarried sibling. When his brother Gideon was in this position, Gideon's date was not the woman he's about to marry. Having no older sibling, the eldest prince, Lionel, danced at his cousin's wedding. Lionel's date, though, was his future fiancée and wife.

The next phase of this social media chatter gets under my skin. Cheery articles debating my worthiness to attend get posted here and there. For one, the press begins to question my royal wedding readiness: *Does she know about etiquette? Has she so much as been to a quinceañera?* Without losing that eerily pleasant tone or resorting to name calling, the media is pretty much saying I'm just an around-the-way girl.

When I get home from classes one afternoon, my text alert rings out. Logic tells me I'm hearing the same chime as always, but somehow there's a shrill tone to it. I pull my phone from my skirt pocket. Skye has sent me a stop sign emoji. My stomach starts churning. I look out the window behind me and see Owen's car pull off.

"How bad is it?" I ask Skye when she picks up on video chat.

"Nothing so bad that everyone won't forget all about it in a couple of days," she says. Skye is walking outdoors. She's holding the phone close to her face to compete with the sounds of cars swishing by.

"Okay, I'm going to check," I tell her. I walk through the house toward the back porch.

"Does that stop sign mean anything to you?" Skye purses her lips with attitude. "It's not worth scrolling through comment after comment."

"Comments about what?" I move my stack of books on the couch from yesterday's study session and take a seat.

"All those little stories you were told would go no further than a mock student newspaper?" she asks.

"Yeah, I remember." My breath grows shallow.

"Well, they're out. The cell phone swap incident, campus police escort out of class, even the Goodie award and prize money reversal."

I groan in response.

For the rest of that week, I come straight home after classes and study on my back porch. When Owen wants to meet up for another campus picnic, I invite him over instead. And it's fun— we end up ordering pizza and eating on the back porch—but I'm still on edge.

One evening, I tell my mom I'm considering not going to the royal wedding, and she practically stands on her head until I agree to go with her to my favorite diner. The diner is our happy place, where we get together to either forget about our troubles or solve world problems. Well, at least problems in our tiny corner of the world.

Once I pick at my eggs and hash browns enough to make a dent, Ma slides her plate over, anchors her elbow on the table, leans toward me, and cues her serious-talk voice. "I know you want to hide from all the critics right now," she says. "It's strange seeing your name in bold type in the tabloids and thrown around on the internet. It's strange for me as your mother, believe you me," she says. "But, Zora, honey, the press is no different than the voices in your head, telling you to doubt yourself. And you, baby, have conquered your inner critic before."

I look out the window at the sun shower pelting down. Ma rubs my forearm.

"That day the press showed up outside? You were such a warrior. I know you can hold steady on that. You got this, Zora."

"Thanks, Ma," I tell her. "I'll think on it."

"You keep thinking, and I'll go on and keep praying," she says.

I decide to take things day by day. By the time Thursday rolls around, I'm looking forward to seeing the camp kids as planned, but I'm dragging my feet to the community center. Ms. Nelson will no doubt have a million questions for me, and I doubt she'll take "no comment" for an answer. But there's no way I can skip going.

"Shall we drop you off at the community center?" Owen asks me during our ride home after classes Thursday afternoon.

"Sure."

A part of me is enjoying being chauffeured around, but another part is missing being off the radar. Okay, so maybe I was never off the radar in Appleton, but that was by choice. Maybe in a way, I'm missing my old low-key life. But Ma, John, and Daddy all agree the Men in Black car ride is the best approach for the final weeks left of the summer program. And the best part about this setup is hanging with Owen at the start and end of each day.

Ma says she's glad she doesn't have to worry about who will approach me on the train ride to school. She secretly can't wait for my school year to start back up, because then she'll know I'm mostly in Appleton.

"You're welcome to come in and meet the kids," I tell Owen. "I'm sure they'd love to hear a little about life as a royal."

"You really do view everything as a lesson to share with these kids," he says with a laugh. "Okay. Text me when I'm cleared to come inside. I know you'd rather have a few moments with them first."

I only take a few paces into the center, when Ms. Nelson spots me.

Mr. Lance at the front desk makes an apologetic face. I brace myself.

"There you are, Zora," she says. She pulls me aside and looks around to make sure there's no one within earshot before beginning.

"Hi, Ms.—"

"Now, I'm not going to get all up in your love life or anything," she cuts me off. "And I've never had eyes for anyone other than boy-next-door types, if you catch my meaning. But I do know that if everything is appropriate in the eyes of the Lord, you're not being disrespected or made to feel less than, then nothing anyone else says should matter."

Wow, that's a relief to hear. Ms. Nelson is pretty much telling the trolls to suck it, and I'm here for it.

"Thank you," I say.

"In any case, he's better than that *lackadaisal* boy with the overgrown 'fro and the tattooed arm you used to walk around with." Ms. Nelson grimaces.

"Um, you mean my brother, Zach?"

"But oooh, girl, you caught the big fish, didn't you?" She stomps away chuckling to herself. I can still hear her tickled reaction bounce off the walls down the hall.

I go in to see the kids and tell them I have a surprise guest. When Owen walks in, the kids greet him as they would any visitor. They have no idea who he is, and this makes a smile spread across Owen's face.

He once told me this is a reason he loves being in the States so much.

"I once spotted the world's most celebrated football player on a busy New York City street, and no one looked twice at him."

"That's because of the identity-hiding helmets they wear during the game," I teased.

"I mean football as in soccer," he said, and then we both cracked up.

In the center with the kids, Owen introduces himself and says that he's a prince of a country called Landerel. Some of the kids *ooh* and *aah*, and they all have tons of questions. Owen talks to them about the obligations and responsibilities of his role as a

234

royal. And he answers that, yes, he does live in a castle but, no, he doesn't live in a fairy tale.

It's a great discussion. Owen asks the kids to think up ways they have obligations to their friends and families.

"I have to feed my cat," says Dante.

"My bed won't make itself, so I need to do it," says Anaya.

"Oh yeah, I have to work on our family puzzle a few minutes each day," shouts Prentice.

"That ain't one." Dante sucks his teeth. "*Oblimations* can't be fun."

"Obligations," I correct Dante.

"And yes, they can be fun if you take interest in what you're doing, or team up with the right people," Owen says. He winks at me.

Then he glances around the room, and he sees what I recently brought in to hang on the wall: a copy of the picture of the Reconstruction-era African American Halstead students.

"Wow," Owen says, nodding to it. "You brought that here, Zora?"

"Yes, the kids love wondering about what became of them," I say. "So, we've been doing a little digging to research them."

"What have you found?" Owen's face lights up.

"This woman went on to graduate Howard Law School, in DC," Anaya says proudly, pointing.

"One student was from Monrovia, Liberia," remembers Prentice.

"The other was a son of a university janitor and graduated summa cum laude and went on to get his PhD," I say.

I go from laughing to tearing up. I turn my back to the kids before they see me, and take a few paces away. Owen puts a hand on my shoulder.

"I'm just moved by their resilience and success so much, it still chokes me up," I say.

He nods in understanding. I think I see emotion welling up his eye, but he blinks it away before I can tell for certain.

"Some of the kids' families and I have been talking about re-creating that photo with the kids posing the same way," I tell Owen. "They'd represent academia's future students."

"That's a really powerful idea," he tells me.

For the rest of his visit, he makes an awesome assistant. He's observant and attentive, offering warm smiles and encouraging words to the kids when they need it. They give him a group hug as he leaves.

"You looked like you were having fun in there," I tell him as we ride back to my house.

"I was," he says. "Your energy was contagious. I love how you treat them with tenderness yet also like little adults."

That makes me happy to hear.

"Seriously, kids remember the feeling people give them," he goes on. "My older sister taught me that. She asked my opinions, my ideas, my help. I try to bring this to my interactions with all children because of her."

"She sounds like an amazing person," I say softly. Suddenly I become aware of the weight of my words in this moment. I don't want to say the wrong thing, but I want him to know I care. I reach out for his hand and lace my fingers through his.

"She meant everything to me." He smiles sadly, then glances my way. "She would like you."

"I guess I'm kind of meeting her in a way, through you."

"Yes." He sits up. "Through me, she'll be represented at the wedding. It would have been *her* night to dance with someone she cares for."

It would've been her time. But now, it's our time. And mine. I can almost see those Reconstruction-era students waving their sign at me. "A Time for Change." For me, right now that means a change of heart. I'll try not to sweat what's said about us on social media.

"Well, then we better represent." I sit up, too. "Let's do it for Emily."

"For Emily." He nods with a smile.

Chapter 28

THE NEXT day, when I'm leaving class, someone unexpected is waiting for me outside in the hall.

"Zora, we never met in person," he says. "I'm Finn Burlington, the student reporter you spoke to over the phone a few weeks ago."

I almost roll my eyes right in his face. But with all my strength, I push back the attitude bubbling up.

"Yes?" I ask him.

"I'm working on a piece for the *Halstead Chronicle*. We'd like to profile you."

"Why?" I ask.

"Well, you've been talked about on local and even a bit of national news, and we'd like to give you an opportunity to speak about your experiences in your own words."

I want to walk away, but that would look like I'm running from something. Why should I? I have nothing to hide.

"I'm sure you helped out a bit in making me newsworthy," I say, thinking of the recently released details.

"Well, I—"

"You all right, Zora?" Matt is suddenly at my side.

"You don't have to answer now," Finn says. "I realize you have a lot going on. But I'll text you my number so you can reach me when you're ready."

"Or not," says Matt.

We watch Finn walk off like his mission is accomplished.

But no. This just won't do.

"Hey, Finn," I hear myself say. Finn looks just as surprised as I feel as he turns around and I walk over to him. "I can meet you Monday at noon at the east entrance of the campus."

"Th-that works!" Even if it didn't work for him, the thirsty, wide-eyed look is not the face of a person who would miss this opportunity.

"Will you be bringing a photographer for the story?" I ask.

"Yes, I can definitely arrange that," he says, giddy that I'm being so cooperative.

The next Monday, when Finn arrives with a photographer by his side, he's perplexed to find me waiting with Anaya, Prentice, Dante, Ms. Nelson, and Owen.

"Oh, Prince Owen," Finn says. "I'm not sure I'm authorized to speak to you as well."

"I'm just here to observe," says Owen as casually as he can muster.

"Yes, Owen was impressed with your invitation for me to tell my story in my own voice," I say. "It's nice when allies stand up and refuse to participate in questioning girls about the guys they may or may not be connected to."

The photographer smiles her approval, but Finn looks at her like Caesar must have looked at Brutus.

"Just one more thing before we get started," I say. Owen picks up the long wooden easel lying on the ground and props it up. I uncover the large, blown-up photo of Halstead's early African American students and place it on the easel.

"I promised this field trip would only last two hours," I say.

The three children pose in front of the brick base of the clock. I check against the photo and give them a thumbs-up. If I could respond to choreography as easily as they do, I'd truly be slaying on the royal dance floor.

For the final touch, I hand Anaya the sign we worked on together. As in the original sign, it reads: "A Time for Change."

"Here are release forms signed by their parents with the correct spelling of their first names," I tell Finn. "Please do not use their last names."

"We are the future of academia," the kids shout as the photographer snaps pictures of them.

A small crowd forms. People clap and murmur appreciatively, taking their own photos with their phones.

"Have you visited the campus archives?" one woman—a professor—asks the photographer. "If they have any more of these early photos, this would make a great gallery show."

I look at Owen, who's beaming proudly at me.

Chapter 29

I'M JUST finishing off my makeup, getting ready for the last day of classes, when that one-ding doorbell rings. I sprint downstairs to answer it. Skye charges in, and I'm instantly enveloped in a bone-crushing hug.

We jump up and down in a fit of giggles, until she stops short and grabs onto her side.

"I sprinted all the way here," she pants. "I need some water."

While she hydrates in the kitchen, we catch up on the stuff we didn't have the time to cover during our short phone chats. Skye absolutely loved her program and is convinced I would, too. She shows me photos of her robotic creation, her robotics classmates, the Atlanta sights, and, of course, her selfies with Zach.

"Aw, look at how much fun you two are having," I say.

She says something unintelligible in a pitch only dog ears could pick up. In fact, I think I can hear a faint howl coming from outside.

I shake my head.

"Oh yeah?" she says. "Let's see you keep a straight face when I mention Owen's name."

I cover my mouth with my curly strands so as not to give myself away too easily. Skye points at me.

"Look at that! And I didn't even mention the part about his flying you first-class to a real-life castle in Landerel," she laughs.

"You have your stuff ready?" I keep a smirk on my face as I change the subject. "C'mon, we have a train to catch!"

"Ugh, I figured you'd be sentimental and want to catch the train on your last day of class," says Skye.

"Maybe you'll get the security chaperone experience this afternoon at the beach."

When we step outside, Zach is already in the car waiting to drive us to the train station. It was the only way I could get my parents to agree to my taking the train instead of my now-usual Men in Black escort.

Skye does a happy hop before running up to give Zach a hug. When they break apart, he holds the front passenger door open for her with a smile.

"You mind if I sit in the back with Zora?" she asks him sweetly.

Here it comes. I wait for him to say this isn't a rideshare and he's not getting paid. But instead he graciously says, "That's cool."

Skye and I chat nonstop on the way to the station. Our train is waiting on the platform for us, so our conversation isn't disrupted by any hiccups along the way. We find two seats and talk

U of A vs. Rutgers vs. Halstead, college campus life, and royal wedding! Of course when we discuss the wedding, we lower our voices. Rush hour commuters don't seem to care about anything but outpacing the clock, but you never know.

When we arrive on campus, I lead Skye right to the library, where Owen and I arranged to meet up before class.

"Best friend, meet boyfriend," I whisper to Skye as we approach Owen, because it's too dorky to say aloud.

"Aah, the boyfriend meets the best friend," says Owen, stepping forward to shake Skye's hand.

"You two belong together," Skye mumbles to me before greeting Owen.

Skye repeats this a few more times throughout our afternoon outing to the Jersey Shore. With classes wrapped up and a strong finish with high marks and college credit toward graduation, there's a lot for everyone to celebrate.

Skye, Owen, Matt, Abby, Perez, Amir, and I, with, of course, Pork Roll Dominic there to guide us, scale the boards (boardwalk) and enjoy disco fries (fries with gravy). We get in a beach volleyball game (the girls beat the guys), and take a dip in the Atlantic Ocean (Abby's first time).

Aside from Abby and Matt, who attend the same school, we're aware that we may not hang out again. So it feels right to drag out this day just a bit. When Owen puts his arm around me as we watch the sunset, I know I've accomplished so much this summer, but it's far from over. And I'm especially glad my time with Owen isn't over yet.

Chapter 30

OWEN LEAVES for Landerel a few days before Ma and I do. Saying good-bye is sad even though I'll see him soon. I guess it feels like the dress rehearsal for when we'll really have to go our separate ways. I'm assuming that will be after the wedding since there's no reason for him to come back to the States. The program is over. But I'm not going to let this get me down. Not when so much excitement is happening.

I'm going to the freakin' royal wedding! In a designer dress!

The evening of our overnight flight to Landerel, Skye helps Ma and me do a final luggage check for everything we need to bring. Then we carry our luggage downstairs.

"Ay, Zora, Ma, Skye," Zach calls to us, holding the front door open. "Let's all wait out front for your pickup." When we head out to join Zach and John, we see it: A crowd has formed outside of our home. But it's not the media. It's Mr. Stanley, Ms. Nelson, Anaya, Prentice, the owner of the Jamaican store, Layla and the rest of the Fredrickson family, and the mayor.

It's the most amazing send-off I've ever seen. I tear up as people wish us a good flight and a great visit.

"Please sneak in a dab or something while you're dancing," says Layla. That gets a good chuckle from the crowd.

"I think I'll save that move for our next block party," I say.

"Don't remind her," scolds Mr. Stanley. "Y'all can hide from her and her block party duties sign-up sheet—I live right next door!" Everyone laughs again.

"Thank you, everyone!" I say. "Wherever I go, I'm taking Appleton with me!"

From our airport ride to the first-class flight, Ma and I are treated like royalty. We start off politely repeating, "We're fine, we're fine," to every offer on the plane for more snacks, an extra blanket, a different movie. But once we're high above the Atlantic Ocean, we stop playing it cute. "We're fine" grows up to be "Thank you, I will have another" and "Yes, please."

In between delighting in the comforts, Ma and I keep looking at each other in disbelief.

"Did you *ever* imagine?" Ma stares wide-eyed at me.

"No, not this." I shake my head.

Neither Ma nor I have ever traveled much farther out of the States than Toronto. And we drove there. Crossing the Atlantic is pretty special for us, but it's too dark outside to appreciate it.

"We're closer to the Motherland than ever before," Ma says. She's always wanted to visit West Africa and walk the land of our ancestors. Secretly, John has booked her a surprise birthday trip to Ghana. Ma is obsessed with all things genealogy, and her DNA results show the bulk of her ancestry comes from that region. I keep the secret to myself, knowing she will be so excited when she gets that gift come September.

I manage to get some sleep in the fancy reclining seat-bed, and before I know it, it's morning. As we begin our descent into Landerel's Glenby International Airport, it already feels like a different planet. The open fields are a special kind of green. And everything about the buildings, highways, and traffic patterns is structured differently. I can't wait to take a closer look.

After we get our luggage, we find our driver waiting for us, as Owen promised. He holds an elegant sign that reads "Zora and Yvette." Mom and I look at each other and grin for the millionth time so far.

Owen said he wouldn't be able to pick me up himself—he's recognized too easily here, no matter how many hats he wears. This is his country; his face is well known in these parts.

It's disorienting looking out the window as we drive through the streets. For one, everyone looks refreshed and revitalized, like they got a good night's sleep. It's about 3:00 a.m. in Jersey and I feel it. And when you throw in the left-side-of-the-road driving and the endless roundabouts, you get the sense that we're far, far from home. But surprisingly, these differences feel more exciting than scary.

The hotel we're staying in is as posh as they come, in a mon-eyed area of the capital city of Glenby. It sits right across the street from what looks like Glenby's version of Central Park. Our driver tells us that the park houses the royal church and castle where the wedding and reception will be held. This is such a world away from life in Jersey.

A doorman in a top hat ushers us in. The hotel is dripping with elegance, and I can't get enough of the ballroom vibe. A friendly hotel representative escorts us to our space on the tenth floor. We don't have a hotel room. It's a hotel *suite*! I'm talking two bedrooms with two private bathrooms. In the main living space, there are what appear to be freshly delivered flowers on the coffee table. It's a delphinium arrangement, the same plant Owen grew at Halstead's greenhouse.

There's a card from Owen with a sweet welcome message for me and my mom. Below his name is the same local phone number he texted me before my flight. I promptly call him using the hotel phone.

"You're here!" Owen sounds so excited.

"Can you believe it?! We're going to check out the area, maybe grab breakfast. Are you able to join us?"

"I—I can't," says Owen.

"You can't?" I ask.

"Royal duties," he says with a groan. "But I booked you and your mom on a great tour of Glenby this afternoon."

"Yay! Thank you!" I bounce on my toes. "Will we see you before or after the tour?"

"I'd love to see you after the tour if that works for you," he says. "There's so much going on here, but I'm planning on making a getaway before dinner."

I wish I could see him sooner.

Ma and I are too excited by all the amazingness to worry about that now. We shower, change into summery-cute yet pedestrian-friendly clothes, and head off on a day of adventure. We grab a quick breakfast and walk a bit of the park, which we learn is called Glenby Green. Soon, we are so sleepy, we have to pinch ourselves to stay alert. Being wide-eyed keeps tourists from looking the wrong way before crossing the street so they won't miss a *lorry* (aka truck) heading their way. In an unrelated story, we think we learn a Landerelian cuss word.

We head back to the hotel, where Ma and I take a nap and recoup. We enjoy a lunch of fish and chips in the hotel restaurant, and then we're ready to hit the tour. We sit top level on a double-decker bus and hop off to visit town squares bustling with charm, museums that rival New York's, historic churches, and universities way, way older than Halstead. We look both ways, three times, at every intersection. Ma takes countless pictures of every last one of these sites. The woman goes hard with her tourist flow.

We're exhausted when we get back to the hotel, but I'm eager to see Owen. Maybe we can have an early dinner together. I call him to find out what time he'll be coming.

"I'm not," he says.

Chapter 31

"OBLIMATIONS," OWEN says, then pauses to listen for my chuckle. But there's only silence. "Duty calls again, and I'm expected to join my family for dinner with Sadie's family. I'm terribly sorry, Zora. I wanted so much to see you tonight."

I go back to my early transatlantic flight refrain.

"It's fine," I say. "I'm fine."

But as the kids in my program would say, duty stinks.

"I'll see you tomorrow, though?" Owen asks cheerfully.

"Tomorrow," I echo.

"Glide, sway, dip, slay," bellows Jethro, our dance instructor.

Owen and I are in a sunbathed dance studio in downtown Glenby, literally bright and early the next morning. I don't have to glance at the mirrored wall to know that we are also a breath away from stepping on each other's toes. At this point, I wouldn't mind causing him a bit of pain. The only reason I get to see him today is because he *has* to be here, and that's not a good feeling. Since arriving on his turf, it's been hard to distinguish what he does out of duty and what he does out of desire.

"Don't look so stiff." Jethro winces like it's *his* feet that are in peril. Such an offense would be a fashion misdemeanor, because his sneakers are as stark white as the walls of this studio. Apparently, you don't get to be the chief royal choreographer with scuffed footwear.

All that social climbing and he keeps his kicks pristine. What's even more impressive is his backstory, which he told us after I said I'd never waltzed before. Jethro is not at all from Landerel. Or any place in Europe. He's from the Appalachian foothills of Ohio . . . by way of Brooklyn.

"Miss Zora, pick up your feet. You will not be wearing running shoes or house slippers on that night, but heels. Where are your heels?"

"Can they be wedges?" I can't get with the toe torture that comes with heels. And I have narrow size sevens! Heels started out being worn by men centuries ago and should've stayed that way.

"We have this one morning to prepare before the grande dame Lady Lois gets here later." Jethro ignores my whiny question. "And nothing less than a tight routine with elegant postures will do. Take a quick water break, throw on your *wedges*, and then let's get back to it."

I'm not as afraid of Lady Lois as Jethro seems to be. Apparently, she's my "handler" while I'm here. To me, her arrival means I get to try on beautiful gowns. To Jethro, it means an evaluation that could cost him his reputation. So I need to get this right.

Owen heads to the same corner of the room and cracks open the water bottles set out for us.

"It's so good to see you, finally," Owen whispers to me, wrapping me in his arms. It's amazing to see him, too, and my stomach butterflies start flapping, but I purse my lips like I don't believe a word he's saying.

"I'm sorry we haven't been able to spend more time alone," he says. "But this afternoon, I've arranged for a visit for you to Sister's Keeper, that impressive community organization you mentioned to me."

I finally look Owen in the eyes. It's like his amazing memory is his superpower, and he uses it to delight people around him. "Really? I can't believe it. Thank you."

"Time." Jethro calls us back to the floor.

"But you're still not off the hook for ghosting me last night," I say.

"It's inexcusable, I know," he says. "I underestimated how in demand I would be. I'm not even the groom!"

Jethro is not here for the chatter. "Positions, please!"

I stick out my chest, and Owen puffs out his. When Jethro starts up the classical piece again, we gracefully respond in kind to the soaring strings and passionate piano. I think of how Skye would approach this dance challenge. I flair out my fingers to add panache like I know she would. This space no doubt holds the spirit of auditions past and future. On another day, there could be talented musical theater hopefuls auditioning in here. I channel their energy, too. I stretch my neck and hold my head high. Owen adjusts to my elongated frame, which elegantly extends his reach, too.

"Better," says Jethro. Owen and I take it. It's the closest thing to a compliment he's given us all morning. Owen winks at me. I put up my fist and he bumps it with his. Jethro catches our celebration.

"'Better' is a relative term, dears," Jethro clarifies. "And considering I'm comparing it to how you started, you have no time to stop and pat yourselves on the back!"

As if on cue, Owen steps on my toe. We avoid eye contact because we can't trust ourselves not to crack up. Jethro cuts off the music and commands us to take it from the top once again.

We run through the four-minute dance countless times. Truth be told, because Jethro starts the music from the beginning every time we make a mistake, we know the opening choreography better than the ending. But we must be doing something right because Jethro's comments go from "Better" to "Yes!" At first, it sounds like Jethro is saying "Worse!" but I tell him it must be a Midwestern accent we're picking up.

"Between the two of us, you think *my* accent is the one that stands out?" Jethro says. *"Mmkay."*

Jethro is about to ask us to take it from the top once more when Lady Lois floats in as if she's on a cloud. She's an imposing figure, that's for sure. And even though she's facing us, we somehow are only able to perceive her profile. It's like she's perfected the art of remaining at an angle. It's a highly aristocratic view of her, which I'm sure is what she's intended. She might as well be a talking coin or a life-sized clay bust.

Jethro rushes to greet her.

"Welcome, Lady Lois." He is almost trembling. "We're honored to—"

"Let's see the choreography," she cuts Jethro off.

Jethro gets to the play button quicker than we expected. The music begins a millisecond later. Owen and I have to throw down our water bottles and race to the center of the dance floor to catch our musical cue.

Even though the music fills the space, there is a deathly silence in the room because of the tension Lady Lois's presence creates.

"That'll do," she says before we've come to the end. Jethro looks relieved; that must be high praise from Lady Lois.

"Miss Emerson, I'll need you to gather your things and come with me," she says. She nods toward Owen, and then leaves the room.

"Where is she taking me?" I ask Owen.

He gives me another hug, even though we're both a little sweaty. "I think Lady Lois has some items on her agenda for you," he explains. "And I have to go meet my brother now for his suit fitting. But I'll meet you later?"

"Later," I say, squeezing his hand.

I grab my bag and walk out of the dance studio, where Lady Lois is waiting in the hall . . . with Ma!

"Are we leaving?" I ask. Lady Lois ignores my question and keeps walking.

"Are we being deported?" I touch my mom's arm and ask under my breath. Ma smiles and taps my hand.

"Your gown sizing, remember?" Ma reminds me. I can't believe I let Lady Lois's intimidation tactics throw me off the fashion scent.

The three of us get into the waiting black stretch town car. Inside, Lady Lois grabs a large binder and a tablet and gets to business.

"Right, I'm Lady Lois, and I'm pleased to make your acquaintance," she says, ignoring the fact that we've been in her presence for the past fifteen minutes or so. "I will be your handler whilst you're in Landerel and I'm here to provide you both with your styling requirements."

As I'm already aware thanks to social media, there's buzz about what I'll wear to the wedding, what style, which designer. I don't mind that buzz so much. There's nothing wrong with a healthy competition among designers who are all vying for my attention.

Lady Lois proceeds to show me proposals from five top designers. I'm in awe. These are designers I've heard of, ones I've followed on Instagram just to get a glimpse of their genius. I can't afford nor do I have the desire to wear designer clothes, but the low-end clothes I buy and wear are sometimes inspired by them.

My mom and I lean in and soak up the beauty of the designs while Lady Lois turns to different pages in her binder to let us feel the swatches the clothes are based on. This is so much fun.

Then we move on to hair and makeup. The survey Lady Lois has me fill out on the tablet will help the hairdresser and makeup artist know how to style me.

"I see here you haven't checked off the available hair styles listed. I'll just put blown out straight," she says.

"Uh, I'd rather wear my hair curly," I say.

Lady Lois eyeballs me over the retro-cool frames of her reading glasses. "I . . . see," she says.

"Zora's hair can be worn in so many beautiful styles, like these," says Ma, ever ready with images to prove a point. Ma holds her phone out to Lady Lois and scrolls through one photo after another of me in different naturally coily styles.

"Yes, well, that settles it," Lady Lois says. We can glean from the haughty purse of her lips that coily coifs aren't her personal taste. But they don't need to be. Ma and I smile at our coup.

As her last act, Lady Lois snaps a pic of me with her tablet. She rides the rest of the way in silence.

When we step out of the car, I whisper to Ma, "This is going to be way more fabulous than I ever imagined."

"Let's hold the happy squeals until we're home." She beams.

"We've arrived," says Lady Lois as she leads us toward a sleek building. "Let's go in."

Sixteen floors up, we enter a designer studio. I'm told that at different appointment times several designers will come to make an appeal to me. Could this be really happening? This place looks like the behind-the-scenes room at a fashion show. A really tall woman with angular features and leggy strides smiles at me as she leaves the studio. I wonder if she's a model prepping for her *Vogue* photo shoot or something.

"Everyone, I'm proud to present to you sixteen-year-old Zora and her mother, Ms. Yvette," says Lady Lois in a commanding voice. The busy staff respectfully pause their ironing, steaming, sewing, measuring, and sorting. Of course, they also start assessing me, giving me head-to-toe once-overs.

"Now, Zora, you are going to hear us commenting on you physically, but we know the confidence and grace you exuded during your dance rehearsal is what truly matters most," Lady Lois says, surprising me with the casual compliment. "This team will advise you in all things fashion, so that you'll have the best designs to match that spirit as well as your personality, personal style, and physical qualities."

Okay. I nod my head in understanding.

"Hello, Zora," says one friendly woman. "Are you ready? We promise to make this fun for you. Let's start with your music choice. Any special requests?"

With a thumping playlist on repeat, people wearing thin measuring tapes like scarves take measurement after measurement. And gown after gown is handed to me to try on, along with the fanciest hair accessories. "Fascinators" they call them. My fitting room is makeshift, but Ma stands guard at the curtain to make sure I have all the privacy I need.

Each stylist is also wearing a sleek black fanny pack containing all of the tailor needs to solve any fashion emergency. They pin the back of the gowns I try on until they fit me like a glove.

Ma puts her hand over her heart or mouth each time I step on the platform in front of the full-length mirrors. I can hardly believe what I'm seeing myself. The gowns give me a Hollywood-starlet-on-a-red-carpet vibe. I look and feel spectacular, though a part of me feels guilty about it. If only everyone I know could experience this. My dad for one would relish this. And Skye. And, of course, Anaya. In fact, all of the kids in the program and at school would, too.

"Zora?" My mom catches that look on my face.

"Ma, how about if we throw an annual Royalty for a Day party back in Appleton? I'm sure my principal would donate the school gym . . ."

"Let's talk about that later, hmm?" Ma says sweetly. "Right now, just enjoy your moment."

"Okay, but on our way home, can we stop at a supply store? There are a few things I need to pick up tonight."

"The moment, Zora," she repeats. "The moment."

After three hours of nonstop fittings with doting designers, we settle on a royal-blue gown that I can't stop staring at.

"Mini squeal now, just because I can't hold it in anymore?" Ma asks.

I nod my head yes. We clutch each other's hands and *squeeee* together when no one is looking.

Chapter 32

THE TOUR of Sister's Keeper blows my mind. We learn about the origins of the place as a shelter for women and children, and how it grew to also help resettle refugees and immigrants in its changing community. We are in the original space where the organization got started. There are offices and meeting rooms here. And lots of old and new framed photos of the people they've met with, right here in these offices. World leaders, spiritual leaders, celebrities, and everyday people. Ma and I take selfies in front of some of my faves.

"Oh, there's Sadie!" I point out a photo of the princess-to-be.

"She used to volunteer here as a teen," says our tour guide. "She lived in this area as a child, and said she always wanted to give back as thanks for what Sister's Keeper did for her friends and family."

The building next door is newer and open to the diverse, heavily immigrant community it serves.

Ma and I sit in on a talk there about the new programs serving the influx of refugee families from war-torn parts of the world.

Once the talk is over, Ma and I head out for a stroll into the sunshine.

Sofia, the royal security woman who drove us here, tries to usher us straight into the car. But Ma and I insist on walking out into the neighborhood awhile.

I'm so glad to be out among the people. The area is so different than where we're staying. Here kinda reminds me of Appleton. There's more of a down-home vibe, with people holding lively conversations in all types of languages on front stoops, music thumping from car stereos, and kids playing in the streets.

"Watch out for the lady!"

A girl of about eight pins the runaway soccer ball—or, I guess, football—with her foot, pausing the street game until I walk safely by. I greet her with a smile and nod my thanks for her shout-out.

A lady.

Wow, that's a first. It sounds so regal. So noble. *Lady Zora.* Or *Lady Emerson.* Maybe *Lady Zora of the Emerson Dynasty.* I'm not entirely sure how the royal court would address me, but here in the streets of Landerel, a kid has christened me a lady.

I feel my spine straighten, my hips sway. Even my shoulder bag is lighter. It's hard to remember what I'd been so nervous about all week. *Lady, you got this,* I tell myself. *You're fierce, and you're from a long line of brave women.*

As I strut by in my restored confidence, one miniature player with scraped-up knees and a scrappy vibe looks impatient. She examines me with squinted eyes and bunched-up lips, not the least bit fooled.

"That's not a lady, that's a *girl*!" she blurts.

Poof! There goes *that* confidence boost. I laugh in spite of my worries, and Ma laughs with me.

Chapter 33

OUR HOTEL suite is a busy scene the next afternoon. One after another, stylists, a hairdresser, and a makeup artist all arrive to give me pizzazz for the rehearsal dinner. There's even a royal etiquette lady schooling me on dining protocols.

A rack of clothing wheeled in holds dress options for tonight. As I thumb through the rack in awe, the glam squad preps their tools while watching the nonstop live coverage of the wedding on TV.

I watch, too; I'm curious to get as much scoop as possible about which designers other people are wearing. Just when I feel at ease about the talk centering on Gideon, there's a news report about Owen.

"Prince Owen is flying above the radar these days, and recent reports paint him as having shed his wild-boy image," the reporter standing on a busy Glenby street corner says. "Young girls everywhere are noticing that he's matured quite nicely. The lucky girl he is bringing to the wedding is an American from the state of New Jersey. But, we'd like to know, what do girls closer to home think of the prince?"

"He looks ripe for a proper snog," says a girl on the street.

"And what of his American girlfriend?" The amused reporter pronounces it "go-u-friend."

"That can't last," the girl replies.

Everyone in the room avoids eye contact with me. I feel like shrinking.

Ma walks in at the perfect time. "Zora, look who's here," she singsongs.

I never thought I'd be so happy to see Lady Lois. It just feels comforting. I walk over to her and actually give her a light hug.

"Oh my," she says. But the gleam in her eye tells me she understands. "I don't normally get such greetings."

I can tell. The room is even tenser than when the news report was playing.

"Chop-chop," she tells me. "You are to go to hair and makeup now."

Soon, I'm settled in a chair chatting with my makeup artist. I ask her about her neighborhood and hear fascinating stories about what it was like to grow up with five human siblings and four canine ones.

When she turns the chair to the mirror, I am loving how beautifully the tones of my lipstick and blush match my brown skin. "Thank you," I tell her.

I stay in the same chair and leaf through Landerelian gossip magazines, waiting for my hair to get done. Cover to cover, the tabloids are all royal wedding everything, with a special focus on the bride's and groom's personal lives before and after they met each other. It's hard not to get sucked into every page.

Not one, but two stylists are working on my hair. They stand at each side of my head and use super-skinny curling irons on strand after strand. I'm faced away from the mirror, so I ask as many questions as I can about what look they're going for.

"It's going to be fabulous, you'll see," says the stylist to my right.

"You have a lot of hair, so four hands are better than two," says the other.

Neither of them have coily or even curly hair, but that's not too much a cause for concern. Some of the top experts in natural hair care are people you wouldn't expect.

After what feels like an eternity, they turn me to the mirror. I almost gasp out loud. It looks like I'm wearing a motorcycle helmet. The shape of this hairdo is nebulous. Layers of Little Bo-Peep ringlets are piled so high, my entire coif wouldn't fit into a selfie.

"You like it?" one of the hairstylists asks.

"I—I don't normally wear it like this," I say.

"Well, of course you don't. This is a special occasion, so nothing normal will do."

"I—you're right, this isn't . . . normal," is all I can say.

"Now hurry and get dressed so you can show your mum the whole package."

The whole package is unfortunately sitting on my head. And it's oddly shaped.

"The car is waiting downstairs. You have ten minutes!" Lady Lois pokes her head inside our suite. She's distracted and on the phone, so she doesn't see me gesturing to her. *What's the Landerelian sign for SOS?*

I drag my feet to my room to get dressed. I had been so worried about the stylists getting my makeup tone wrong that I didn't think of my hair.

"Are you all dressed?" Ma knocks on the door.

"Come in," I grumble.

Ma scans me from the toes up. My kitten-heeled pointy mules are looking fierce. My legs have a tanned glow. The copper-and-black polka-dot dress is a retro wonder. Its flowy skirt and mid-century belt are snatching wigs out here. The flawlessness of my makeup—crushing it. And then . . . record scratch.

Ma's face when she sees my hair confirms everything.

"Okay, don't panic," she says. "I have extra hair pins."

"I'm going to need lots. We're talking a *lorry* load of pins, Ma."

Ma pins the front half of my hair into a French roll. She does the best she can, but I'm still not feeling this hairdo. I kiss her good-bye but wish more than ever she was coming with me to this rehearsal dinner.

"Remember to curtsy upon meeting the queen, just as we rehearsed," Lady Lois says. She stares at my hair, train-wreck-gawker style, as we get into the black car to drive to the dinner. It's tough to hear her around my noise-canceling curls.

At least I get to hang out with Owen tonight. I feel like I haven't seen him in forever.

The car navigates a smooth twisty road through the enormous park until we enter a canopied entrance to what must be the royal grounds. I grab my phone and get my camera ready. We come upon a peaceful pond, which reflects its foresty surroundings. I try to capture the leafy reflections, but a large white bird with a yellowish head and long beak swoops down at that moment, sending ripples through it. Once we cross a charming old brick bridge, the sight of Highbury Castle poking through the trees grabs my attention. It is breathtaking. I can't stop snapping pics from every angle. I turn my phone from portrait to landscape and back again. I zoom in on the brickwork, the stained glass windows, and the iron doors. The early evening sun perfectly outlines all the Gothic filigree details on the castle's peaks.

"Oh, wow! I can't imagine what it must look like inside!" I say.

"Our first stop is the reception location in the East Wing of the palace," says Lady Lois.

"Is there a difference between a castle and a palace?" I ask.

"Technically this is a castle, originally built as a fortress. But it's had some upgrades over the centuries, like its decorative windows," says Lady Lois.

If I had Wi-Fi in this car, I'd email Anaya these photos. She's obsessed with drawing castles. There's a budding architect in her, I think.

The car drops us off, and we enter the East Wing's marbled halls and are led to the grand banquet. It faces the pond, and the view through the floor-to-cathedral-ceiling glass wall almost knocks me on my booty.

Are these rich people kidding me right now?

I can't imagine the epic cookout the whole of Appleton would love to have right outside. The marble-top patio table would no doubt be the scene of Daddy's spades game challenge to John. That would easily draw a crowd.

Inside the hall, the tables are already elegantly dressed and waiting for the big day tomorrow. There's no faux-wood-paneled dance floor framed by lighted trim like there was at Ma and John's reception. It's all marble everywhere. I hope the heels I wear tomorrow won't slip.

As if reading my mind, Lois gives me the rundown for tomorrow: what cues to listen for, who to look out for, and where to stand right before the dance.

"Where will I be seated?" I ask.

She points out a table near the wall. As soon as I see it, I get a sinking feeling I know the answer to my next question.

"Where will Owen be seated?"

"At the second table from the bride and groom," she says.

It's cool. That makes a lot of sense, I tell myself to let the nervous fluttering in my stomach fade away.

When we arrive at the Wilhelm Drawing Room for dinner, I'm struck by the textured wall covering and stunning oil paintings hanging on the walls. Though it's a large room, the decor is much more intimate. There are soft chenille settees and chairs angled in the corners, and the long dinner table looks set for a Thanksgiving meal. The lighting has a candlelit tone to it, giving everyone's faces a warm glow.

Everything seems to be in full swing by the time Lady Lois and I step in. People are mingling and chatting it up, and Lady Lois makes her exit. If it didn't look like I was wearing a fuzzy pillow around my head, I would stand a chance at entering unnoticed. But who am I kidding? People would notice me even if my hairstyle were not an issue. Aside from the bride and her father, I'm the only other brown person around for miles.

Owen. Owen. I scan the room for his ginger hair, but there are a few decoys.

"Zora, you made it." Owen touches the back of my elbow, and I turn around with a start.

"Owen!" I smile. He wraps his arms around me and kisses my forehead. I'm glad he doesn't seem put off by my unfortunate hairdo. "Do you need anything?" he asks softly.

"Some water would be great," I say.

Promptly, Owen flags down one of the waiters, who delivers me a glass of sparkling water.

"Thank you," I say to the waiter, and then to Owen. I lean my head on his shoulder for a moment.

"Owen?" the queen beckons from a few paces away.

"Come with me. I'd like to introduce you to my mother."

I really don't want to budge from this sweet spot. Nothing about the judgy look on his mom's face makes me want to meet her. I'd love nothing more than to carve two comfy foot grooves into the floor and settle in.

Owen takes my hand to coax me forward.

The queen looks younger than I'd realized. She can't be too much older than Ma. She wears a conservative but slim eggshell dress and her blond hair is in a sleek bun. Her husband, Victor, always seems to be in the opposite corner of the room from her. Like now.

"Mother, may I present Zora Emerson of New Jersey," Owen says proudly.

"It's a pleasure to meet you, Queen Mildred," I say.

I reach out my hand and then take it back quickly, remembering the curtsy protocol. Recovering, I position my right foot behind my left and dip slightly. When I stand upright and reunite my feet, I lose my right mule. The queen's mouth forms an O.

"Is this the American girl we've been hearing so much about?" Owen's brother Gideon asks as he arrives with Lionel. The brothers are good-looking, blond versions of Owen, though of course I think he's cuter than both of them. I shake hands with each of them.

The queen takes this opportunity to pull Gideon, and unfortunately Owen, to another part of the hall. Owen gives me an apologetic look over his shoulder.

But his eldest brother stays to say hello. "Jolly good to meet the American girl my brother can't stop prattling on about," says Lionel with a devilish grin. "Welcome, Ms. Onyx Santiago," Lionel adds, referring to Owen's favorite R&B singer. I've had enough practice at Halstead to know how to deal with condescending comments tinged with bigotry. So I stay on the offense, just in case.

"When I'm not on tour, I go by Zora." I don't miss a beat.

"An American with the dry wit of a Landerelian? I approve," says Lionel. "I should not tell you this, Zora, but our brother is smitten—the likes of which we haven't seen."

I smile into my drink.

"Yes, we do hope someday you'll grow to like him," continues Lionel.

"Aw, well, I'm warming up to him." I smile. "Slowly." We share one last guarded chuckle before he strikes up a conversation with newcomers to the hall. Feeling more at ease, I take a stroll around the room, glass of sparkling water in hand. Sadie and Gideon seem like a cute couple. I pause a moment to find the bride-to-be. She's surrounded by well-wishers, and she maintains a gracious smile and gentle head nods. She looks amazing in a struc-tured crème dress.

Just like Ms. Earley, Mr. Stanley, and other elders from Appleton, I am a witness to history as I stand here in this room. A biracial woman is joining this royal family that reaches back through centuries of European rule. Here she is, just as proud of her African heritage as her Landerelian.

When we're called to the dinner table, I'm relieved to see I'm seated next to Owen tonight. His reassuring arm bump and warm smile are back where I remember them. He whispers into my ear about some of the craziest people in the room, filling me in on hilarious royal backstories. But he's not even finished eating before his mother summons him away to greet some special guests.

After dinner, people continue to mingle in the room. I'm trying to hide out in a corner when Sadie, the princess-to-be, wanders over to me.

"How are you, Zora, is it?" she asks in her sweet Landerelian accent.

"Yes!" I say nervously. "Hello—and congratulations to you."

"Welcome to Landerel," she says. "I'm happy to have you here."

"My mother and so many American women of color send their best wishes." I smile when I think of what Ma's reaction will be to this story.

"Well, please tell your mother thank you. I can feel their love and support, and it truly is appreciated."

A woman who is dressed like a guest but is clearly on the clock says, "Pardon. If I may—" and walks away with Sadie.

I know this woman is working at the queen's behest, because the queen eyes her as if checking whether the mission is accomplished. It appears as if—and this is not too far-fetched to wonder—they're trying to keep the few brown people in here from clumping together in one place. Maybe this Sadie snatcher is like the royal answer to *Showtime at the Apollo*'s Sandman. Sandman only hits the stage if you're getting booed, and he'll gleefully yank you off with a long hook.

Having had a little practice mingling with standoffish people at Halstead, I make my way around the room. When I join a small gathering of chatting people, the conversation stops. They all look at me like a human fart.

Now I'm starting to think the order to keep Sadie from me is less about brown grouping and specifically about *me*. Just to check my theory, I approach another clique. They respond to my greeting, but their voices trail off soon into silence. They act like there's nothing else under the Landerelian moon to talk about among the group. Sure, they are less obvious with their shade, but it's shade nonetheless.

I hear an American accent close by, and the sound makes me so happy, I want to do the *Fresh Prince* Carlton dance.

"I'm Austrian," the girl says when I greet her, dousing my enthusiasm.

"Oh, cool," I say awkwardly. "I guess I was thrown off by the American-sounding accent."

"I was educated at an international school in Austria, but I was born and raised there."

"And that's cool," I repeat. "I guess what I meant was, like, hearing a familiar accent kind of—well, I know it doesn't mean— oh, never mind." And I walk away.

I find Owen escorting an elderly man out the door.

"Perfect timing," he says when I walk up to him. "I think that's the last of my hosting obligations."

"Well, I hope so, because it seems like your mom put a shun hit on me, and everyone knows."

Before he can respond, Royal Sandman is back.

"Pardon," she says, clearly ready to drag Owen away.

"Wait just one minute," I cut her off. I turn to Owen. "You see what I mean?" In the same nasty-nice formal tone I've been hearing, I tell the woman, "I'd like a word with Owen, if I may." Two can play that game. She stands aside as Owen and I walk to the corner of the room.

"Zora, I think you're mistaken about her," says Owen in conflict-resolution mode. "That is Ms. Dunigan, whom I've known since childhood. She always has everyone's best interest at heart."

"Oh, I'm imagining things?" I feel my inner Kenney coming out. To heck with waiting for an appropriate time and place to have a meltdown.

Owen looks surprised.

"I'm not saying that. I don't mean to come across like that's what I think. Can we start this conversation over? I think the stress of my being back is—"

Then Sandman appears, like our chat time has expired. Oh really? I'm about to go full-blown Kenney, when—

"Zora, join us."

It's Sadie, waving me over. She is chatting with three women, and when I walk over to them, they introduce themselves as friends who met at school over a decade ago. In the next few minutes, these girlfriends are making me giggle and teasing me about Owen.

They're cool. *Sadie*'s cool. My temper cools.

I glance at the queen and her sidekick Sandman and think, *Not today, Your Highness. Not today.*

An hour later, the party is over and Owen is still otherwise . . . engaged. He breaks from posing for family photos to give me a hug good night. He looks sorry I'm leaving, but a bit relieved at the same time. *I wonder what that's about . . .*

Regardless, it's time I leave and get a *head* start on tomorrow. Literally. I plan on an emotional do-over so that I have a much smoother outing at the wedding.

$$\text{⤜⟶}$$

"Baby, that is gorgeous," says Ma when she sees my hairdo the next morning.

Last night when I got back to the hotel, I went into action. I co-washed my hair, flat-twisted it, and used Ma's flexi rods on my ends. This morning, I finger-combed it loose and, voilà! The flat-twist roller set *always* comes through for me. It just took some remembering about the many times it has.

In fact, I had to recall a number of things, like . . . I got this, and I'm built for this life of challenges, triumphs, and everything in between. So what if my mule slips off my foot in front of the freakin' queen, or if I'm on some official royal shun list? I survived it. The sky didn't crash onto Earth. I moved on. Massaging my scalp in the shower helped jog my memory.

I admit, ever since I started at Halstead this summer, my self-doubt stock has gone up a thousand percent. Before this, the biggest change I've had was when Ma married John and we moved from Appleton's rougher East Ward to the other side of the Garden State Parkway. But in every case, the people I connect with are just people. No matter who they are or what the size of their bank account is, they turn out to be no different than the characters I'm used to dealing with in my old neighborhood.

There is no way I've flown this far just to be a wallflower. I came here to represent. I came here to dance at the reception. That's what I'll do.

Now when I look in the mirror, I see a glammed-up version of Zora from around the way. In a killer royal-blue gown. Rocking the dopest hairstyle. Topped by a fascinating fascinator. Memory fully restored.

Ma looks beautiful in a soft-rose fitted designer dress. The hairstylists were happy to use their curling rods and portable hair dryer when she instructed them how to style her locs. Curly tendrils cascade to her shoulders, and a faux-diamond-studded accessory adds sparkle to the side of her do. She has special tickets to sit right outside the Chapel of St. Margery, where she will be among the first to view the newly married couple emerge.

You would think we personally know the bride and groom, we are so excited. As we climb into the car and drive toward the royal grounds, I watch Ma's face as she experiences all of the awe I felt when I rode to the castle yesterday. She keeps shaking her head, amazed.

"Have you ever seen anything so—?" she asks.

"I know," I say, smiling.

Today is a lot less quiet. There are cheering throngs of well-wishers lining every inch of the drive, until we enter the royal grounds.

We get as close as cars are allowed, and walk the rest of the way up an unpaved circular driveway in front of the castle's west entrance. It's a gorgeously sunny day, and invited guests and chapel ticket holders are greeting each other and offering compliments. Ma and I spot some major celebrities, but we play it cool. We're sure we're also walking right by Landerelian superstars only locals would recognize.

A dapper attendant checks our passes and points Ma to a charming garden lined with white chairs.

"This is me," she says. "And ohmygod I think I've gone to heaven. Look who I'll be sitting near."

I look over Ma's shoulder at a group of African women in traditional dress. They kind of look familiar. "Are those the women you read about?" I ask.

"Yes, they traveled here as a symbol of the two merging societies," she says, breathless.

For a second, I feel like the parent dropping her off at the first day of school.

"Go, see if you can sit with them," I say. I'm happy for Ma.

I turn and make my way inside the chapel, when I'm stopped in my tracks by the sight of a person that definitely *is* familiar.

Kelsey is staring right back at me.

Chapter 34

"WOW, I almost didn't recognize you," says Kelsey. Her under-whelmed tone makes it clear she's dragging my Halstead student look.

"Hello to you, too, Kelsey." I roll my eyes.

Kelsey and I are handed programs and ushered into the old chapel. It's crowded and slow-moving in the entry foyer.

"Where are you sitting?" I ask her, half hoping she'll be far away, and half hoping we'll be seated together. Like her or not, she's a familiar face when I can really use one.

"Well, I was originally going to sit with my father, ambassador to Landerel."

"Interesting, don't think I've ever met anyone with the first name Ambassador." I smirk at my own joke.

"But," Kelsey continues, unfazed, "a dear friend asked me to keep his girlfriend company."

Oh.

Once we finally clear the foyer, my eyes adjust to the darker interior and I see I'm in the company of giant saints peering down from stained glass windows. Side by side with the centuries-old architecture is state-of-the-art camera equipment. The wedding is being televised across the globe, and the TV crew members do their best to be invisible in black tuxes.

There are at least four sections of church pews, the first two of which are reserved for family and members of the wedding party. Kelsey and I are led to the middle of the second block of pews. Our guide checks our passes one last time and gestures for us to be seated.

"After you," I tell Kelsey, because I want the aisle seat.

I can't help but notice most of the faces here are like Kelsey's—haughty and a bit distant. For a second, I catch my own face tightening up in that same mold, but I shake it off. Standing on the edge of that slippery slope makes me wonder if Kelsey was once more connected than detached. Was there a time she felt she had to change in order to adapt?

Right there in the aisle seat of that pew is where I find my calling. If I could make a living watching people file in and then reporting my findings to Skye, I'd take the job. It's thrilling! This must be what it's like to have great seats at the New York Fashion Week shows. All of the amazing dresses, suits, accessories, and, of course, hats. I recognize a "schoolmate" of Gideon's from last night's dinner. He is winning every title in a jacquard high-collar jacket and matching turban fit for Indian royalty. Speaking of headgear, it turns out there are a million and one ways to accessorize hats and fascinators. So far, I've spotted ruffles, feathers, satin ribbons, silk flowers, netting, gemstones, buttons, pins, and even porcelain figurines. In most cases, the more elaborate, the better. I see one fascinator that looks like a windblown, inverted parasol.

I come my closest to catching the Holy Ghost when my eyes land on a thing of exquisite beauty. A woman walks in with the African version of the fascinator. The bursts of color, the vivid patterns—what an amazing surprise. Behind her, there are more people with African-inspired accessories, be they handbags, tux lapels, pocket squares, and, best of all, elaborately tied headdresses. *Squeee!*

It all makes me wonder what the setting would be if this were a royal wedding in Africa. I think about the article Daddy had texted me, "Trace Your Lineage to African Royalty." I read it, and learned about the Benin Kingdom. Just like the stained glass saints in this chapel, the Benin people brought divine faces to life through art. Except theirs were carved into busts, masks, and tool handles made from precious materials.

Once everyone is seated, the pre-wedding procession begins. The heavenly voices of the boys' choir's echo through the space. Cheers rising from Ma's garden crowd outside alert us that VIPs are on their way down the aisle.

First to walk down the aisle are Owen's parents, Queen Mildred and her husband, Victor, the prince consort.

And then there's Owen, escorting the bride's mother. Owen's royal wedding suit rocks my world. He is wearing a luxe black tux with a touch of sheen to it. It's a retro classic and he's wearing it with suave style. Owen's on the right side of the aisle, the same side I'm seated. As he comes closer, he keeps his gaze forward, where his brothers are. Just as I wonder if he'll pass by without noticing me, Owen glances at me peripherally, and then does a double take. It's not at all an exaggerated gesture, but here in the land of emotionally conservative folks, it stands out. I hear soft chuckles behind me. Kelsey looks over her shoulder and fixes one of her glares on the person tittering.

When the crowd cheers again, it's for Gideon and his best man, Lionel. Wearing black tailcoat tuxedos and white gloves with a fly modern twist, they walk side by side down the aisle.

After Owen seats Sadie's mother, he greets his brothers at the head of the church. They chat in hushed tones, and smile at relatives in the first few aisles.

Seeing them all together makes me think of Emily, the sibling who is missing. The only daughter of the family isn't here physically to witness this day. And if *I* can feel this absence, I can't imagine what Owen must be going through.

The flower girls and ring bearers are about to make their way down the aisle now. I happily let them distract me from a tearful moment. But immediately I start tearing up when I see the little biracial girl included in the procession. How amazing for brown girls watching back home to see themselves reflected in this way.

I wipe my tear on the sly, but Kelsey notices. She takes a peek to confirm what she's suspecting, and I roll my eyes when she looks away. But then she turns back to me with a tissue from her handbag, and I'm surprised by the gesture.

The garden crowd goes wild, which can only mean one thing. The bride has arrived. We stand and prepare to fawn over her. Sadie's father walks her partway down the aisle, and then she walks up to her groom on her own.

Her gown is simple elegance in a silhouette-hugging design. Her wisps of dark wavy hair are worn in a low bun, and her tiara sparkles yet doesn't overpower her look. She's stunning. By the expression on Gideon's face, he agrees.

The ceremony takes us through a journey of two cultures. We hear Landerelian chamber music alongside the gospel music of Landerel's Black community and the jubilant drumming of Sadie's ancestral home. There's hushed murmuring from people who don't seem to approve of these program choices, but that's to be expected.

When the newly minted Mr. and Mrs. exit the chapel, they are met with joyful, unabashed African ululations from the women in the garden crowd. It's such a touching moment that I tear up again.

Chapter 35

I COULD tell that people were curious about me at the wedding, and now that they see me here at the reception, they're certain I'm the American girlfriend they've been hearing about.

Photographers outside of the chapel snapped a few pics of me alone, a few of me with my mom. It was a surreal experience being asked for a photo by a gaggle of suited and booted paparazzi. Now, in the fancy hall in the castle, Ma is hanging out with her newfound friends from the African delegation, and I find myself staying close to Kelsey. Thankfully, we're seated at the same table for dinner.

"Thank you, Kelsey," I tell her as we sit down at our places. "I didn't think I'd need a tissue during the ceremony, but I was blubbering all through it."

"Glad I could help," she says without much of a change in expression. But I can tell she means what she says.

"Owen asked you to sit with me, huh?"

"Yes, he knows how harsh people in his circle can be."

"Apparently, I can be just as harsh, because I misjudged you," I say.

"I haven't exactly made it easy for you to like me," she says, her shoulders softening a bit.

"Let me guess," I say. "You're the one who told that student journalist about everything." I finally put my suspicion out into the universe.

Her mouth pinches. "I may have spoken to him a couple times." She turns to face me more fully. "But I was never trying to steal Owen for myself. Seriously, he's my friend. And that's all."

"Just trying to protect him, right?" I say sarcastically.

"Well . . . yeah, kind of." Kelsey picks up her glass, but puts it back down without taking a sip. "Owen has a lot on his plate, and it's hard to be close to him. It takes a lot of guts."

"Which you didn't think I had."

"I didn't doubt you had guts," she admits. "But Landerel is . . . a lot. But you handled the press really well back in New Jersey. And you've been doing well at this wedding. I *may* have misjudged you, too." She pauses, but then murmurs, "And . . . you *may* be a decent match for Owen."

"Gee, thanks," I chuckle. Uncomfortable with the sincere moment, I crack, "We'll see if you still think so after I try to dance with him in front of all those cameras."

"You'll be fine," she says, rolling her eyes.

And right on cue, Lady Lois is at my side. "Zora," she says, "it's time for the dance."

I look at Kelsey and she shrugs. "Go kill it."

Lady Lois walks me over to Owen, who is standing next to the grand piano in one corner of the room, looking fly in his tux.

"Hi, Zora," he says, his eyes lighting up at the sight of me.

"Hi," I answer.

"You look beautiful," he whispers.

"Thank you. You look good, too." I feel awkward, like we haven't truly spoken to each other in ages.

I turn my attention to the musicians. There's a DJ, a full band, and a string quartet and piano player. They each take turns providing the sounds, and right now calls for the strings and piano.

Lady Lois asks us to continue standing shoulder to shoulder until we're announced. Owen moves his hand closer until the back of his hand grazes mine.

Our herald—the man who announces us— takes great pride in affecting what I imagine is the traditional Landerelian accent. He's rolling his "r"s theatrically, and seems to harness everyone's anticipation in his announcement. He's mesmerizing. This will be a tough act to follow.

"Her Majesty the Queen requests your attention as her son Prince Owen performs his *Seanghilder* dance, accompanied by Ms. Zora Emerson."

Owen ushers me to the dance floor. All eyes are on us. We barely have time to talk, but I manage to say it:

"For Emily."

Owen's breath catches in his chest. "For Emily," he agrees.

The strings begin, and we extend our dancing legs without

stepping on each other's toes. I imagine a tiny Jethro sitting on our shoulders, calling out reminders. When I elongate my frame and limbs, Owen responds in kind. We glide, sway, dip, and slay as Jethro intended.

Cameras are flashing from different corners of the hall. I try not to look at anything or anyone or I may trip myself up. I'm concentrating too hard on my feet to truly appreciate the feel of Owen's arms around me.

When the dance is over, the entire banquet hall applauds, and a few people let out whoops. Owen and I pose for some photos before he walks me back to my seat. Just like that, it's over.

"No lie, you two looked incredible out there," Kelsey says.

Another person walking by our table says the same thing.

"Actually, it felt pretty amazing," I say, my adrenaline still pumping.

"How do you feel, Owen?" Kelsey asks.

"Brilliant," he says. "I couldn't have done it without Zora." He turns to me. "You are a beautiful person inside and out, and I thank you for being here."

We look at each other and smile, shaking our heads about the wild ride we've been on.

The DJ gets on the mic and calls everyone out to the dance floor. The giddy bride and groom start everyone off, and the guests gradually join them.

"Zora, will you dance with me again?" Owen asks, and I swoon inwardly.

We do the two-step and, with the cameras occupied elsewhere, manage to talk and dance at the same time. It's our first private conversation in close to a week.

"I have some big news," Owen tells me, and I wait, wondering what he has to say. "I've decided to attend Halstead University in the fall," he says, a big smile crossing his face.

My heart jumps. For real? "Ohmygod, that's huge!" I yell, forgetting where we are for a minute.

"Yes, and my mum does not approve. She's afraid I'm doing it because of you."

"Me?" I can't believe what I'm hearing.

"Hence her tepid reception, which you may or may not have noticed." He grimaces.

"Ah," I say. "That would explain her efforts to keep us apart these past days."

"Yes, that as well," he says. "I'm sorry I haven't been around much while you've been here, Zora. But I promise we'll make up for lost time when I'm back in the States this fall."

I'm still in shock. "You're really going to live in Jersey, huh?" I ask.

Owen nods, beaming. "And while I did admit to my mum that you being Stateside *is* a perk, I am doing this for myself. I loved my time at Halstead this summer. And I really appreciate the privacy it affords me. It's invaluable."

"You call being hounded by the press privacy?" I ask.

"It doesn't hold a candle to what I face here," he says.

I nod. I can see that.

"What do you think of it all?" Owen asks me eagerly.

"I'm so happy," I admit. "For selfish reasons, of course. But also for you. You've made the choice you wanted to make."

"Appleton hangouts, here I come." He smiles and leans in close to start to kiss me.

A royal official in a tux and a name tag walks over.

"Prince Owen, the queen is requesting your presence for the tribute."

"We'll be right there," says Owen.

"The queen is requesting only you."

Owen frowns. "I'd like Zora to come."

The man walks away. He must have convincingly tattled on Owen the way my Walk Me Home kids do to each other, because the queen herself walks up to us.

Uh-oh.

"Lovely dance," the queen says, acknowledging me.

"Thank you, Your Majesty," I say. Is that right? I know Lady Lois told me what to call the queen and it's flown out of my brain under her haughty gaze.

"Owen, shall we?"

She gestures to the side exit.

"Mother, I'd like Zora to attend as well."

"You'll see her when we return, dear," she says with a tight smile.

I look like I'm following a volley at a tennis match.

"Zora is my guest, and I invited her here because she's special to me," Owen says firmly. I feel a small thrill at his words. "I'd like to share this moment with her. Emily would have loved her, Mum," he says quietly. "I know in my heart, she would approve of Zora being there."

I hold my breath until the queen finally blinks first, the edges of her mouth softening. She nods at her son and gestures in invitation to the both of us.

Whoa.

Owen takes my hand in his, and I give it a squeeze. We follow the queen down a corridor to a tiny chapel dedicated to their family. There is a large painted portrait of the Landerel royals on one wall.

The rest of the family, including Sadie and Gideon, are gathered in front of a covered column flanked by two tall candles. Once we join them, a chaplain begins the short dedication ceremony. The column is uncovered, revealing a sculpture of Emily, Owen's sister. It's a bust, in marble, reminding me of the family's long European traditions. But she looks so alive, a small smile on her lips, her hair swirling as though in a light breeze. She looks . . . free.

Owen's jaw tightens when he sees the sculpture. The chaplain begins saying a prayer. Owen drops his head as the tears flow down his cheeks. He squeezes my hand back when I reach for it.

After the prayer is over, Owen and his brothers light one of the candles and his parents light the other.

Following the contemplative moment, Owen and I make for the gorgeous outdoors. The sun is beginning to set. We head out on the tiled terrace and keep strolling until we're far enough from the banquet hall entrance. Other couples have nabbed private spots here and there, but we find a tranquil area overlooking a sweet corner of the pond.

"Thanks for including me in that," I say, snuggling up next to Owen.

"Of course," he says. "Having you here has meant so much to me. And now my mum can see that, too."

"Hopefully she'll come around to the idea of you living in New Jersey," I say.

"So you're about to start senior year. Do you think you'll be applying to Halstead?" Owen asks. "It's a great school."

"I'm thinking about it," I admit. "I have a lot to accomplish first, but Halstead might see an application from me. Now that I've visited your stomping grounds, I can see why you like the campus," I say. "For one, the library looks like a castle, so I bet you feel right at home there."

Owen nods. "In the future, I'll make sure to keep out of any private conversation I overhear there," he chuckles. "Unless it's yours."

I tip my head back and laugh.

"Sounds like a plan," I say before we seal that deal with a kiss.

The next day, Owen rides with me and Ma to the airport. He helps us bring our bags in, and gives Ma a hug good-bye.

"Wait. Airport selfie!" I say to him. Ma stands off to the side, smiling, to give us a last moment to ourselves.

"Are you going to post this?" Owen asks as I take out my phone.

"Of course not. Do you want the *Halstead Chronicle* tracking me down for the story behind it?"

Owen and I put our heads together, and I snap our picture.

"Actually, I might join the *Chronicle* as a reporter this fall," he says. He's not joking. "What do you think?"

"No comment," I say with a laugh. Owen holds me close and we both crack up together between kisses.

"See you in a few weeks," he says, waving as I walk off to join Ma.

I give a little cheer as I link arms with Ma and we make our way toward the security screening.

From the fancy airport lounge, I text our selfie to Skye. I smile with my whole heart when I see what she texts back.

Cute couple! Two of the most royal people on the 🌍. ♥

Acknowledgments

This book is a celebration of women who help women. Of triumph after false starts. Of recognition and inclusion. Of open windows and open doors. Thank you, Adrienne Ingrum, for making literary sparks fly from day one. Utmost gratitude to my friend Julia DeVillers for the introductions, invitations, and in-couragement. A special thank-you to Sarah Mlynowski for your superhuman kindness and generosity. Here we go, Laura Dail! You are a game changer, and I'm thrilled to have you as my agent. Thank you to my star editor, Aimee Friedman, for making this storytelling experience so exciting! So many thanks to Olivia Valcarce for editing with heart. Loving hugs to the most special Zora in my life. Merci, family and friends, both living & in spirit, for the love and support. And a soul-deep thank-you to my princess Olivia, my prince Lincoln, and my royal crush Bernard.

About the Author

Debbie Rigaud grew up in East Orange, New Jersey, and began her writing career covering news and entertainment for magazines like *Seventeen, CosmoGIRL!,* and *Twist.* Debbie now lives with her husband and children in Columbus, Ohio. Find out more at debbierigaud.com.

YOU MAY ALSO ENJOY . . .

"This effervescent romp bounces between playful fluff, witty humor, and happily ever after sincerity, and romance fans will be gleefully hooked."
—*Booklist*

What's better than one deliciously cozy, swoon-worthy holiday story? FOUR of them, from some of today's bestselling YA authors!

"Love is in the air and on the airwaves in this sweet romance . . . West delivers banter with plenty of sparks."
—*School Library Journal*

Books about Love.
Books about Life.
Books about You.

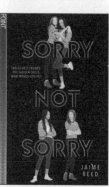

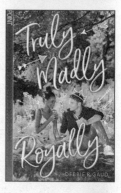